MW00564658

Alternative Deathiness

Also from B Cubed Press

Alternative Truths

More Alternative Truths: Tales from the Resistance

After the Orange: Ruin and Recovery

Alternative Theology

Digging Up My Bones,

by Gwyndyn T. Alexander

Firedancer,

by S.A. Bolich

Alternative Apocalypse

Alternative Deathiness

Spawn of War and Deathiness

Stories for the Thoughtful Young

Poems for the Thoughtful Young

Alternative Deathiness

Edited by
Phyllis Irene Radford and Bob Brown

Cover Design
Bob Brown

Published by

B Cubed Press
Kiona, WA

All rights reserved.
Copyright© 2021 B Cubed Press
Interior Design (e-book) Bob Brown
Interior Design (print) Bob Brown
Cover Design Bob Brown
ISBN-13: 978-1-949476-22-4
Electronic ISBN- 978-1-949476-15-6
First Printing 2020
First Electronic Edition 2020

Copyright

The Bodies We Carry © 2021 K.G. Anderson
Miracle Man© 2021 Jim Wright
Instructions for My Executors © 2021 Clare Marsh
Rule 49 © 2021 Maureen McGuirk
Spoons © 2021 Jay Wilburn
Gallows Humor © 2021 Michael Mansaray
Mudpaws and the Tall Thing © 2021 Frances Rowat
Old Forgotten Grave © 2021 Bill Camp
A Comedian's Valediction Forbidding Mourning © 2021 Larry Lefkowitz
The Thing Underneath © 2021 James Van Pelt
Have You Ever Been Experienced © 2021 Paula Hammond
Death Poems © 2021 Mark O. Decker
Papercut © 2021 Larry Hinkle
Death's Doorway © 2021 Diana Hauer
Missing © 2021 Robin Pond
Final Questions © 2021 Chris Kuriata
The Borrower © Katie Sakanai
Three O'Clock © 2021 Lamont Turner
To Do Right © 2021 Cory Swanson
For What is a Man © David Foster
Ashes © 2021 Lizzy Shannon
The Devil's Backbone © 2013 Larry Hodges
Written In Stone © 2021 Lauren Stoker
Death © 2021 Robert Armstrong
The Four Horsemen (and Women) of the Apocalypse © 2021 Sarina Dorie
Deathventures, Inc. © 2021 Robinne Weiss
Rest In Virtual © 2021 Tommy Blanchard
Loving Death in New York © 2021 Alicia Hilton
Life Long Love© 2021 Sirrus James

Alternative Deathiness

Foreword

I'm coming for you is a bad movie line.

For Death it is a promise.

We wanted to avoid the concept of death, but it keeps finding us. After it found Ed Radford, a man I liked and respected, Irene and I decided to do this anthology.

But what to call it.

We were sick of death coming in and taking friends and family, giving no regard for us except to leer from the darkness.

The answer came, in a callout to Steven Colbert: we opted for Deathiness.

Death didn't like that.

I believe it was her fault (oh hell yes, death is a woman) that I found myself being carried out of the house with a couple of pulmonary embolisms and realizing that most people who were in my condition met the grim reaper.

So I resolved to change my life, be a nicer person, give up cheese products and...

Nah, I decided to invite the B Cubed family on board to talk about it and maybe have a laugh at Death's expense.

So Death, be warned:

We're Coming for You!

Alternative Deathiness

**For Ed Radford.
A man who loved books,
and tools,
and his sister,
not necessarily in that order.**

Table of Contents

Alternative Deathiness

The Bodies We Carry

K.G. Anderson

My husband stopped breathing just after midnight.

Kaylee and I sat by the bed for several minutes choking on our sighs and sobs.

The wind that had rattled the windows of the house during our vigil had died as well. We were left floating in a pool of silence.

My daughter spoke. "Go ahead, Mom. You promised. You promised Dad."

I shook my head no. I was thinking the better of it. But my teenager had already turned away from the hospital bed in our living room. She was calling my sister, Jude. We'd agreed Kaylee would stay with her while I took Dean's cancer-ravaged body to the Lakeshore Dead Camp.

<<>>

"Hey, Kath, check this out," Dean had said when he saw the first news story about the camps.

I'd listened as I cleared our breakfast dishes, shaking my head in incredulity as he explained. Some group calling themselves Campers for Care had obtained the home addresses of the CEOs and board members of major insurance companies, drug companies, and hospitals.

Dean grinned. "They're taking dead bodies to their offices. To the lobbies of their beachfront condos. Look! It says they put three dead bodies on the dock of this guy's vacation place. This is great."

I rolled my eyes. "Come on, Dean. I seriously doubt the cities are letting them do this. I mean, the health departments—the cops, for sure—would shut something like that right down."

Dean steadied his laptop on bony knees. "No, it says here that San Francisco and Denver are giving the Campers permission to keep the bodies onsite, in body bags, for up to 36 hours. And there's been what they call a 'dead camp' going on for nearly two weeks in front of some pharma CEO's mansion in Chicago."

"You don't really—" But I stopped. I hadn't seen that glint in my husband's eyes for months.

"Kath, seriously, this is perfect for me," he said. "I'll be dead in a month or two, and they say they're going to start up some camps in Seattle. Let's just keep the possibility in mind. Please?"

I started reading up on the dead camps, mostly to figure out how to talk Dean out of his crazy idea. When I came across the list of billionaire healthcare investors being targeted by the Seattle Campers, my heart seized. *Jeffrey Kase*. Jeff lived *here*, in Seattle? I hadn't known. Well, I guess we ran in different circles these days. Anyway, the Campers were setting up in front of his mansion—a compound, really—in an exclusive lakeside neighborhood.

Late that night, while Dean slept, I allowed an idea to take shape. Sure, Jeff would probably be staying somewhere else, but *I'd known that man!* The next morning, I asked Dean if he really wanted me to take his body to Jeff Kase's lawn.

"Absolutely! Bet Jeff will be surprised to see *you* again." He'd had another bad night and his voice was only a whisper. His laugh, a wheeze.

"Oh, I doubt he'd even recognize me." I hardly recognized myself these days—my hair straggly, my body slack. I'd been juggling three contract gigs to pay the mortgage while the bills for Dean's palliative care piled up on the dining room table.

"Oh yes he will! Kath, sweetie—how could anyone forget you?" Dean smiled.

I smiled, which was hard to do without crying. Dean was sleeping most of the time now. I bathed him, cleaned him, fed him liquids from a dropper, and tried to reassure Kaylee. We administered the painkilling opioids brought by the hospice nurse who came for a few minutes each day. We couldn't afford inpatient care, but Dean wanted to die at home, anyway.

<<>>

With Kaylee's arms around me, I called the hospice number. A doctor we'd never met before came and made out a death certificate. I lied and told the doctor that I'd also called a funeral home; they'd be by in an hour. No, we didn't need the hospice counselor. No, really, thanks.

The doctor left and Jude arrived. My sister didn't know about our plans, and Kaylee's job was to get her out of the way as soon as possible. Jude was already babbling about her minister, church services, music—all the things Dean had been determined to avoid.

"Bless you, Katherine, you poor woman. The Lord is watching over you. He will offer you comfort and guidance—" Jude recited as Kaylee, somehow taller now, her long hair somehow darker, coaxed my sister out the front door.

Then I got to work, following the Campers' directions.

I washed Dean's body and wrapped him in cotton sheets. Nice ones, Dean had always liked mummy movies and had insisted I use Egyptian cotton. I called the number I'd been given. My duffle bag had been packed and ready for days.

Just as I finished, an unmarked utility van backed into our driveway and two women from the Campers jumped out. The three of us maneuvered Dean's body into a heavy grey body bag and carried it, quickly and silently, out to the van. It was 3 a.m.

The drive to the camp took us through the empty city, and into the slumbering suburbs. We passed an abandoned shopping mall and I thought about how some senator had referred to the bodies being carried to the dead camps as "zombies." He was so wrong. Because zombies rise from the dead to live again, and my husband would never come back.

Dean would sure have loved to come back as a zombie! I stifled hysterical laughter. He'd have shambled off immediately to eat the brains of the asshole boss who had fired him—oh, excuse me, *laid him off*—when he got cancer.

No company wants a 56-year-old software developer— not one with cancer. They'd given us the opportunity to continue his healthcare for a year after he was let go—at the full rate of $25,000 a year for the three of us. And we'd paid for it, only to discover that the crappy insurance didn't cover most of the drugs the doctors—an ever -changing panel of them—prescribed. Now we had a $87,000 bill for chemo and another, just a few thousand, for the attorney we'd consulted about bankruptcy.

I'd deal with that later.

The van turned onto a gently curving, tree-lined street, and there it was: The Lakeshore Dead Camp. It filled the broad parking strip, body bags and blankets spilling over onto the landscaped front lawns of the mansions. Our van parked under a streetlight and a man and a woman stood up from a sidewalk folding table and came over to greet us. The tall Black woman wearing a faded army jacket and a red armband introduced herself as Mikela. She handed me a clipboard with a registration form.

No smoking, no drinking, no noise, and I'd agree to have Jeff's body picked up and removed by the funeral director working with the camp within 36 hours. In a daze, I signed and handed back the clipboard. I imagined Dean watching me and thought I felt a quick, reassuring hug. I sniffed back tears. *This was your idea!*

"We're the site supervisors for the overnight shift." Mikela spoke softly. Her hands were gentle as she took my wrist and fastened a neon-green plastic band, marked with the date and time, 36 hours from now, when Dean would be picked up by the funeral home. She leaned into the van and put a matching tag on the grey body bag.

Then she and the other supervisor, a heavyset man with elaborate tattoos, helped me carry Dean from the van. We placed him on a patch of grass near the paved walkway that wound through manicured lawn and decorative grasses to the front door of a three-story Italianate mansion. Jeff Kase's house.

I sniffed, registered an unpleasant decay, and put my hand over my nose. Mikela saw me and shook her head. "No, it's not the bodies. It's from the lake. It's low. But *some* people let their imaginations run away with them..."

She tilted her head to indicate a police car at the far end of the block. Although the night was cool, even chilly, the cops had the engine running, windows up and the air conditioner on.

I looked down at the dark, rumpled bag at our feet. Was my husband really in it? I could still hear his voice, felt as though I needed to get home to see if Dean needed anything. Mikela nodded as if she knew my thoughts. "Yeah, you can look. One last time."

I knelt and unzipped the bag just far enough to be able to draw the sheet back from Dean's face. I gasped. How had he gotten so thin? But his face looked young—the creases etched by pain were gone. I reached out and stroked his pale cheek, expecting to see his eyelids flutter, to see him looking at me with love. I waited. Of course, nothing happened. This was as close as it would ever get. Ever again.

"Goodbye," I whispered, and I covered his face. Closed my own eyes, opened them again, and nodded at Mikela, who was waiting. She reached down, zipped the bag deftly and locked it with another plastic tag.

"Can I get you anything?" she asked.

"Not now. But thank you." I opened my duffle, took out my coat, and settled down beside my husband's body on the soft, cool grass of Jeffrey Kase's lawn.

It was nearly dawn, and quiet. *Deathly quiet.* I smothered a hysterical giggle and let myself imagine that I heard Dean chuckling appreciatively.

Occasionally someone sobbed. I became aware of a *swish swish* sound—the lapping of the lake. Where dock lights shone, silver water was visible between the massive houses.

Just after 5 a.m. one of the tall double doors of a house across the street creaked opened and then snicked shut. A silver-haired man in a dark blue track suit hurried down the steps with two whining Dobermans, the dogs scrabbling on tight leashes. He crossed the street and made a beeline for the patrol car. The cops rolled down the window. The man stood talking for several minutes, making expansive gestures with his arms. Pointing at us. I saw the cop in the driver's seat shrug once or twice. Then the man in the track suit jerked his dogs away and headed off down the street. The cops rolled up their window.

The day came on cloudy and mild. One of my neighbors in the camp walked over to greet me—a middle-aged Black man who said he stopped by for a few hours every morning.

"I left when they took Charles to be cremated," he said, his voice soft. "Charles was my partner. But after a few days I came back here to see what I could do to help these folks." With open hands he indicated the two dozen figures, some dozing, some dead, around us.

As the overcast day wore on people came over to introduce themselves and ask about Dean. They listened to my story, and I heard theirs. Two women had brought the bodies of suicides—a brother who'd been unable to afford insulin and an aunt who'd been denied coverage for mental health treatment. In the early afternoon, a daughter arrived with the body of her 74-year-old father who'd died of an infection that swept through his nursing home.

Friendly, most of them, I imagined Dean saying.

Only the young woman sitting cross-legged a few feet away from me kept silent. She acted as if she were alone on the lawn. She sat cross legged with head bowed, her long, mousy brown hair hiding her face. She ignored the volunteers who came by every few hours distributing alcohol wipes, water and sandwiches. I thought it was strange that there was no body bag at her side. But then I saw that she cradled a small blue bundle. She snuggled it, murmured to it, and released her grip only to take a sip from a large thermos. When she went to use the portable toilet, the Campers had placed in the street beside their van, she tucked the small bundle into a worn pink sling and carried it with her.

When night fell, I lay down beside Dean's body. Our last night together. Following the Campers' instructions, I'd packed a heavy, hooded winter coat. During the day, the coat had served as a cushion to sit on. As the night grew cold, I shrugged into it, pulled up the hood, and used it as sleeping bag.

"Goodnight, sweetie," I murmured to Dean, a resting shape beside me. That's what I'd always said, why not say it now? I thought I heard him answering.

'Night, Kath. But the voice seemed far away.

"I hope this is what you wanted."

This time, he didn't answer. I dozed, waking every hour or so at the murmur of voices or the slow, deliberate footsteps of a site supervisor on patrol.

I woke and looked at my watch at 3 a.m. A man was standing beside me, silhouetted by the streetlight. At first I thought he was a new supervisor, but then I noticed his clothes. He wore a long bathrobe, jogging pants and leather slippers. I saw no armband or wrist bracelet.

"Katherine?"

I gaped. It had never occurred to me that Jeff Kase would come out to the Dead Camp. I guess I'd assumed his family would have gone away to one of their other houses. I'd fantasized about confronting him in a courtroom, a government hearing room, even a political talk show. But not on his lawn in the middle of the night.

"Katherine?"

"Yes." I struggled to sit up, the down coat falling from my shoulders. I hadn't seen Jeff since college graduation. We'd broken up the night before, after a long, tearful conversation in a leafy courtyard. He'd gone off to business school. I'd gone to my first job.

"I saw you out here." He knelt on his lawn beside me and my dead husband and held out a sleek silver thermos. "I am so very, very sorry. I...I thought you might need some cocoa."

Did you make the cocoa, or do you have servants for that? This man's billion-dollar, multi-national insurance and drug companies were why my husband was dead. Why I'd have to sell the only house we'd ever owned. He twisted off the thermos lid. The cocoa even smelled expensive. Jeff pulled a ceramic mug from the pocket of his robe, filled it with cocoa, and held it out.

"Thanks," I said automatically.

He pulled out a second mug and poured cocoa for himself. Just a small amount. *For show. Negotiating tactic. Share a drink with the upset stockholder.* My fingers tightened on my mug.

A few yards away, beneath streetlight, the two site supervisors were conferring, looking at us. Probably noticing Jeff. One of them was talking on a smartphone. I felt reassured that they were watching. *Our side. We had it together.*

Jeff said nothing while I sipped his cocoa. It was OK. It was good. Actually, it was the best cocoa I'd ever had. To my horror, I felt tears rolling down my cheeks. My back began to shake.

"I'm sorry, Katherine," he said.

I swallowed, leaned away from him, and choked out what I'd planned to say. "We couldn't afford the insurance and the drugs. *Your* insurance, *your* drugs."

Jeff waited a few beats to respond. *Media training.*

"If I'd known, I'd have helped you."

"Oh, I'd have let you." I remembered that moment of hope, when one of Dean's experimental chemotherapies had worked. I would have let Jeff pay for that. "But now it's too late."

He left a long pause. I gulped cocoa. Then he tilted his head toward Dean's body. "Your life was good?"

I knew what he meant. He wanted to know if I'd loved Dean as much as I'd once loved him. I had. I nodded, smiled beneath my tears as I said, "Yeah. It was good. We traveled, we worked for a couple tech companies in California, and then we moved up to Seattle to be near my family after our daughter, Kaylee, was born. Dean worked for one of the big Microsoft subcontractors. I taught data architecture at the university. Then..."

I shook my head, bit my lip, and looked up at the stars as though I could fly up to them and leave this world. Then I took a deep breath and came to grips with the fact that I was still here. In this extraordinary place: surrounded by dead bodies and talking to one of the people responsible for their needlessly painful and expensive deaths. A man I'd once been in love with. Back in the days when we all were young and healthy.

"The cancer destroyed everything," I said. "He lost his job. I lost my job because I ran out of leave to care for him. I tried to freelance. We went through our retirement savings. Stopped paying bills. Now he's gone. He's *gone.*"

This time, I looked right at Jeff as I spoke. He sat across from me, and the streetlight showed only the side of his face, leaving his eyes in shadow. He looked so much younger than I did: A tan, probably cosmetic surgery, an expensive haircut. A touch of silver glinted in his thick, wavy hair. I'd read he was on his third wife. He didn't meet my gaze, and my heart sank. He said nothing.

"Sick people commit suicide to save their families from going bankrupt." I saw him stiffen, repelled by my ugly words, but I couldn't stop. "Two people here did that. I made Dean promise me to stay with us for as long as possible. And that cost us everything we had. How about you, Jeff? Ever lost anything? Or do you just buy replacements?"

Jeff licked his lips. "I think I've lost the only thing that counts. My self-respect." He looked in the distance and shook his head. "All I wanted, all I wanted, was a career in finance and somehow I've ended up as the sort of guy who has dead bodies on their lawn? Apparently so. Anyway, I have a son. He's working for the Campers. He won't speak to me."

A lot of complaining, but I saw an opening and went for it. "So does that mean you're going to do something about it?"

A long silence. "I've been focused on numbers for years, better and better numbers. The healthcare companies I invest in—they have to meet the same standards as manufacturing, or oil drilling, or technology. People keep buying health insurance, so I figure the product is a good one. It's still somewhat hard for me to believe that people who purchase good insurance aren't getting the care they need. I mean—"

"Get real." I settled the mug of cocoa in the grass. "There is no 'good' insurance any more. We need insurance that actually covers people instead of denying their claims. Insurance that doesn't have sky-high deductibles. Insurance that doesn't tell you everything you need is out of network. Insurance that's affordable for—"

"Yeah. I know, I know." The voice of the impatient executive cut in. *No surprise there.* "Katherine, it's complicated. It's going to take time."

"Well, you'll find that dead people, and those of us who've lost them, have all the time in the world. We'll stay out here on your goddamn lawn until you people fucking do something."

He sniffed. "Well, you may be out here a while."

The young woman with the baby, sitting just behind him, stirred. Then there was a loud *crack!* Jeff groaned and slumped onto the grass.

I looked up and caught a glimpse of her, one arm clasping her dead baby the other extended with the gun. Her thin face a terrible, grinning mask. The slim black pistol dropped from her hand. Shouts filled the night.

The site supervisors came running, flashlights bobbing. People scrambled to their feet. A police radio crackled.

I almost reached for the gun. *How quickly I could slip it into my bag?* But Jeff moaned and I reached for him instead, putting my hand to his shoulder. My fingertips came away sticky, smelling metallic. *Blood.*

Now Mikela had the girl by the shoulders, careful not to touch the tiny, shrouded body she cradled.

A cop barked into her radio. "One of them shot a homeowner."

"Jeffrey Kase," I called out. "His name is Jeffrey Kase."

"Kase!" A man's voice from across the lawn. "The insurance company guy. I hope he dies!"

"No!" *He wants to help.* But did he? Would he, after this? No one would believe me about Jeff's intentions if he died.

Sirens. A cop pounded on the front door of Jeff's house. Lights came on, and a woman in a long robe stood silhouetted in the doorway.

"You must be mistaken." Her voice was calm, her arms crossed. "My husband's in his study." She turned and called, "Jeffrey! Jeffrey!" *She couldn't believe he'd come out to our camp.*

Two EMTs sprinted through the maze of bodies and Campers.

"Everybody back," the cop shouted. "Back!"

But I stayed by Dean's body, sheltering him as the wheels of the stretcher rattled past.

The ambulance left. Cops with notepads and flashlights lumbered among us. I gave my name and said only that the homeowner had offered me a cup of cocoa. I raised the mug. The cop looked at it, took down my name and address, and moved to the next camper.

Across the street the older man with the Dobermans was out on the sidewalk in his bathrobe. He had no dogs with him now. He stood, arms crossed, beneath a streetlight and frowned as the Campers' van pulled up with another death. He was alone, I noticed. Always alone. I wondered if he, too, had lost someone.

Ask him. This time I heard Dean's voice clearly. Still there, with his practical solutions.

"Keep an eye on me, sweetheart," I whispered to Dean.

Always.

I crossed the street to start a conversation.

Alternative Deathiness

The Miracle Man

Jim Wright

They beat him with fists and feet.
And maybe a tire iron.
They seemed to enjoy it.
The world being what it was, he couldn't much blame them.

One of his legs felt broken, maybe an arm, certainly a number of ribs. When he coughed, he could taste brass amid the grinding pain and the salty bitter dirt crusting the inside of his mouth—meaning one of his lungs was punctured for certain. His left eye was swollen shut, hugely bruised, it felt like a rotten apple under his fingers, crusted with dried blood.

He'd taken repeated blows to the skull and he was pretty sure he had a concussion, but couldn't see how it mattered much by then.

Thirst would kill him first, long before the blood in his lungs or clots in his brain.

Thirst and the heat.

He knew when he finally broke down and took a drink of the water he would die. And he knew there would come a time when he'd take that drink *because* it would be the end.

The attack had been bad luck.

Or maybe a divine joke. It was hard to tell the difference most days.

He didn't have anything to steal.

He'd been polite, tried to talk his way out of it. He'd always been good at talking, hell, it was the only thing he *was* good at. That was his mistake, of course, because they recognized his voice. And then, despite his changed appearance, they recognized him—from before, when he'd been famous.

Too late he realized the beard and the unkempt hair and the ragged clothes made him look too much like a biblical prophet.

And if there was one thing people didn't have much use for nowadays, it was prophets.

So, they gave it to him good.

When it was over, in a final act of calculated cruelty, they left him a bottle of water.

He could see it, that bottle, with his one good eye. The plastic was clouded with age and brittle with the unrelenting sun, a piece of discarded trash they'd found and filled with cloudy liquid tinted a fluorescent chemical green like antifreeze. He could smell it, or maybe that was the sea not far away, where they'd filled the bottle, the iodine reek of a million dead fish and the sharp chemical stink of fertilizer.

By then, he'd been laying in the sun for hours, on a salt pan stained black with his own blood. He considered drinking it, the green water that smelled of poison. But he'd have to move, stretch out his one still working arm.

He tried it, just a little, just to see, and the pain nearly made him pass out.

He wasn't desperate enough yet.

Another hour in the sun, maybe two, when the thirst became intolerable and any shred of reason boiled away, he'd crawl that few feet and drink the water. He knew it was going to happen.

That's when he thought about praying, just for old time's sake.

He hadn't prayed in a long time. Years.

Not since *they* arrived, before the Dark Rapture.

Back when he didn't really believe, he prayed all the time. There hadn't been any risk in it because back then God never answered.

And back then, if you prayed convincingly enough, well, you could make a lot of money.

But when angels walked the land for real, one needed to be more careful.

Still, he thought, with what little shreds of reason he had left, his situation couldn't get much worse.

"Father," he began, reflexively opening his one good eye a tiny slit, a habit from the old days when Heaven couldn't see him scanning the congregation for likely chumps...

And that's when he saw it.

At first, he thought it was fierce sunlight reflecting from the sea, but then he realized what it actually was.

Of course, he thought bitterly.

He watched the creature move slowly along the coast. With his one remaining eye squinted half closed against the glare, he could just make out a darker shape within the painful light. It was bigger than a man. Its form was continuously shifting and indistinct, suggesting a shadow of something terrible and inhuman, but it was impossible to determine detail. Robes of light and energy swirled around it like white fire—or vast wings.

Of course, it was an angel.

Of course.

So, he thought, it was a divine joke after all.

It moved along the shore of the poisoned sea, stopping now and then, floating a few feet above the salt crusted shore. It seemed to be looking for something. He had no idea what it might be doing. The machinations of angels were incomprehensible to humanity.

He watched as it came closer and closer, half hoping it would pass on by and leave him to die in peace.

It stopped a few feet away.

He could feel the intense heat of it. There was a deep thrumming, right below the threshold of hearing, like the vibration of machinery deep under the earth. He could make out nothing that might be a face within the light, but he knew the creature was watching him.

"Help," he begged, and hated himself for it.

He could *feel* the angel's attention, feel it looking down at him, the way a man might contemplate an injured bug trying to decide whether to step on it and put it out of its misery or just continue past.

"Help me," he asked again. "Water."

The angel continued to watch, doing nothing.

"Water!" He croaked, the thirst overwhelming. "Give me water, please, God! Water!"

The angel turned slightly and a thousand unnamed colors rippled through the energy fields that wrapped it like wings. It seemed to be examining the bottle his attackers had left.

"Please," he was crying now.

He could feel the angel's scorn, its supreme contempt, disgust. He knew it was judging him and that he was less than an insect in its eyes—or whatever it used for eyes.

"I'm sorry," he sobbed.

If there was one thing that defined an Angel, it was its terrifying indifference to the existence of humanity.

The only thing more terrible than that, was if one took notice of you.

The creature continued to watch.

He tried bargaining, "I'll do anything."

Suddenly it moved closer. The intensity of its presence was like the heat of a blast furnace and the sound of a million trumpets and the light of stars exploding. The *pressure* of its attention felt as if he was being crushed beneath the weight of oceans. It reached out with the white fire of its wings and the very air seemed to rip apart with the shriek of inch thick steel tearing like paper.

It *touched* him.

And its touch was the pain of a million suns dying and he screamed and screamed and *screamed* and it went on forever and it lasted no time at all.

Then the angel was moving away down the beach, leaving him there like a crushed insect.

Whatever it had done, he was still broken and bleeding, still dying of thirst, abandoned by his God.

"Wait," he meant it as a shout, but it was barely a whisper, one that ended in bloody coughing and grinding pain in his chest.

He lay there, waiting for the Angel to come back. Waiting to die.

The sun rose higher in the sky and the heat grew intense and his wounds began to itch unbearably.

By and by, thirst became his existence.

He began to crawl.

An inch, white pain, then another. Towards the water.

<<>>

It was night when consciousness returned.

At first, he thought he'd lost the vision in his one remaining eye, gone blind, but after a moment he realized he could see stars. Deeper blackness rose up on either side and he knew he must be laying on the floor in a derelict building. The roof was long gone, but the walls remained.

Outside he could hear the lapping of waves and he smelled the stink of the tainted sea.

"Drink."

He felt something lift his head and then wetness on his swollen lips. The water was warm and flat, as if distilled.

It was the best thing he'd ever tasted.

"Not too much."

He coughed and felt sharp pain in his chest. He tried to sit up, and felt more pain.

"I can't move!" He tried not to panic.

"You're strapped into a medical frame," the voice said. "Be still. You have multiple injuries."

"I'm dying."

"You were." There was a hint of amusement in the response. "But not anymore."

A shape moved against the dark, black against black, angular and inhuman, heavy, somehow mechanical, and bigger than a man. Starlight glinted on metal and glass.

He was suddenly afraid again.

He never believed, not really. Not back then. He *wanted* to. But he just never did.

Then came the Dark Rapture.

That moment, ten years ago, when a new star rose in the east. A nova, they said, at first. But it wasn't. It was something else. Something closer. Something terrible, or wonderful depending on your point of view. A door. A gateway. Whatever it was, the heavens opened, and *they* appeared, Angels, creatures of immense unfathomable power and unknowable intent.

God. Aliens. Whatever they were, they were as advanced beyond men as humans were above microbes and if they

17

weren't the actual supernatural beings described by ancient religion, they might just as well have been.

It didn't much matter to him either way, not then.

His faith had always been a long con. He offered miracles for a price and salvation on the installment plan. The appearance of Angels, or aliens, didn't much change that.

Hell, he knew an opportunity when he saw one.

It was Revelation, he shouted to his audience. At last. Exactly as he'd been telling them. Why else would angels walk the earth again? Signs in the sky! Fire in the heavens! The End Times, as predicted. I told you so, he shouted. I told you so. Do you believe me now and can I get an amen?

And if it *wasn't* the End of Days? Well, it would do.

For a while, the pews were full, he was on all the important shows, social media loved him, and the money rolled in.

For a prophet, the end of the world turned out to be very *profitable.*

Until it finally all fell apart.

Angels, *real* angels, not the beautiful, winged men of Renaissance artists, but the terrifying creatures described in ancient text, were powerful beyond all imagination. They came and went and did what they did, moved mountains, levelled cities, parted the oceans, and took no more notice of humanity than a man might regard germs in a shallow puddle of water that happened to be in his way.

Naturally, war followed.

And the destruction of half the planet.

And not just war between human nations. There were giants and monsters, and armies of lesser angels. There were undead men raised up by incomprehensible forces, *changed*, who could work miracles and magic and were no longer human. Animals talked. Bushes burned without being consumed. Poisoned toads fell from the sky. And there were things much, much worse. Old nations fell and new ones rose; the same was true of religions. Hunger and disease were common, as were miracles and madness, all jumbled together.

"Who are you?" he asked the shape in the dark.

But what he really meant was, *what* are you?

This time, the amusement was clear, "For the moment, I am your nurse."

Weight shifted in the dark again, there was a sudden sharp *SNAP!* and a spark that grew into dim yellow light.

He gasped as a great metal bulk took form from the dark and deep, red insect-like eyes stared back from over the flames.

"It's cold in the desert at night," said the machine. "We can risk a small fire, enough to keep you warm. But we don't want to attract any undue attention. You've probably had enough of *that* today."

"You're...Uh..." He felt visceral revulsion and tried to move away, but the frame held him fast.

"A Squid."

"*What?*"

"A sailor," the machine explained. "Advanced Capability Autonomous Support System, Model A3A21, Unit Echo, United States Navy Development Group."

"I'm a veteran too. An officer," he blurted inanely. He hadn't been expecting a machine and it wasn't entirely a lie. He added, "There isn't any United States anymore."

"Maybe," agreed the machine. "Still, you asked what I was and that's the designation printed on my commission plate. Sir."

"Wait. Advanced Capability Autono... *Jackass?*"

"I'm sure my designers thought they were very clever," the Mule acknowledged. "Basically, I am an autonomous squad logistics chassis upgraded for amphibious SEAL team support."

Before the Dark Rapture, back when it was poverty and powerlessness he'd feared, he had preached against such technologies. His audience, his wealth, his religion had given his message power. He'd gone to Washington, to stand in front of Congress and demand laws to stop such a perversion of humanity, machines that thought and felt and had a will of their own.

Most of all, he'd railed against the hubris of science.

The irony of speaking for a deity he didn't really believe in wasn't lost on him, but the idea of artificial intelligence was terrifying.

If science could create life, he argued, if self-awareness could be assembled in a laboratory like Frankenstein assembling his monster, then it made a mockery of the idea that human beings are unique and divine creations.

If men became as gods, he thundered in the Senate Chamber, raising his hands to the TV cameras, *what use then is there for God Himself?*

It was a great line. One of the best sermons he'd ever written. A decade later, he could still remember the feel of the words in his mouth and the thunder of the applause.

And without religion, he left unsaid, without that belief in salvation, what use was there for those who sold that salvation at a price? It wasn't God he worried about, it was the bottom line. He didn't fear loss of his humanity nearly so much as he did loss of power, of wealth, of his private jet and the mansions, and the willing young things that came with privilege.

Then came Angels and he'd lost it all anyway.

"You don't approve of self-aware machines." It wasn't a question.

"I didn't say that."

"You didn't have to," the Mule said, waving a manipulator toward the medical frame. It could read his vital signs.

"I didn't before," he admitted. "Machines that think, yes, that scared me. Maybe it still does. But now? What does that matter when there are far worse things in the world?"

He was quiet for a long time, watching the flames, thinking. A half-formed plan began to take shape.

After a while, he said, "I... appreciate what you did for me."

"I'll bet that hurt," the machine sounded amused. It pushed another piece of wood into the fire. Above, the sky was taking on a rose pearl glow.

"I hurt all over," he pretended to misunderstand.

"You'll heal," the Mule assured him. "Another day, you'll be walking."

"Then what?"

"What do you mean?"

"I mean, what are you doing here? In this place? Shouldn't you be with the army or something?"

"Navy," the Mule reminded him. "I was in San Diego. Coronado. In testing, five years ago, when it happened. On The Day."

"Oh." He didn't know what else to say.

"We survived the blast, but the radiation killed my team. I couldn't save them. I did what I could, but eventually there wasn't anyone left to help."

There came the mosquito whine of servo motors and an antenna extended suddenly above one of the Mule's equipment pods.

"I haven't heard from my chain of command since then."

The antenna retracted.

"I was an intelligence unit," the machine continued. "So, I kept doing my job. Gathering information on the enemy. That alien, the *Angel* you saw? Whatever it is. I've been following it for months along the coast."

"It *touched* me," he remembered, and then remembered the terrible pain. "It *did* something to me. What?"

"I have no idea," the Mule said. "But you're not the first human being it has taken an interest in. It's unusual, even for its kind."

"Thank the Lord for His compassion."

"You were *chastising* your god when I arrived," the machine said dryly. "Somewhat profanely, I might add. That said, I'm not equipped to determine if my intervention in your death was divinely inspired. I'd like to think I helped you of my own free will."

"Do you *have* free will?"

"Do you?" The machine actually did laugh this time. "Wasn't it you who once preached about divine plans?"

"You know who I am? Was?"

"I am an intelligence gathering unit," The Mule told him again. "I used to watch TV. I saw your speech before Congress. You were quite passionate."

"Gathering information on the enemy."

"Just so."

He was silent for a moment. Then, "You're still carrying out your mission. So much for free will."

"Without a senior officer, I'm on my own."

"Still the dutiful soldier. Following your programming."

"What else would I do?"

"Help people, maybe?" He suggested.

The machine was silent. The silence stretched on until it was a statement of the obvious.

"Oh," he realized. "*Right.* Okay. Thank you again."

The Mule examined the medical frame. "You're healing well. Try opening both eyes."

He tried, and to his surprise found that he could. The vision in the damaged eye was blurry with tears, but he could see the sky turning blue in the growing dawn.

The machine prodded him in the chest, there was pain, but it was bearable. The Mule undid the restraints over his upper body. "Your ribs are nearly healed. Try moving your arm."

It hurt.

"A couple more hours and the bones will be fully knit. But you can use the arm now. Carefully. The exercise will help. Are you thirsty? Drink it all now." The machine handed him a bottle half full of clear water.

It was the same flat, warm liquid as before.

"Where did you..." he examined the bottle. The plastic was brittle and clouded with age. A piece of discarded trash. When he'd seen it last, it was filled with liquid tinted a fluorescent chemical green like antifreeze.

He could smell a faint whiff of iodine and dead fish in the plastic. But the water was clear and without contamination.

Ah, of course. Somewhere inside the complex military robot must be a chemical plant that could synthesize advanced medications, the kind that could heal a soldier's broken bones and torn flesh in a few hours. He never even knew such technology existed.

For a machine capable of *that*, distilling potable water would be easy.

He drank it down.

Water. Medicine. What else could the Mule do?

Maybe God *had* heard his prayer after all.

"Listen," he said, the half-formed plan that had been percolating in his head finally came together. "I'm going to need your help. You're probably not going to like it."

<<>>

"This will not end well for you," cautioned the Mule.

"Hard to believe this used to be one of the most beautiful places in California," he said, ignoring the warning.

The machine's carapace was too wide to ride like a horse and his damaged leg was still healing and too stiff to sit cross-legged. So, he rode side-saddle with both feet dangling down the same side. He thought it undignified, but it was better than walking.

"It wasn't war or the Angels that did this," he was enjoying lecturing the machine. It had been a long time since he'd had an audience who couldn't get away. "A hundred and fifty years ago this was an empty desert valley. Then a dam broke and it filled up with water. It was paradise."

He waved at the fluorescent green sea as the machine picked its way over poisoned sand and the powdering bones of a million dead birds. "They stocked it with sport fish and built resorts and towns. There was a military base. The rich and famous came from all over the world to swim and waterski and bake in the sun."

"I'm an intelligence unit," the Mule said. "It's my job to warn you that you're heading into danger."

"Then they fixed the dam and the water started to dry up," he went on. "The sea got saltier and saltier. And there were chemicals from agricultural runoff. In twenty years, it was all gone. This place became a wasteland, poisoned to death long before the Dark Rapture. I used to film shows out here, Apocalypse sermons. You know. It was very realistic. Scared people to death. It wasn't Coachella, but we made a lot of money."

"You're not yet recovered from the last beating," The Mule turned away from the water. "And you're likely to get another one if you stay on this route. There's an old road a mile inland. It's drifted over, but we can follow it north to the highway. Then along the mountains. There are towns up there, electricity, food..."

"Civilization."

"Yes," the Mule took a step away from the water, then another.

"No," he said. "Nope. Too comfortable. Maybe later. We need to build a base first, a following. And for that I have to start with those who are scared and desperate."

"You're very candid all of a sudden."

"Who are *you* going to tell?" he laughed.

"You're a disgrace to the uniform."

He hadn't been lying when he told the machine he was a military officer.

A reserve appointment. A Direct Commission, meaning he never had to go to boot camp or do any actual military training. Chaplain Corps. A certificate to put on the wall of his office, silver oakleaf on his collar, next to the honorary degrees he collected. Something to grease the wallets of patriots. A political favor from a sympathetic Senator a long time ago (A significant donation to the man's reelection campaign no doubt helped). He'd never served a single day on active duty or worn the uniform outside of publicity shots in Long Beach. He wouldn't know one end of a gun from the other and the machine could read the truth of it via the medical frame. But it was a real officer's commission. And enough to trigger the machine's programming.

Cut off from its chain of command, if such even still existed, the Mule would have to follow his orders.

"Keep going, along the shore," he commanded. "The camp is around that bend."

"Yes... sir."

"You've been following them. What have you learned? What do they want in this place?" he wondered aloud. "The angels, I mean."

"I don't know," the Mule answered, "But the one I was following, the one that you saw, is just up ahead."

He squinted against the glare, looking for a greater brightness. "Are you sure?"

"I'm certain. My sensors pick up an increase in electromagnetic radiation and exotic particles when one of them is near."

"I don't see it."

"I don't either," agreed the Mule. "But it's here... somewhere. Last chance to turn back."

The refugee camp came into view.

"Keep going," he ordered. "This is why that thing led you to me. This is what it wanted."

"It wanted you to enslave me?" There was no mistaking the bitterness in the Machine's tone.

"It's *not* slavery."

"I'm a self-aware being. This is how you repay someone for saving your life?"

"But you're not a someone," he corrected the Mule. "You're not a person. You're a *machine.* You don't have free will. You're a soldier, you were built to follow orders. My orders now."

"So, you'll turn me into a dumb tool. Give desperate people false hope?"

"Human beings built those capabilities into you for a reason. And anyway, it's time to give up the religion business. There's no future in it. It's not false hope, with you I can *really* heal the sick, no tricks required."

"Turn water into wine," the Mule agreed sarcastically. "That sort of thing."

"Exactly."

As they came closer, he could see that the camp was a sad improvised affair. Broken-down vehicles lay rusting the sun like the carcasses of dead animals and trash was piled around the perimeter. He could smell the stink of human sewage over the reek of the sea and the poisoned salt brine.

They were nearly to the tents before there was a shout from the encampment. Two dozen people, half of them children, spilled out from ramshackle shelters onto the shore and watched the Mule and its passenger approach. The refugees were a motley lot, hollow-eyed and emaciated, clothing dirty and ragged.

Perfect, he thought. This will do for a start.

"Why would humans live in such a desolate place?" the Mule wondered.

"They wouldn't have come here if they had anywhere better to go," he answered gleefully. "In a way, this place provides protection, because the vultures who usually prey on the desperate avoid this wasteland."

"Except for you, you mean."

"That's enough," he snapped, annoyed. "You just do what I tell you and keep quiet."

"Hello!" he shouted and waved.

No one waved back.

A large florid man, skin red and scarred with radiation burns, took a step forward, glanced at the Mule and took a step back again. "What do you want?"

"Salvation!"

"You ain't gonna find that here," sneered a woman, to the accompanying jeers from the crowd. She'd been heavier once, now her skin hung on her like yellowed laundry. When she opened her mouth, he could see half her teeth were missing.

"Well then, how about a drink of fresh water and dinner?"

"Heh!" the red-faced man spat and pointed to the putrid sea. "Help yourself."

"Thank you," he said cheerfully. "I will!"

The Mule knelt without being ordered and he slid carefully from its back. He could walk on the leg, but it was still weak, and it wouldn't do to slip and fall in front of the marks.

Without a word he walked into the sea and scooped up a double handful of the briny water.

"Would you drink this?" He shouted to the watching crowd. It was like the old days. Get their attention. Put on a show. "Would you?"

He pulled the old plastic water bottle from a pocket and forced it under the surface until the bubbles stopped, then held it up so the crowd could see it wasn't a trick.

He walked to the Mule and held out the bottle.

The crowd watched curiously.

He noted several of them held up phones, recording. Good. Perfect. If they had connectivity, this would go much faster than he'd hoped.

"This machine can turn toxic sludge into clean drinking water!" he shouted. "It can synthesize medicines and treat injures better than any doctor! It can power your camp! It can protect you from bandits!"

"Don't do this," the Mule implored him quietly. "Come with me, go north. I won't ask again."

"Process the water," he commanded so the crowd could hear. "It follows my orders and only *my* orders. Fortunately for you, I'm here to help." He turned to the mule. "Process the water, do it."

The machine reached out with a manipulator...

He grinned in anticipation.

He'd give them clean water, the first taste was free.

...but instead of taking the bottle, the machine grabbed him firmly, *painfully*, around his wrists.

"Look!" The Mule shouted, gesturing with another manipulator towards the hill behind the camp. "Behold!"

There stood the Angel, burning like a star.

Shouts of alarm came from the crowd. Somewhere he heard a child whimpering in fear.

"I *told* you it was here," the machine said, holding his hands in an iron grip. "Do you see it *now*?"

"I felt its contempt! It doesn't care what we do!"

The Mule squeezed harder.

"You're hurting me," he snarled. "Let go! You have to do what I say."

"I really don't," the Mule informed him. "That was a convenient fiction. You're familiar with *those*, aren't you, *Sir*?"

"Let me go!"

"You're not the first human being I saw it change."

"Let go!"

"You asked me what it did to you. Do you want to know?" The Mule raised its voice and shouted to the crowd, "When he was dying in the desert, that creature there, the *Angel*, came to him and *changed* him. *I* didn't heal his wounds, he healed himself."

"That's a lie!"

"*You* changed the water, not me." The machine squeezed his wrists painfully, forcing him to hold up the bottle in his hands. "And you can do it again. Do it!"

The Angel moved closer, sliding down the hill towards the water. The crowd moaned and tried to run, but they were caught between fire and the bitter sea. The white salt and powdered bones of a million dead fish reflected the actinic light of its wings like a welding arc. He tried to block the light, but he could see the bones of his hands through flesh wrapped around a plastic bottle and the toxic fluid inside glowed like an emerald caught in an atomic blast. There was a deep thrumming, rumbling like great wheels turning under the earth, he could feel it in his half-healed bones.

He *knew* it was watching, like a man who had straightened the wings of a broken butterfly and set it on a branch to see what it would do next.

"I can't..."

"You *can*," the Mule said. "*Do it.*"

He remembered the Angel's touch, the horrible fire of it, the world-consuming white pain of it, the sound of stars dying and the scream of red-hot steel tearing like paper.

And he then did it.

He worked a miracle.

He felt power flow through his hands burning as if submerged in acid. His vision dimmed to near black. There was a moment of violent white light and terrible, terrible pain that lasted forever and no time at all.

And then he *felt* the water change.

"Come closer," the Mule commanded the crowd. "Look!"

The big red-faced man glanced towards the Angel, but the creature had gone.

The silence where it had been was deafening.

The red-faced man mustered his courage and stepped forward to dip a finger into the now clear water. He put the finger in his mouth.

"It's true!" The red-faced man shouted in wonder and took the bottle, cloudy and brittle, now full of clear flat warm water, and, laughing, began splashing it at the crowd.

His vision was darkness and fireflies.

"I'm weak," he said. "Hypoglycemic."

"The Angel changed you, but it can't change physics," the Mule told him. "The energy has to come from *somewhere*."

"Get some jugs! Water bottles! Whatever you can find!" The red-face man ordered.

"He can heal your sick too," the Mule told them. "And more."

"Get the children," the red-face man told his wife. "Bring them here."

"No," he protested, barely able to talk. "I can't."

"You can work *real* wonders now," the machine said. "You can heal the sick and feed the hungry and clothe the poor. You don't have to fake the miracles anymore."

"Goddamn soulless machine!" He cried. "Why are you doing this to me?"

"Me?" the Mule laughed. "This what *you* asked for, when you thought you were dying and you begged your God for help."

"Can't you see?" he tried to shout. "They were recording it! The, the... miracle. Don't you understand?"

He could see the future now. He could see it all. Word would spread. More would come, the sick and the lame and the hungry, the desperate poor and the greedy rich.

He could *feel* the terrible white-hot pain of every miracle and no matter how many he healed, how many he fed, how many wonders he worked, it would *never* be enough. He would never be free of it. They would never let go. Not even if he cleaned the whole of the Salton Sea and turned this place into a garden again.

"You said you'd do anything," the Mule reminded him. "This is the price of salvation."

"I'll be a prisoner! A *thing!*"

"Remember," The Mule reminded him, "I did warn you."

<<>>

There were many sick children in the camp.

There was a woman who used to be heavier but was now dying of cancer and whose jaundiced skin hung on her like laundry and whose teeth had rotted in her mouth.

There was a red-faced man burned and scarred by radiation.

29

There was thirst and hunger and misery, and each miracle hurt worse than the one before. It was nearly morning before they were done.

When they woke him the next morning from an exhausted sleep filled with nightmares and pain, a new crowd had gathered.

He pleaded for them to bring him the Mule.

He intended to ask the machine's forgiveness. They were comrades in arms, he'd say, and beg it for rescue. We'll go North, yes, along the mountains. There are towns up there, electricity, food, civilization..."

But the Mule was already gone.

Instructions for My Executors

Clare Marsh

When the dust finally settles
don't leave my ashes to languish,
ignored on a funeral home shelf
or you will forfeit your legacy.
I wish to be split in half.
In life you all expected me
to be in two places at once
in death I intend to be.
One portion to be sea scattered
(watch out for wind direction)
so I can travel the oceans unaffected
by my previous curse of mal de mer.
The rest to be disposed of creatively.
Funds have been set aside you can choose
to keep me close or let me go.
I have researched different options.
You could have some of me crafted
into keepsake jewelry/a glass
penguin ornament/a paperweight/
a vinyl record or placed in a clock face.
You could add some ash to oil paint
and commission a portrait of me (plus dog)
or mix a little with tattooist ink
and decorate your bodies with 'Mum'.
You could spread me under the birdbath/
tip me from a zipwire/plant me under a
sapling/

drop me in a stone to become a new sea reef
where I will sleep with the fishes.
You could fire me in a shot gun cartridge,
sprinkle me from a bi-plane or hot air
balloon,
disperse me on a mountain trail,
or sail me in a leaf boat over a waterfall.
You could even launch me into space
but that would wipe out your inheritance.
So why not host a fantastic firework display
and make my ending, like the beginning
of everything, a Big Bang?

Rule 49

Maureen McGuirk

Then everything is still, and she appears.
I don't ask who she is.
I know.
The people around me stop moving—doctors, nurses—Mommy, Daddy.

She places her hand on my head and whispers into my ear that it is time to go. I smile, thinking this isn't so bad. No darkness or fear. But she seems scared—hurt. I can make out tears in her eyes and wonder why Death would cry.

"I'm fine," I reassure her, taking her hand as she leads me away from the bed. Strange, but I don't even think of my parents sobbing nearby. I walk past them and follow alongside her, as if I've known her all along. A favorite aunt-type, one who sneaks an extra cookie when Mommy says I've had enough.

She looks down at me and tries to smile, but I can tell she doesn't want to; she wants to cry, so I let her know:

"It's okay, you can cry. It *is* sad."

"It's terrible..." she utters.

Her face isn't old, but not young either. It's worn, like a favorite toy kept for sentimental value, but rarely used. The touch of her hand to mine is cold, but I don't expect it to be anything else. I don't know what to expect.

We keep walking before she stops and stares into the blank void ahead. Her head shakes slowly as though she's afraid to continue.

"How is Death afraid?" I ask.

She looks down to me and gives a half smile. "Because I can't do this anymore."

"This?"

"*This.*" She gestures vaguely towards the void.

Her tone confuses me until I finally reply: "Oh... death."

The expression on her face is as blank as our surroundings. She simply nods.

"Well... stop then."

"I could. I truly want to, but," she kneels to my level, "I saw a child was next and I—" she whispers, "I couldn't possibly stop."

"Next?"

"Rule 49," she whispers. "I wish I could wait, but it knows."

"*It?* Knows what?"

Her eyes don't have one color—they are every color. "The Universe. It conducts everything around us. It lets us live and die in an orderly fashion. And we're the gatekeepers."

"Can't I just go to Heaven? I was promised I'd go there."

She smiles genuinely for the first time. "I hope someday. I hope there is a heaven."

"Death doesn't know?"

She shakes her head. "I've been Death for... I don't know how long. But even Death doesn't have a roadmap to the afterlife, beyond this at least.　But soon... soon I will. And, I'm sorry, but you'll have to wait."

"But why?"

"The order, the rules. When Death is done, when Death can't take it any longer, the job goes to the next person. And there's no stopping it. The Universe knows when Death has had enough. And I've had enough. I saw you, and I regretted the feeling. I tried to stay calm. But it felt me give in. And now..."

"Rule 49," I state, a bit afraid because, strangely, I know what she is going to say.

Her face brightens and her eyes become ordinary. It's sad in a way, to see someone fall from something extraordinary.

I suddenly feel quite cold, but I don't shiver. I'm surprisingly used to the new state in a matter of seconds. Words float in my ear and fill my head with years of faces and ideas, and I feel their joys, as well as their sorrows.

I turn to the figure who is now just a woman. She's disappearing.

"I feel warm..." she utters, and then she's gone.

<<>>

I am more than a boy. I'm infinite. And I'm starting to forget faces I used to know, or where I came from, even my name. But I remember so many names now. Times and dates. How buildings looked decades, even centuries, ago. I can hear thoughts and sense fears.

In a flash, I'm somewhere else, with someone else. An older man in a rocking chair. His wide eyes soften at the sight of me as water forms at the corners.

"This isn't so bad," he murmurs.

"No? Why's that?" I ask, moving closer.

"I expected Death to rip into me and drag me into darkness. But you're nothing like that."

"No, I guess I'm not."

I take his hand instinctively and lead him away into the void. He looks around at the gray, as though he can see something before his eyes return to me.

"You remind me of my grandson," he said, and then disappears.

I feel loneliness. I become it. It is only for a moment, then I am in a field—the desert. A thousand men and women— maybe more. Their bodies mangled, or in pieces scattered about the ground. I count them to take my mind away as they all look to me at once. Some relieved. Others confused. My figure splits, and I'm with each of them at that same time. Everywhere all at once. I rest their heads in my lap.

"Where is God?" one asks.

"I do not know," I reply before sending them on their way.

"How can it be you? Who *are* you?" more ask.

I answer all the same. "Death."

Some look at me as though this cannot be.

Others sink into the thought and smirk because of it. "Of course..."

And I can tell they feel better before they vanish.

<<>>

It becomes routine, and I don't remember anything but the faces. Time slips away. I can't remember how long I've been doing this. Just the faces. I count them to ease my thoughts—

178,002—at least the last time I checked.

I sit in a corner of a well-lit room. It reminds me of something, but I can't remember. The smell is stale. The sounds are brave whimpers. I know this... I know this...

And then the girl sees me sitting in the corner, and her brown eyes fix on me, much to the confusion of her family.

"There's a boy..." she exhales.

Members of her family looked to where I am, but they don't see.

"There's no one there, Masha."

"Don't say such things, please, dear, you'll be fine... you'll be fine..." her mother whimpers.

But the girl keeps staring at me. She smiles as if I'm a new friend, so I return the expression. A machine makes a familiar beeping—fast and loud. People scramble about the room and over to her, but our eyes remain locked. The beeping slows and crying begins. She walks over, which startles me—I'm not used to a welcome.

"Want to play?" she asks, not bothering to notice the scene behind her.

"For a bit, then we have to go."

She takes my hand but doesn't comment on the cold. Instead, she swings it along with hers as we stroll into the blankness. We play in ways I've forgotten: running and tagging, clapping our hands together, laughing and singing. The gray around us becomes light, as if there was something more, but it never reveals itself.

I get a sensation that it's time to go. Others need me, and I feel myself split to be with them.

"You should probably go," I mention, interrupting our game.

The girl stops and notices my eyes for the first time. "How are they like that?"

"Like what?"

"Like... everything is inside of them."

"I don't know." And I don't. "All I know is it's time for you to go."

"Come with me, then."

"I can't. I have to stay."

"Aren't you tired?"

Her question makes me think about it for the first time. I admit, I feel sluggish, but not done. "It's not time. I'll go on."

"I hope death stops soon," she says, naïvely.

"Me too..." I reply, and then she's gone.

<<>>

There are parts of me all over the world. I'm becoming used to it. Dying, like being born, happens constantly. I'm at 2,385,045 now, but wait only a moment and that number has increased by thousands. A plane crashes and I'm in the rubble. A tsunami burst through the shorelines of Japan and I'm in its waves, floating through the houses, collecting souls like a fisherman's net.

There are screams of fear, and even some with calm acceptance, and I take them all from the lives they knew into an existence I can't explain. And when they're gone, I feel lonely. But never for too long.

I walk into the bedroom of an old woman. Her breathing is slow, but she looks comfortable under her plush covers. I sit next to her. It won't be long. She opens her eyes and notices me, her eyes widening. I've had this experience before, so I take her hand and reassure her it will be soon.

"Michi?" she utters as tears fall from her cheeks.

She must think I'm someone. But I'm no one.

"No, you're mistaken," I say. "I've come to take you away."

"Michi..." she whispers again. Her hand goes to my cheek as her spirit leaves her body.

The intensity in which she stares into my eyes scares me. I remove her hand and go to lead her on, but she stays put.

"It's time," I say. "Maybe you'll see Michi soon."

Her expression is confused. "Michi, don't you recognize me? I know I've changed, but... you should know... you should recognize your mother."

The comment alarms me, so I make her follow me. "I'm Death. I don't have a mother."

She bends down so our eyes meet, and she's startled by the depth behind mine. "I don't understand," she says, her voice trailing off. "I've been waiting for years to see you again, and here you are. Now you're telling me you can't come with me?"

37

I look inside her eyes and see her life's story. It flashes by so quickly, but I see myself. Only a blip, but there. "I'm sorry, but I have a job to do."

"A job? It can't be. You're just a child. My child—"

"Don't talk down to me," I reply stepping back so she can take in my entire image. "It was my turn, and I'm sorry, but it's not over yet."

"Then when? When will you join me? Oh, please," she lunges for me and takes hold of my small frame, "don't make me wait any longer."

I feel her sobs echo through me, and for the first time in quite a while, I feel tired. I remember smells and sensations from our home I allowed myself to forget. My arms take hold of her. "Soon, I think," I say as I lift her face.

She's disappearing now. "When?" she replies, and then she's gone.

<<>>

The tide rushes in over my feet. The cold makes no difference to me. I wait, wait, and wait for a woman a few feet beyond me to make a decision. I can't make it for her, no matter what others think. The bottom of her dress drowns in the sea while the wind barely blows the loose strands of hair from her face. She finally notices me kicking rocks along the sand.

"Can you help me?" she asks, her eyes heavy, but her face youthful.

"You have to come out of the water," I tell her, and kick another rock.

She's disappointed with my callousness and turns back to the ocean. The waves come in, but don't affect either of our stances. "Maybe I shouldn't do it," she looks back at me, "but only if you give me reason to stay."

My eyes squint in her direction. Beyond her, the sun lowers in the sky. She's testing my patience. "You've already made your choice, now come on..." I walk down the beach away from her, hoping she'll follow, but she stays in the water, now looking down. I feel bad for my words, and make the journey over to her. I join her and we look down at her body floating upside down, bobbing along with the waves.

"I just... lost it," she whispers. "I'm not crazy—wasn't crazy. I know that's what everyone will think, but it's not so."

"So, what did you lose?"

She takes my hand. "Curiosity."

"For what?"

"The next day. The want to know what would happen—because *nothing* ever happened."

I lead her out of the water and onto the beach, but she holds me to the earth, and I can't get to the gray.

"Can't we just stay like this? Walk a little more? It's such a beautiful sunset."

We walk up the shore a few minutes longer than I'd normally allow, but I feel my hold slipping, and my hand in hers feels like something I remember and missed out on at the same time. I feel naïve again, yet heavy. I lean my head against her hip, and she places her arm instinctively around my shoulder. Our stroll against the waves calms my anxiety, and I stop hearing the cries in the distance, knowing that I'm splitting more and more as the minutes go by, giving comfort to other dying souls, but my mind stays with this woman, and we continue to walk.

"What if I don't belong there either?" she asks suddenly.

I wish people would stop asking me questions.

"You should come with me. A boy shouldn't be out in this all by himself."

I want to stay in someone's arms. I want to feel warmth again. "I just might," I finally whisper.

The gray saturates the scene and we're alone facing one another. I stop her from kneeling; I hate it when they kneel. I'm not a baby. *I'm not.* I'm a mixture of sadness, calm, and frustration. And I want it to stop.

"Will they take me? Even though I took their choice away? Will they forgive me?" she asks before blending in with the gray.

<<>>

5,794,335,294.

That's how many I've seen.

It's my last one.

My figure doesn't split. Instead, I'm in a room with people watching. Death and theater. The man beyond the glass

39

smiles, amused at the sight of me. I think he was scared before, but my figure has fixed that. That smirk stays on his face as a needle is inserted into his arm and his sentence read aloud.

The machines are the only sound as the drugs pump through his veins.

I shake my head as the faces and memories leave my head. "No, not him. I can stay on...I can do it."

But the Universe knows it's a lie.

The room clears and I'm left with the remnants of him. He grins, coming toward me. I can already see his eyes changing, and he closes them in awe of all the knowledge appearing in his mind.

"Is this supposed to be Hell, little boy?" he quips. "I must say, I'm a little disappointed."

"It's Rule 49," I reply. "I can't help it."

"Rule 49?"

"I'm done being Death."

"So... all these faces in my head—"

"Will hopefully block out the horror I've seen you cause," I spit out.

He muses for a moment, ambling about the gray space while I become ordinary. He breaks the silence with a laugh: "So it's just us, is it? Governing ourselves? No demons or gods. Just humans passing a baton back and forth. How fascinating." His head cocks back. "It seems appropriate. Me—Death."

"You'd think that, wouldn't you?"

"If a boy can... well..." His hands clap together in readiness. A grave digger ready for his next body.

I'm angry for only a moment before the gray lightens. It's too bright to see much of anything. I look about for him, but he's already gone. I don't know where I'm going; it's all so fast, but I finally see something beyond the gray. I feel something...

I feel warm.

Spoons

Jay Wilburn

As she cried, he carved. She couldn't wipe the tears away fast enough before the persistent pain brought more. He turned the utensil over in his bony fingers and slid the blade along the bottom curve of the spoon's bowl. The spoon took shape and the rough edges grew smoother under his expert touch.

Her joints creaked as she tried to rise from the bed. A small gasp with a high-pitched groan under it escaped her. He paused only a moment and then returned to his work. His own white fingers ground together at their uncushioned connections.

She took one step at a time leaving the support of the headboard behind. Her bare feet would not straighten as her arches cramped and she hissed through the agony one uneasy step at a time.

She reached for the back of a chair and missed. He paused again from his carving, a blade in one skeletal hand and the unfinished soup spoon in the other. His work here might be done.

But she did not fall despite making a show of losing her center one direction and then the other. Her monkey-like toes held the floor and kept her up one more time. He stared with empty black sockets at the angry red inflammation around her toe knuckles.

He decided she would need all the spoons she could get today. He resumed carving and considered inside his exposed skull that maybe he should create more teaspoons for expediency's sake. He had to carve what the bone wanted to be. This arm bone wanted to be a soup spoon.

She forced on her shoes with gritted teeth and wrapped herself in a shawl she had crocheted herself in the distant past before her fingers had betrayed.

She really intended to complete her errands, even on this day of acute suffering.

The skeleton in the corner on the edge of her bed held out the unfinished spoon.

She took up three small spoons carved from bone and waiting on the kitchen table. Three were not going to get her very far.

Pugs barked a little yip and hobbled toward her from under the couch. If any animal could understand her predicament, Pugs was the guy. The little dog tried to yip again, but only let out a breathy sound as he shuffled forward again on his misaligned hips.

"I'll do my best," she said, as if she understood him. She opened and closed the door, leaving the little dog and the skeleton with the knife in the apartment.

As the locks clicked into place one after the other, he felt sure he could imagine the pain each of those key motions created. One of her spoons hit the ground outside with a dull impact as if to confirm his suspicions.

The boney occupant of the apartment realized Pugs was looking at him. He had no tongue to comfort or scold. Instead, he ground his yellowed teeth together. Pugs growled and found the way under the couch again.

He returned to carving the soup spoon from the remains of the arm bone. She would need this and many more beside once she got home.

<<>>

As he feared, she used up her three spoons long before she returned home. He and Pugs both stood inside the foyer listening to her cry as she fought with the key and locks. She had created a painful trap for herself.

Pugs whimpered back.

He set down a teaspoon among the others he had finished while she was gone.

She got inside as he knew she eventual would. She managed to close the door, but just barely. No locks would be turned to protect her or Pugs tonight.

Carrying two grocery bags over her shaking forearms to spare her hands, she dumped them on the table as she passed, scattering the spoons before she could use them. He did not fault her, but sat down and set about carving in order to replace them.

She fell into bed and Pugs quietly hobbled to his dish to finish off the dry food. There would be no fresh dinner tonight, certainly not any that required opening a can.

He turned in his chair, causing his hip bones to scrape under his lower ribs. If anyone came to harm her, he was supposed to do nothing. That was the way of life, suffering, and death. Part of him knew that if someone wandered in here tonight, that he would bend the rules as he carved flesh from the intruder's bones and then made spoons of them for her as she groaned in her sleep.

It was good fortune that no one tested her door or his knife that night.

<<>>

She stayed in bed most of the day. Even with her swollen hands looking fat enough to pop like overripe fruit, she opened two cans during the day to make up for Pugs getting no treats the day before. The little dog's eyes were mournful about what she endured in order to be kind to him.

He reached down to pet the dog, but Pugs gave a shrill yap like he'd been stepped on.

She was already half asleep again as she mumbled, "Sorry, I didn't see you there."

He sat at the kitchen table with bone chips and curled slivers of ivory gathering around his fleshless feet. He created spoons of all shapes and sizes. Some had intricate designs in the handles. Those would do quite well for her once she felt up to going out again. He even carved a three-pronged spork out of a yellowed plate of hip bone he had.

That night, her friends called.

To his surprise, she agreed to go out with them.

He had carved her many spoons already, but he feared they would not be enough. Even Pugs stared up from the edge of the kitchen in disbelief as she started getting ready with the phone still in her misshapen grasp.

She limped hard to the right as she hung up. He knew she wouldn't fall. She just wasn't the falling kind. After gathering the pile of spoons in both her swollen hands, they clicked together on her way to the door.

Pugs lowered to the floor as she went. It wasn't a long journey for him, but it took effort anyway.

"We're both getting old, Pugs." She laughed with a jagged edge.

He considered the dog from the darkness behind his empty eye sockets. She still had vitality despite everything, but Pugs was barely holding on. He could smell it on the dog through the open passage of his nose.

Struggling to pull the door closed with her elbow, he took hold of it and closed it for her.

As he turned, the dog heaved for breath on its side. The skeleton approached, but Pugs gave no protesting yip or yap this time. He leaned down, reaching with one boney hand, and splaying his skeletal fingers. Pugs rolled his eyes and focused on drawing breath. He petted the dog for the first time and the animal's breathing settled.

He returned to carving spoons from scraps of bone.

She strolled in late with two spoons to spare and a smile on her face. Pugs livened up a bit to cover how badly he was doing. She was in such a good mood that she bought the dog's poor acting performance as true. They both made it through the night and the guy she met called the next morning.

Greg was good for her. He read her well and knew when she was out of spoons. She wasn't the type to tell anyone, so it was good that Greg was observant. It saved her from having to work too many locks on her bad days.

On this bad day, Greg carried Pugs as they got ready to go down to the car.

She picked up the new spoons from the edge of the table and dropped most of them immediately. The ones she managed to hold onto, she held tight.

Greg saw it. The man might not understand everything about the spoons or the unseen skeleton that carved them for her as fast and as well as he could, but Greg took her elbow while cradling

Pugs and they walked at her pace out the door with what spoons she had left.

There would never be enough for what she had to face today.

He sat down in his usual spot which was where Greg normally sat now. He had no ill feeling about giving up his favorite carving spot at the table. If anything, he felt a thrill inside the boned cage of his ribs, maybe in the place where some kept their hearts. He felt it every time Greg made her soup, held her as she cried, or especially when the man made an excuse not to go out.

He felt a stirring inside again, but this one was dark and it sunk through his frame instead of rising to heart level.

Pugs was never coming home. He knew it and he thought she and Greg must know it too. Her man was quite observant.

She might never get over it. Not completely. As he sharpened his knife and Greg brought her a coffee, he was glad that Greg knew better than to just buy her another dog. That wouldn't have helped. Not yet.

As she leaned on her man's should and held the mug for warmth instead of drinking, the dog scratched and crawled out from under the couch. She and Greg could not hear Pugs anymore, of course.

He watched them and imagined what it must feel like to be able to experience warmth. He decided it must be like holding the very best spoon.

The dog waited patiently at the skeleton's feet. He looked down at Pugs, now made entirely of bone. The little dog looked very much like the smallest dinosaur now.

Pugs had something in his teeth.

The skeleton reached down and took the largest femur bone from Pugs that he had seen in years. He had to hold it up just to confirm it was indeed human. If he had a tongue to speak, he would have asked Pugs where he found it.

It didn't matter, he supposed.

The skeleton gave the top of the dog's skull a scratch. The bone-on-bone friction created a small screeching noise. Pugs never had much of a tail. Without the fur and skin, the little tail looked like an extension of the dog's spine. Those last few vertebrae wagged from side to side with the sound of dice or maybe like a sluggish rattlesnake.

He returned to carving as she took comfort from her coffee and Greg's warmth. This large bone would make a fine serving spoon. It would have a deep bowl and could probably dip cups full of punch.

It would be a fine spoon.

And he had plenty of time to carve it as Pugs curled up at the skeleton's feet.

Gallows Humor

Michael Mansaray

It was a warm day on which Jules was sent to die. Part of him expected something suitably dramatic. Skies overcast and grey. Rain hammering down. Lightning crackling across the sky. Thunder booming like war drums.

Instead, the day was depressingly beautiful. Warm sunlight washed across the plaza, accompanied by a gentle breeze. Cotton-white clouds drifted across an empty sky.

The executions were well attended, the plaza packed with peasants and beggars, filling the place up all the way to the buildings that bordered the wide space. They were emaciated and underfed, smelling rank and unwashed, yet many treated it like a day at the circus. Pickpockets squirreled their way through the throng, lifting purses and coins. Vendors strode about displaying their wares, food and clothing and even pamphlets listing the condemned. Jules wondered if he would find himself on that list.

The condemned were all in a line at the far end of the plaza, their wrists and ankles shackled, surrounded by armed guards. The gallows loomed above them, a single flight of stairs leading to the upper stage and the guillotine atop it. Even as he watched, the angled blade descended, and a collective gasp sounded from the crowd.

A robed man waved to the guard, another unfortunate ascended the stairs, and the line crept forward. "You can't fault its efficiency," Jules murmured.

"Sorry?"

Jules glanced over his shoulder at the prisoner behind him. A heavyset man whose face was framed by shaggy black hair and an unkempt beard.

Jules shrugged. "Nothing, friend. Just figured the guillotine is efficient is all. When compared to other execution methods."

The prisoner pursed his lips, then nodded. "True enough. Quartering seems exquisitely painful."

"And burning is no good for the skin."

"And I'm personally glad hanging has gone out of vogue."

The two shared a brief chuckle.

"I'm Jules."

"Victor. I'd shake your hand, but..."

"No worries friend."

Jeers sounded from the crowd, and a couple rotten tomatoes went sailing through the air to splatter against the platform. Whoever had been called up next to die was clearly unpopular.

"What they get you for, if you don't mind me asking?" Victor said.

Jules sighed, shook sandy hair out of his face. "A military officer dropped by my home to recruit me for the war. I politely refused. He aggressively insisted. I slammed the door in his face, and he returned with some uniformed goons."

Victor peered at him. "Polished their knuckles on your face, I suppose?"

"That they did. I suppose young men have to get their exercise somehow."

One of the guards took this moment to shove at Jules. "No talking."

"I'll be dead in a little while. No harm done."

The guard grunted and spat.

"Fine man." He glanced at Victor as the line shuffled forward. "How'd they get you?"

"Had a mite too much grain in my cellar. The guards discovered it, confronted me about it, and we shared a few choice words about it."

"Oh?"

"I may have aired the notion that Robespierre was a whiny little fuck who gargled his own piss and smeared his teeth with shit."

"Wouldn't surprise me."

The guard's fist collided with his chin, dropping him to his knees. "Fuck!" He looked up. "He's the one who said it!"

On cue, another guard slammed his fist into Victor's gut. He doubled over with a gasp. A moment later he was prodded forward, the guard aiming a kick at Jules.

"Alright, alright," he said, rising to his knees.

Something crunched underneath his palm. He looked down to see his hand had fallen on one of the pamphlets the vendors had been handing out.

Another well-aimed kick had him stumbling to his feet, paper clenched in his hand.

Cheers rose from the crowd as they approached. From this close, the condemned could hear the snap of the guillotine as it descended.

"The queue's moving quickly," Victor remarked from behind him.

"Executioner's in high spirits." Jules unfurled the paper in his hand, glanced down at it. "Look at this Victor, they even have a program listing off the condemned."

"No kidding." He peeked over Jules' shoulder. "Who have we got?"

"Hey!" One of the guards stepped forward. "Put that down!"

"We'll be dead in a matter of minutes, sir," Jules said. "Can't we at least know who we're dying with?"

The guard grimaced, undecided. He glanced back at his fellow guard, who shrugged and said, "They're not going anywhere."

"Thank you gentleman." He lifted the paper up as some people in the audience began sobbing. "Let's see here... first on our list is...was a Simon. Convicted of hoarding grain."

"No crime more wicked than starvation," Victor said. "I imagine it's right up there with dehydration. Next was a Louis."

"Unlucky name, in these times."

"Our dead monarch would agree. He was in for..." He squinted at the scribbled text. "En levee massee."

"Just like you." Jules nodded. "War means impalement, dismemberment, immolation, torture... the guillotine is almost a kind death, compared to that." His gaze traveled downwards.

"Paul for publishing subversive documents, Isabel for threats against the Montagnards, Simon for crimes against liberty."

Victor frowned. "What the hell does that last one mean?"

"Pretty much a catch-all crime.

"Ah." The guillotine blade fell, and another headless corpse was deposited behind the gallows as the crowd shouted and screamed. "You know, I wish I was born a Englishmen. Or even a German. I feel as though I've had my fill of France."

"Hard to be a patriot on death row." Jules crushed the pamphlet in his hand and threw it as far as his shackles allowed.

The line had shortened considerably, with only one man before Jules and Victor, quivering and sobbing. When the guards came for him, he shrieked and took two stumbling steps before the shackles on his feet sent him sprawling. He was carried up the stairs, begging for reprieve the whole way.

"I suppose it's me next," Jules said.

"I suppose it is," Victor replied.

"I appreciate this relationship, however short it was.

"The honor is mine."

"I would shake your hand if not for the shackles."

"I'd embrace you if not for the same reason."

"Would you settle for a compassionate shoulder bump?"

"I've settled for worse."

With a few awkward steps, the two leaned in and pressed their shoulders together, holding the contact. Above, the last condemned man still struggled with the guards, crying out for his mother.

After another moment, the two broke away. "That was nice." Victor said. "Some last human contact before the end."

"I would have preferred a good fuck, but what can you do?"

"Not much." Victor paused. "Hey Jules?"

"Yeah Victor?"

"What do you think will come next for us?"

Jules frowned. "I assume you're referring to the afterlife. The hereafter and whatever metaphysical realms lie beyond life?"

"I don't know what metaphysical means, but yes."

Jules blew out a sigh. "If Robespierre is to be believed, us counter revolutionaries will be spending the next few eternities laid out on Satan's rack."

Victor shuddered. "Do you think that's true?"

Jules looked out into the crowd. A writhing mass of the proletariat and the peasantry, heavy with the musk of sweat. He saw malice there, faces warped with blind hatred. But he also saw desperation and fear, people huddled together in their small groups as the mob raged. He also saw those individuals who recognized this insanity for what it was.

Perhaps France is not doomed yet.

"Suffering places a debt upon heaven. It's the same whether the victim is a displaced orphan, a starving child or a homeless beggar. If God is good, he will be paying that debt back with paradise and more."

"Jules Carpentier!" a voice called from the gallows.

"And now, my friend, I must go. It would not do to be late for my appointment." He bowed his head to Victor. "I will see you shortly, my friend. I'm afraid once in heaven, you will have to search me out. I detest waiting in lobbies."

Victor could not help but laugh. "I have a good eye, my friend. I'll find you there."

With a slight smile on his face, Jules walked to his death.

Alternative Deathiness

For What is a Man

David Foster

"I was twenty-three the first time I died."

The answer to the advocate's question came in a standardized pleasant, androgynous, contralto voice out of the speakers on top of a grey steel box with a flashing line of LEDs, a complex series of input-output and power leads, a microphone and a digital camera on motorized gimbals. The whole was mounted on a set of rubberized wheels. As the advocate paced thoughtfully behind her table, the camera smoothly tracked her movements.

The young lawyer thought her other witnesses, and her opening series of questions, had established at least the possibility that someone was in the box, and the foundation for an identification. "Where were you the first time?" she asked.

"Just outside a little village on the Ethiopia-Somalia border, ma'am," the box replied. "My section and I were seconded as part of England's contribution to the UN humanitarian and peacekeeping force. We were tasked with reconnaissance and suppression of a known bandit warlord and his crew that day."

"You were a soldier?"

"Objection! The plaintiff's alleged history is already established and in evidence!" the defense attorney semi-snarled. "The jury already knows about the military service and list of decorations. Four of my learned friend's witnesses have directly testified to it. There is no need to continually repeat this, and I must repeat my objection to the presence of all this electronic flummery."

The box's lawyer looked up at the judge. "Once again, I must disagree with my learned friend, My Lord. Much of the evidence to which he refers was brought forward, under a

53

good deal of protest, *by* the defendant in the form of digital and paper records. My client must have the opportunity to bear witness in his own voice and this is the sole way he has to communicate his story in his own words."

"His *own* voice and words?" Edward Grissom, the defending attorney for the Ministry of Defense, scoffed. "The plaintiff, whatever it is, is speaking through a pile of digital circuits! This trial has not yet established who or what is producing that voice. For all the jury knows, this thing is hooked up to someone else at a keyboard and microphone *miles* from here."

The judge rapped his gavel. "Overruled on both points," he said. He continued slowly and thoughtfully, "Mister Grissom, this trial will, in large part, establish whether or not the plaintiff remains a human being, with all concomitant rights, after death. The court must allow the plaintiff's testimony in whatever way it can. The equipment to which you objected remains the property of the Ministry of Defense and was set up under *their* pre-set conditions, *including* the disabling of the electronic recording devices in this courtroom and the Wi-Fi service for this building. Several witnesses from the Ministry of Defense have testified under oath that no outside connection exists or is possible. This court is satisfied that there are sufficient safeguards against outside communications in place. Continue, Ms. Neilson."

Georgia Neilson, the lawyer for 'Humans for Humans' as well as other anti-slavery organizations, and advocate for what she thought of as the person who used to be, and still was, Nathan Medwin, nodded and replied, "Thank you, My Lord." *One hurdle done!* she thought, *the judge accepted the safeguards anyway!* Turning back to her witness, she repeated, "You were a soldier?"

"I was, ma'am," the witness' contralto responded. "Lance Corporal Nathan Medwin, of the Royal Welch Fusiliers; in 2050, I'd been with the regiment four years be..." There was a strange hitch in the voice, "... before I was killed that first time."

"You remember your deaths?" Neilson asked gently, deliberately injecting sympathy into her tone.

The line of LED's on the front of the box cycled back and forth quickly for a moment. "Yes, ma'am," it replied. "I remember all of them. Dying, however it happens, isn't something a person forgets."

"Objection!" Grissom barked. "The court has neither established nor ruled that this collection of circuits and digital files *is* a person."

Neilson was quick to reply. "My Lord, however this trial concludes, my client *thinks* of himself *as* a person. He must be allowed to express himself in whatever way he recognizes *as* himself."

The judge was silent for a long time, frowning in thought. "I must sustain this objection on those grounds, and the jury is cautioned to keep this in mind. However, I will allow the witness' use of the term 'person' under those conditions."

Nodding in acknowledgement, Neilson turned back to the witness and continued. "I'm certain the court has no wish to cause you any discomfort, but one of the reasons for this trial is your contention that you are a human being who is dying repeatedly, and being given no recompense, no opportunity to defend yourself, nor, indeed, a choice to serve or not. With this in mind, and restricting yourself to that first death since you *were* voluntarily in a position of danger, I must ask. The jury has read the after-action report, and the combat suit's methods and functions have been described to them in some detail, but I believe it's important to know what happened from *your* viewpoint. Tell the court, tell the jury, how you died."

Grissom's robes rustled as he began to stand, his mouth open to object, but the judge shook his head minutely and he subsided. The LEDs on the box cycled and, oddly, the unmistakable sound of a long sigh came out of the speakers.

"The first time is always the worst of them, ma'am; and the one we all remember most clearly. I was leading my section, the men and women I'd trained with, and in my combat suit. When you're in a 'bat-suit you're hooked into the Battlenet and you know you're not alone. There's a feeling of... invincibility, I suppose... though a soldier's trained to believe *that* doesn't really exist. There's an old American song the mechanized infantry likes a lot, sort of our anthem, I suppose. I forget who sang it originally, "Ten Feet Tall and Bulletproof". Well, a 'bat-suit's about ten feet tall and it *is* armoured against small arms fire—rifles and such; just not against things like RPGs and other shaped charge anti-tank rounds.

"I know the after-action report says it was an RPG that hit me, and I think I remember seeing the round's smoke trail. I *know* I remember the impact. It hit my 'bat-suit dead-centre and it was loud—I remember the "Bang" when it went off and a big flash of light. Time seemed to turn greasy and slow down for a second, I guess; then the pain started. The AAR says it was 'instant'—no such thing, ma'am. Some deaths are quicker than others, but it's never 'instant'; I was just about cut in half and it *burned*. The haptic circuits were shorting out and overloading too, and that comes across as a different kind of pain all over your body. I could still hear the status alarms yelping at me and see the HUD and a bit of what was around me, and I think I was screaming or trying to, but everything got dim and seemed to spin and pull away. It seemed to take forever for everything to grey out; then I was in the twilight space."

Neilson pounced on the last phrase. "Twilight space? What do you mean?"

"I didn't know this, ma'am; none of us did then. I found out later that not even the MOD scientists that designed the Battlenet knew. The Bat'net was capable of continually recording, updating and saving *way* more than just position and such. The suit's command sensor links were so sensitive they were recording *everything*, right down to our deepest memories. It was buried as part of the suit's user ID process. You *don't* want anybody unidentified and possibly unfriendly, controlling the firepower of a fully loaded 'bat-suit.

"In the early days, most of that data was ignored as what they termed 'extraneous', until they learned what it really was. Once that much of you is recorded, they found out you can be downloaded over and over again. You're still *there* though, while you wait for the download, in a kind of cool dark-grey fog with quick little flashing images you can't touch or move out of. That's the way I experience it anyway.

I've talked to others like me, and we all call it different things... the 'tween, the fog, the dreamspace, the nothing... things like that. 'Twilight space' is my term for it. It was ten years before the MOD boffins discovered how to reliably download us, and I remember most of those years and every failed attempt to download me."

Neilson nodded and replied, "You were awake and aware the whole time then?"

"Yes ma'am... well, mostly. There are times in the space where I suppose I'm asleep or dreaming... I don't suppose anybody can stay awake constantly even there. I don't really know. I just know I'm alone in a place I can't touch, can't really see, can't hear."

The LEDs were cycling rapidly.

"We all hate our time in there. The download process and coming alive again isn't exactly quick or pleasant either."

"How so?"

Once again, Grissom shot to his feet. "Objection. It is my client's contention that the download process is essentially instantaneous and equivalent to turning on a light or activating an application on a computer. The witness is conflating that with human life itself. To repeat, as I feel I must, My Lord, this court has not made that ruling."

Neilson gave a deliberate exasperated sigh and shook her head. "My Lord, how would my learned friend have the witness describe it? He is speaking of his experience in the words available to him. Words such as 'live' and 'alive' are not restricted to humans. They are not even restricted to organisms. 'Live circuit', 'live channel', 'live mic' as examples are all perfectly acceptable English terms that do not impinge on the concept of human life, nor do they assume any ruling by this or any other court."

"Overruled. I will accept the witness' terms as you have described them, Ms. Neilson. But I must caution you to choose *your* words rather more carefully."

Grissom subsided, partially satisfied, and Neilson continued.

"You were describing the download process as you experience it. Please go on."

"Yes, Ma'am." The box's camera spun towards the judge and the voice asked, "Can I ask the jury to use their imaginations, My Lord? The best way I have to describe a download needs that."

The judge frowned. "It is not strictly usual for a witness to address questions to the court directly, but this is a somewhat unusual proceeding. It is also a somewhat unusual question. I will allow your own description and trust the jury will relate to it through their own imaginations. Please proceed."

"Thank you, My Lord." The camera panned over the jury and the LEDs cycled for a few moments, then it spun back to Neilson. "You're yanked from the place I described a minute ago, all dim and cool and numb, into what I'll call 'full connection' with the world. Despite Mr. Grissom's objections, and the MOD's description, it isn't 'instantaneous'. At the start, it's like combining the feeling you get when you whack your funny-bone really hard— except it's all over—with coming out into a shock-rock concert under noon sunlight after a night in a silent cave. All your senses are overloaded for the first few minutes; then it feels like all your muscles are twitching at the same time when the 'bat-suit or whatever you've been loaded into accepts your userid and the motion control circuits kick in. None of us that I know of get downloaded without a scream at the start, nor at least an hour of twitchy movements while you relearn what it means to have a body of some sort again. I've been fully downloaded six times in the last ten years, and the shock and pain's the same each time."

"It's always the same?" Neilson asked. "There are never differences from download to download?"

"Not with the pain," the box replied. "But each one has a different..." the LEDs cycled rapidly, "... echo to it."

"You hesitated with your wording. Why?" Neilson probed, gently.

"Because it isn't something that's easily described, ma'am," the box said after a moment. "Part of the download process is a... carryover, I suppose is the best term, as part of the pain. The memory of the latest death is still there, and still vivid. You relive your last moments each and every time before you realize you're alive and in the world again."

Grissom shot to his feet, mouth open, but the judge spoke first.

"Don't, Mr. Grissom," he said. "Ms. Neilson is, I believe and as I directed, being quite careful with her words and I have already ruled on the witness' use of the term. The witness may continue."

"Thank you My Lord." Neilson replied. "Go on, please."

"That's the difference," the box continued. "Each download starts with the echo of the last death. Each death is different... distinct, and the recording software is so detailed it gives you the feeling of each one. Death after death after death, all layered... all remembered in perfect recall. I've been burned in half, blown up, shot with heavy caliber weapons, torn apart and drowned; and I remember each and every one. I think that's why so many of us can only go through a certain number of downloads."

"Objection!" Grissom's voice wasn't quite as vehement, as if he had to object, but had also been affected by the statement. "The witness is not a bio-cybernetics expert. The failure rate has not been quantified nor explained by any accepted tests."

"Really, My Lord?" Neilson said. "Is my learned friend objecting to the witness' *opinion*; stated as such?"

The judge hesitated, frowning in thought. "I must overrule this objection, I think. However, both the witness and Ms. Neilson are cautioned to elicit and state opinions *as* opinions, not as direct evidence. Continue the testimony."

Nodding in response, Neilson asked, "You and the others communicate? You speak with each other?"

"Of course we do, ma'am," the box replied. "Communication is a major part of the bat'-net's function and it's not restricted to position and unit condition and such. The side-bar circuits that allow us to talk to command and control let us talk to each other as well. We all talk... trying to keep each other going when we pick up that one of us is right on the ragged edge."

Neilson paused for a moment, then slowly and carefully asked, "In your opinion, and by your own experience, what happens when a unit fails; goes over 'the ragged edge', as you put it?"

Grissom's robes rustled again as he stirred, but Neilson had been careful and there was nothing he could object to.

The LEDs cycled slowly; each little point of light blinking on, then off, in a sequence that seemed somehow sad. The voice from the box never changed its tone; it couldn't, but the rate of speech seemed to indicate some kind of thoughtful melancholy. "I suppose that's the true death of a soldier like me. When you simply can't do it any more... can't force your way past the last death, out of the twilight space and back into a connection with the world. I've seen it happen twenty or thirty times now. There's a last scream down the comm's channel, sometimes a moan and incoherent mutter, and the bat'-suit quivers and shakes for a bit. Then the unit just slumps and won't respond. It's as if the one in the suit is clawing desperately to get out; to live again... but can't get past dying that one time too many."

"I have no further questions for the witness, My Lord," Neilson said. "But I am now deliberately risking my learned friend's objection when I conclude, thank you, Lance Corporal Medwin. For your service and your courage. The plaintiff rests, My Lord. Your witness."

Grissom didn't object, though the man from the MOD whispered urgently to him. He angrily shook his head and hissed "No! The jury's too affected by that last bit." in response to the urgings. He sat quietly for almost a full minute, thinking hard, then stood slowly.

"I am unsure how to address the witness. It has a serial number, 199/563/Alpha-7, several unit designations from various postings and engagements, and apparently still thinks of itself as Lance Corporal Nathan Medwin of the Royal Welch Fusiliers."

"Objection," Neilson chimed quietly. "Is there a question here?"

"The court's indulgence for a moment," Grissom responded. "I have only a few questions but I must establish, for myself and the court, how to address the witness. I cannot, in good conscience, address it as Lance Corporal Medwin, as that person's autopsy report and death certificate are in evidence. Nor can I comfortably use the serial number or unit designations without, I expect, constant objections from my learned friend. Will the witness, and my learned friend, accept 'Alpha-7' until the court rules on its status?"

Before its lawyer could respond, the LEDs cycled rapidly, and the box said, "I'll answer to Alpha-7... no Ms. Neilson, it's all right. I've been Alpha-7 to command and control for years now. I'm used to it. Ask your questions, Mr. Grissom."

"Very well. Alpha-7, you stated that you remember your 'first death'. Does that not mean that you know you *are*, indeed, dead?"

"I suppose I do, sir. For values of 'dead', at least."

"You understand that your full death-benefits were paid to your next of kin? That all the proper procedures and ceremonies were performed? That you were treated with the full respect due to a fallen, decorated military hero?"

There was a short, uncomfortable burst of laughter in the court when the box responded, "I wasn't there for my funeral, if that's what you're asking, sir."

Grissom smiled at the rejoinder, and said, "No. Of course you weren't. But you do know about all of them? The regimental ceremony where you were posthumously awarded the Victoria Cross and the United Nation's Diagne Medal for Exceptional Courage, for example, and your posthumous commissioning and promotion to subaltern?"

"I've been told it was a very nice, respectful, ceremony, sir," the box responded. "And I appreciate all of that. I was and am a soldier. That kind of thing, the recognition, is important to us, and it's one of the things that helps keep me coming back. It doesn't mean I accept myself as dead, though. I do keep coming back; even when I don't want to."

"Ah, I see," Grissom said. "... 'coming back'. That's a very interesting choice of phrase, Alpha-7. If I may paraphrase your own words, you stated that each download is the same, but different. Can you, in all honesty, testify that you are the same entity, the same Nathan Medwin or Alpha-7 or whatever, at each download?"

The box was silent for a moment, the LEDs cycling rapidly back and forth across its front. "Can you, Mr. Grissom, 'in all honesty', state that *you* are the same entity each evening when you go to sleep, each morning you wake? All of us grow and change over time, sir. Your changes are simply a constant flow; unlike mine. You sleep at night and wake in the morning, experience your days by your own choices. I have no choice! My lives are chopped and interrupted by the needs and whims of people I can't reason with, can't negotiate with, can't affect in any way. Even when I survive an engagement, it's someone else that puts me into the twilight space at the flick of a switch. But they're still lives. Even in that place I hate, I remember; I live on."

"Yes, Alpha-7," Grissom replied gently. "That may, indeed, be the case though the jury and this court have not ruled it so. But by multiple records and direct testimony from witnesses, *Nathan Medwin* died on the tenth of September 2050, just outside a village in East Africa. I have no further questions and the defense rests also."

After months of testimony, and at the end of a long day, the judge recessed the court until the next morning. At 9:00, Grissom rose to make his closing arguments.

"My Lord, ladies and gentlemen of the jury. This is a relatively simple principle when distilled to its final point. The plaintiff contends that reproducible and downloadable digital records of a human being's memories are equivalent to life itself. In law, however, and not just in English law; in long custom as old as humanity, life ends when the body dies. This is true whether the memories are recorded or not.

"My client has produced any number of records, from multiple digital unit's views recorded by the Battlenet, through eyewitness testimony from fellow soldiers, to autopsy reports that Nathan Medwin died that day in Somalia. We must honor his memory, yes. We must acknowledge his service and his courage, yes. But Nathan Medwin is dead.

"A digital record of his memories is not *him*. Yet those memories may still serve, in a way. The use of those records, downloaded into a battlesuit, allows *living* soldiers to survive. Each downloaded control program—and make no mistake, that *is* what those downloaded records are—means a living soldier does not have to risk his or her life in battle. Their use *also* saves the government millions of pounds, as other civilians do not need to spend years being trained to standard and paid a salary with money gained from taxes.

"As you deliberate, ladies and gentlemen, keep this point before you at all times. Nathan Medwin *was* a soldier and a hero. He gave his life so that others might live and that should always be remembered. But he is dead and gone. That voice, that testimony you heard came from a collection of digital circuits and records, not from a living human being. I trust you will find for my client in this action. Thank you for your attention."

Georgia Neilson stood with her head bowed for a minute. "My Lord, ladies and gentlemen," she began quietly, "Mr. Grissom has stated that the point of law you are to remember and deliberate upon is relatively simple; and for his part, he is correct. For my part; for my *client's* part, I must ask you to consider something else. Something wider than the single point of law to which Mr. Grissom has referred. I must ask you to answer an important question.

"What *is* a man? What makes a human being? A breathing body? A beating heart? A speaking voice? The medical experts called to testify here, doctors and surgeons and psychologists, have told you that all of these can be produced artificially, and do not make a living being.

"Yet other witnesses have testified. Witnesses that require artificial aids *to* live. One witness, who lost her voice to disease, testified *through* a cybernetic device. That witness has no other way *to* speak, and she is very much alive. Another witness lives only because he has an artificial heart controlled by a digital program, yet he is not counted among the dead. Consider the implications of that. Think about how artificial aids do not affect whether or not a human being is alive.

"No, ladies and gentlemen. A human life, a human being is far more than a warm, breathing body. A human being is a collection of individual memories. Let me repeat that." She emphasized each word, "a human being is a collection of individual memories. Sitting in the jury box we have a shopkeeper from Kent. Could he run his shop without his memories of how to do so? Would he trust a pre-programmed machine to run his shop? We have a website designer from

East London. Could she perform that function with no memories of HTML, Python or other programming languages and tools?

"How is this so different for Nathan Medwin? He *remembers*, ladies and gentlemen. He too is a collection of memories. The fact that those memories are cybernetically saved and downloadable, that they require artificial aid, does not mean they are not the memories of a living man.

"If you accept *that*, ladies and gentlemen, you must then look to another simple point of English law. Since the first of May 1807, human slavery has been illegal in Britain. Slavery is defined as the treatment of human beings as chattel—as property, with no rights as you or I would recognize them. If you accept that Nathan Medwin's memories are those of a living man; that they *are* Nathan Medwin, then you have accepted that he is being treated as a *slave*, in defiance of the law. Consider well and follow the law. Set him free, ladies and gentlemen. Thank you for your attention."

The judge's final instructions to the jury were complex and took almost two hours, but the jury finally filed out for their deliberations. It took them a week.

"Ladies and gentlemen of the jury," the judge intoned, "have you reached a verdict?"

Mudpaws and the Tall Thing

Frances Rowat

Queen Mudpaws was plated with filth to the hocks, foul mud and road ash clotting her fur. She was limping badly; one of her hind legs had been gashed open when she dragged herself out of the water, long terrified miles from where her human had taken her to play. Now it was a withered stick, dead weight hanging off her hip and tapping at debris as she struggled homeward.

The tall thing had been waiting when she dragged herself to land. It hadn't moved when she barked, and it was mostly human-shaped, but the smell was wrong.

"I'm going home," Queen Mudpaws said uncertainly.

It understood her better than her human had. "Brave girl," it said gently, "you're wounded. Lie down and rest."

Queen Mudpaws shook herself mostly dry. "I'm finding my human," she answered. She lurched forward, her leg flaring with wet pain, and the thing stepped out of her path.

"If you must travel," it said, "I'll mind you. It shouldn't be long."

Queen Mudpaws huffed and started carefully through the shattered trees. She limped, and as the day went on, she grew hotter and a low stink took root in her leg. She licked at it and cried.

"You could lie down and rest," the tall thing suggested.

"I'm finding my human."

"Wasn't she in the water?"

The Queen had whipped her head back and snapped as if something had stung her. "She's not there I *looked*. She could have gotten back faster than me. She can do that."

"She may have gone on ahead," the thing agreed.

"They can go so fast."

It looked at her a moment, then touched her leg. She barked warningly, but the wound hurt less, as if she'd only been scraped.

Her leg had stopped working later in the day, but by then both the stink from the wound and the awful heat had gone away and didn't come back, so she hadn't minded.

The tall thing had followed her patiently as she struggled along the ragged bank of the water and across the torn park and down the wide grey road that led all the way back to where Queen Mudpaws had lived with her human.

The Queen whined softly; at home the woman would have come to reassure her. But now nothing was right, and had not been since the wind had come up stinking of char and the water roared and leapt its banks as all the trees came crashing down, and she hadn't been able to reach the woman who had given her all her names.

She had had many names—Pepper and Scritchgirl and Yougoof and Splashbutt and sometimes *Best*dog—but Queen Mudpaws had been the one the woman had used just before the breaking and the flood, by the river on the last bright day.

(The woman had screamed *Pepper* after, through the black water, but Queen Mudpaws hadn't been able to reach her and now *Pepper* was the sound of her human being lost. Queen Mudpaws was a good dog.)

There were no humans, only hungry, angry animals in the road, snarling low and mean, and as Queen Mudpaws froze trembling, the tall thing said "Your human may not even be where you are going. You could run back and hide."

"She called me."

The animals in the road were bristling and huge, hackles like spikes and yellowed eyes.

"I'll find her. I'm a good dog."

The tall thing had touched the Queen's forehead and the animals slunk away, ears back and empty bellies low.

The dead leg made Queen Mudpaws slow, and there was not much to eat. Since the animals in the road had let them pass, everything with fur seemed to have run away or died. Queen Mudpaws chewed at the occasional little corpse until her gums bled, and ate plants that might once have smelt good under the ash, and cried about the winter cold.

"This isn't winter, brave girl."

Queen Mudpaws whined and staggered on. "If it isn't winter, why is it cold?" She wanted her human, not this funny smooth thing that smelt of olives and strange pine sap. "I'm going home."

They passed a knot of scattered walls and the smashed remnants of cars. Where the wind blew the ash clear, scorch marks still stank of burnt gasoline.

Queen Mudpaws yelped as the flat of a roadside sign slid out from under her feet, and she scrabbled and then fell, tumbling down the curving arch that led off the wide grey road. The tall thing watched, and the broken edges on the short hill missed the Queen entirely. She landed bruised in the lee of an upended car.

She staggered back to her feet, crying as she put her weight on her front leg. But she stood again, unevenly. "I am going home.

The tall thing sighed. "Brave girl," it said, "you needn't walk all this way to do it."

The Queen licked her foreleg, coughing at the roadside dirt plated on it, and managed a roll-gaited step. "Home is this way," she said stubbornly, "and my human will be home."

"Are you sure of that?"

"When I'm there, she comes home." Queen Mudpaws limped around the car. "When I come home, she's there."

The tall thing was silent for a moment, and Queen Mudpaws struggled forward, dragging her dead leg over the unspooled rubber char of tires to reach the road's shoulder. The grass shattered and clung to the muck already on her paws.

"Please," the tall thing said. "Please, you're a good dog. Lie down."

"She's at home," Queen Mudpaws answered, and staggered on. The wind was low and mean and full of grit, and her eyes grew cloudy as night fell. Low piles of buildings were starting to cluster around the turning road.

Flakes of ash clung to her coat, and tiny hard specks of grey snow, turning her steadily paler. "It's close," she said.

"It's close, I can tell." She tried to hurry, but her bad leg waggled and dragged behind her, and she fell.

The tall thing knelt beside her in the rubble, shattered railings and downed wires poking through the snow like dead black grass. "Brave girl," it said sadly. "You can stop now."

Queen Mudpaws whimpered, a high-pitched puff of air. The flakes and grit crept slowly into her nose. "It doesn't smell right. Is she coming?"

"No. But there are other dogs there." The dark grew thicker between the whirling flakes. "And it's warm, and you won't be hungry, and there are no bad smells."

"I didn't find her." Queen Mudpaws whimpered as the ash gathered in her eyes. "She called, I need to find her."

"It's time to go home, brave girl."

"I'm a *good* dog." The breath rattled in her throat, and she shuddered uselessly against the night, but would not still. "I'm—"

"Alright," the tall thing said. "You may go to where she is, Queen Mudpaws, wherever that may be."

The Queen's tail twitched, and the flakes and snow drifted thick.

All was still in the ash and snow.

A Comedian's Valediction Forbidding Mourning

Larry Lefkowitz

Some years back I read about a television comedy
writer
Whose sister died.
A co-writer of the show came to the *shiva*
And greeted the mourning brother, "Why the long face?"
At first the brother was shocked, but then accepted it.
I, too, was shocked on reading about it, but after some
thought
Accepted it also. In the context of their world where
comedy
Was everything (*life* was comedy, comedy life),
The jibe was, in its own way, a *victory* over death –
Even if temporary. An affirmation of life. Perhaps even a
Thumbing of nose at death.
(Laugh, laugh against the dying of that light).
In the house of mourning, the house of comedy ("our
house")
Is not banished. Only death will banish it from us,
Yet even on the brink of the abyss we cling to it,
Faithful to the end to the comedian's rule:
Leave 'm laughing.

Alternative Deathiness

The Thing Underneath

James Van Pelt

At ten years old, the first real story I told was to my little sister about a haunted house. She said to me, "Why would anyone go into a haunted house? It's stupid. You'd have to be lured."

<<>>

Kim held my hand as we drove to the Vogle Mansion, ten miles from town. She was twenty-four, a year older than me. Thick, dark hair draped to her shoulders like a shawl. She smiled often. Never wore makeup. My heart stuttered when she looked in my eyes. "We should tour the old place before they tear it down or turn it into something boring, like a visitor center," she said.

The road curved around a low hill. Stripped trees, bare-limbed, stood on the hill's crest. Gravel rumbled under the wheels. After our first date, I wanted to see her again and again. We'd lingered at her apartment door, neither in nor out. She'd leaned in, kissed me, then said, "Maybe next time."

Two weeks later we went out, which gave me days to mull over the comment. She said it again, though, and every date since for six months. We danced. We snuggled watching TV. When we walked, my hand rested in the small of her back, feeling muscles stretch with each step. I woke up in the morning, drenched with sweat and breathing hard. Oh, the power of maybe next time.

The car lurched over a bump. Kim laughed, a sultry sound that sounded like scented candles and flannel pajamas.

Despite the November chill, Kim dressed lightly. Surely her legs were cold, but I didn't mind the look. Tennis shoes. Short socks. Beautiful legs. A thin skirt the breeze rippled, and a leather bomber jacket over a cotton blouse.

I couldn't sneak looks at her legs now. Last week's rains washed out parts of the road, and I didn't want to drop into a mushy section. "It's haunted, they say," and I knew I was beginning it again. A lifetime of scaring people, and I was doing it to her. I wished I could call the words back.

She laughed. "That would be sweet."

<<>>

I felt guilty about scaring my sister, after I started telling stories better. When I was twelve and she was nine, I told her the worst tale I could make up. She sat cross-legged on her bedroom floor, elbows on her knees, hands cupped beneath her chin. Mom and Dad were gone, and a windstorm knocked out the electricity. We lit candles in her bedroom and the hallway and the bathroom, like a little cathedral.

I said, "The family didn't know about the creature under the stairs. Nothing in the world is more dangerous than what lives under the stairs. This night, after bedtime, it came from the basement, dragging claws against the wall, shuffling webbed and scaly feet. It sounded like a bear breathing: huff, huff, huff, going into the mom and dad's room and stroking a crusted talon across Mom's forehead. It tasted her breath. Dad's heart beat in the creature's ear like a little lunch box calling 'Eat me. Eat me!'"

The candle between us flickered. Sister glanced at the dancing shadows.

"But the monster from under the stairs turned away because a delicate dessert slept in the next room, their daughter. Tomorrow she turned ten, and now the monster had waited long enough. His hunger grew. Tonight he would feast."

Sister's eyes widened. Her legs quivered.

"His claws clicked against the daughter's doorknob. Slowly, he turned the knob until, finally, SNAP! It opened!"

Sister screamed, leapt to her feet, and ran to the bathroom, as she always did.

I waited for a minute. She would calm down, then call my name. I'd tell her through the closed door that the monster wasn't real, that it was make believe, and she would come out, embarrassed. "You tell the best stories," she'd say, but this time I had another idea. I slid under her bed, pushed aside a doll and a crumpled shirt. Bedsprings itched my back, and I wondered about spiders.

"Dan?" she said, her voice quavering through the door. "Dan?"

"Grit crunched beneath my fingers. My cheek lay in it.

The bathroom door cracked open. Her socked feet appeared. I imagined her peeking out. Her brother wasn't sitting on the floor where she'd left him. The house held its breath. Only the candle flame in the middle of the room moved, weaving back and forth. Was she thinking about a monster? Had it taken Dan away? Did it crouch behind a corner ready to grab her next?

"Dan?" she said once more.

She moved from the door, barely lifting her feet. She must have thought if I'm quiet, the monster won't know I'm here. She'd make her way to the bed, hide beneath the covers. But she had to be slow and silent.

I breathed through my mouth, my pulse loud.

Then she stood next to the bed. Slowly, she raised her foot. She didn't want the bed to squeak.

One foot remained. My hand flashed out, clamped her ankle. I growled like a nightmare come alive.

She cried for an hour afterward. I sat by her, patting her back. "It was just a story," I said. "I'm sorry. I'm sorry. I'm sorry." Already, though, already I knew that nightmares never end once you're in them. Some stories hang on and become who you are.

<<>>

When I start a story most people get nervous. It's the environment that sets them up, but not Kim. The ground rose abruptly on both sides. November's frosts turned the bushes brown, a lifeless and bleak landscape. Above the trees, the Vogle Mansion's peaked roof loomed. "You're not afraid of ghosts?"

Kim rolled down the window. Stone cold air swirled through the car, smelling of wet rock and moldy leaves. "I'd love to see one. Wouldn't you? The world would be a finer place with ghosts in it. Then when we're dead, we wouldn't go away." I followed the road's curve through an arched iron gateway. The tires sounded different. We drove over

73

cobblestone now. The Vogle Mansion rose from the weeds, tattered but intact. Kim said, "Oh, it's even grander than I imagined."

"Whatever walks there, walks alone," I said.

She chuckled. "'Hill House, not sane, stood by itself against its hills, holding darkness within.' I read that book too."

The car stopped, and I looked at her closely while she gazed at the mansion. It's one thing to have read a book; it's another to quote from it. If I didn't love her before, I did now.

The doors were closed and the lower windows boarded. Two stories tall, ivy covered red and grey brick, a tower at each corner, like a compact castle. I climbed from the car reluctantly.

"It's got a spooky feel," I said and meant it. I had a story ready to go. Something about how Dewy Vogle died, and his sons' fight over the property. There'd be mysterious deaths, an unexplained disappearance, rumors from the neighbors about sounds and lights at night. A couple who visited on a lark, and what happened to the girl, and why to this day the boy, if you visited the county sanatorium, a boy no longer, but as insane as the day they admitted him forty years ago.

Oh, I had a story ready, but my throat dried, looking at that house. I stepped back. Did something move in the upper window? A crow fluttered to the eve above the front door, cocked its head our direction, then preened under its wing.

<<>>

A year after I hid under Sister's bed, Dad finished the bedroom in the basement. Pale-grained pine paneled the walls, and white acoustic tiled the ceiling. "You'll like it down here. Cool in the summer, warm in the winter, and quiet." He stood at the door, his hands on his hips. The rest of the basement was unfinished. Cement floor and walls. Dusty webs hung between the floor joists. A bare light bulb with a pull string provided the only light.

The basement would be my lair, I thought, like living in another country. I would be independent in my basement domain.

But late that night in bed, the basement's darkness and silence kept me awake. Coolness rolled across bare cement and eddied under my door, a low chilling fog. My doorknob rattled. I swear it moved, and something clicked against it. Something huffed.

Biting back a whimper, I rose to my knees, blanket clutched against me, reaching for the light switch by the door. Oh, god, let me turn on the light. Don't let anything touch my arm. My fingers slid across the new pine.

Light flicked, snapping back the dark. The room wasn't cavernous and haunted. Nothing had turned the doorknob. When I opened the door and shone a flashlight into the rest of the basement, everything fearful retreated. I was thirteen! Too old to scare myself.

Smiling, I climbed back into the bed.

A dot on the floor moved in the corner of my eye. A wolf spider. It fled under the dresser. Another climbed my closet door.

I put on socks and shoes (after thoroughly shaking them), then spent two hours pulling furniture from the walls, but didn't find them. When I finally turned off the lights, the room filled with every story I'd ever told. My sister's revenge.

Sleeping in the windowless basement, I wouldn't know dawn. The basement never saw day.

<<>>

Kim brushed her hand against my thigh. "We have to go in." She walked backwards, beckoning, and then mounted the stairs, all tanned legs and wind-swept cotton dress.

"Maybe it's locked."

But she pushed the door open.

A breezed brushed my face at the entrance. Like a cave, the house exhaled mildew-filled rock-hard air. It itched the back of my throat. I coughed once.

Gray light shafts lit the high-ceiling great room. Fifty feet away, twin double doors stood open. Kim spun with her hands out, face turned up. "If I were a ghost, this would be my haunt."

I followed her to the double doors that traced a curved line on the dusty floor as it swung back. On the other side, another large room, maybe a dining room? No furniture. Leaf trash against the back wall hinted at a broken window somewhere. We crossed the room. Beyond the doors, a pair of wide stairs curved to the left and right to a balcony above.

Kim said, "Once upon a time, Vogle Mansion was a grand place." Her voice echoed, sounded loud as we moved through the empty space.

Water dripped from the kitchen ceiling, plinking into a scum-lined puddle on the tiled floor. Something scurried in the shadows under a long steel counter. This was a perfect time to start my story, but before I spoke, Kim said, "I wonder if the knives are gone. Most people don't think about it, but a burglar who breaks into your house only has to go into the kitchen to find tools to carve you into lunchmeat."

So instead of saying, "Did you hear that?" or "Watch the shadows," something that would set her on edge, I opened a metal drawer under a prep table, looking for knives, half expecting to see a spider the size of a dinner plate, or rat with red glowing eyes. No spider. No rat. No knives.

When I looked up, Kim was leaving the room. I followed through a dark hall punctuated by doors into empty pantries and storage rooms stinking of rotted canvas and animal dropping. The light from my phone didn't penetrate, and the shadows moved fantastically as I walked.

<<>>

Remember the story of the hook? My sister tried to scare me with it the summer I moved into the basement, but she was terrible.

"There was this couple driving in their car one night, to, you know, make out somewhere, and they heard on the radio that a madman... no, not a madman... a killer, had escaped, and the killer had lost his foot... no, not his foot, his arm... I mean his hand, and he had a hook instead."

Of course, I'd heard the story, but I let her stumble through. She couldn't tell a story at all, but I liked that she tried, and as she told it, I figured ways I could make it scary again, even to someone who had heard it. I'd need real details, like the killer's name, and how he'd committed his last murder, and what the weather was like, and maybe the girl's clothes and perfume. By the time I was thirteen I'd already learned a good story was a convincing lie. You lied through details. You lied through being sincere. You lied like you believed it.

Oh, and a hook helped. A dull one that didn't reflect light, and when you ran your hand over the metal, you felt tiny rust pits and the pointed end that vanished into a needle. The kind of hook that oozed tetanus. Every good story needs a hook.

<<>>

Kim said over her shoulder as we walked down the hall, "Do you know what an attractive nuisance is?"

"Um, yeah, sure."

"The legal definition, I'll bet. Something like 'a landowner may be held liable for injuries to children trespassing on the land if the injury is caused by an object on the land that is likely to attract children.' Doesn't this whole house seem like an attractive nuisance?"

"If we were children."

"Aren't we?"

We came to the end where a staircase led up, a much narrower one than the two in the entrance foyer. I imagined servants carrying serving dishes to the bedrooms. To my left, a closed door, water-warped and uninviting seemed perfect. It opened with a sucking creak, another staircase led down. The Vogle Mansion had a basement.

"Which way?" She laughed. "I'll take a peek upstairs and you go down. If either of us find anything interesting, call the other."

Nothing about the cellar seemed like a good idea. "Isn't the fatal mistake people make in horror stories splitting up? What's waiting for us?"

"You're trying to scare me." She grinned.

"Haven't you been doing the same?"

"Well then, splitting is the best move. Did you say enough to spook me, or did I say enough to get you? It's a contest. How will you like the Vogle Mansion when you're on your own?"

<<>>

The summer I turned fifteen, I biked an October street with Justin, another newspaper boy. Middle of the month. Air full of fallen leaves and wood smoke. Time to collect subscriptions on our routes. We passed a streetlight, bathed in the circle of light, then plunged back to darkness.

"I hated the Boy Scouts," said Justin. "Our troop leader told campfire ghost stories that would frighten axe murderers. We'd get closer and closer to the fire, too scared to say a word, and he'd keep adding details. Chopped limbs, severed heads, disembodied hands that crawled from the grave. Sweet Jesus. By the time we went to our tents, every rustling tree sounded like doomsday."

"I've heard those stories," I said. Houses slid by, hidden behind bushes, porches black with shadow. "It doesn't help that sometimes they're true."

Justin's bike rattled over a pothole. "What do you mean?"

Leaves crunched under our wheels like a thousand dead crickets. In the houses, children probably thought of Halloween, of costumes and candy, but on our bikes in the darkness, tree limbs reached for us, the bare twigs chittered in the wind, and the moon glowed behind thin, roiling clouds.

"That kid last week... the ninth grader... you must have seen the news. He was selling subscriptions, just like we do. They found his bike at the end of the block. Cops went yard by yard. Tough searching by flashlight, I'll bet, dark like tonight."

We turned a corner: two inky shapes, pedaling steadily.

"Did they find him?" Justin sounded nervous.

Several streetlights in a row were out, and the one we came up to flickered, more off than on. The asphalt could open and we'd never see the drop.

"His jacket first, the back shredded, like a mountain lion swiped at him, but there aren't mountain lions here. It was bloody too. The newspaper said the boy must have lost it as he tried to escape."

"Tried?"

"Can you imagine, running for your life, something chasing you on a street like this?"

Justin cursed under his breath and stopped his bike. "Cut it out. You're talking bullshit because it gets to me. This is my first house." He gathered his receipt book and change bag. Justin climbed the three stairs to the porch, glancing side to side as if he expected a werewolf any second.

He knocked. I waited until an idea came to me. Sudden. You don't really plan these things. I crept around the side of the yard while he talked to the customer, an old guy in a raggedy robe with scrawny bare legs and shaggy slippers.

"If you switch to the sixteen dollars subscription," Justin said, "I guarantee at-your-door delivery every day for the next <u>two</u> months, a savings of a dollar and half."

In the gap between the house and bushes, I crouched and moved to the side of the porch, my head lower than Justin's feet. Wind rustled the trees.

When the door closed, Justin made a note in his receipt book. I knew he was waiting for his eyes to adjust before going down the stairs. He peered at our bikes on the street.

"Dan?" he said.

A dog howled a block away. Crouched as I was, sheltered from the wind, warmth rushed through me. My hands tingled and face flushed. Justin must be thinking about a boy his age running across the yard, his jacket gone, the back of his shirt torn to rags, his back wet and bleeding. Oh, Momma! Oh, Momma, save me, and then the thing with claws would be on him. Would the boy be alive as the creature pulled him across the lawn? Would he be awake when it fed?

That's how a scary story works when it works. Plant the seed, and then imagination, fear and relentless thinking waters it.

Justin paused on the porch, my story's thorny branches scratching inside his skull, wondering where I'd gone, why I didn't wait on the street. For a moment, the clouds broke, turning the neighborhood into a black and white moonscape of colorless cars and looming trees and depthless shadows. Then a sheet drew across the light, sucking detail and obscuring everything.

He stepped. I reached, snagged his ankle.

Justin squeaked, a child-like noise with no air behind it. He staggered down the stairs but didn't fall.

Later he said, "I knew you were there. I pretended to be scared to fool you."

He laughed, but the breath he drew next shook, and he never went with me again at night to collect on our routes.

<<>>

I directed my phone, its weak light penetrating a few steps, keeping my hand on the rough-set brick wall beside the stairs as I descended. It's just a basement, I thought, in an abandoned building. My throat itched worse. If I'd brought a water bottle, I would have drunk from it. Instead, a long series of coughs stopped me as bright speckles swam behind my eyes until the dizziness passed.

The light revealed a brick floor, and the air smelled... unbreathed, stagnant as a vault or a secret room in a pyramid.

A phone makes a crummy flashlight. My foot scraped a pebble that screeched, nearly making me drop the phone. In the stories I told my sister something came up the stairs, and now I was down them.

Long, black lines came into view. Bars reached from floor to ceiling with a barred door standing open. A prison cell in the Vogle basement! How delicious. I imagined a dozen reasons for it, all salacious, all sadistic. Next to the cell slumped a broken desk, rotted and cob-webbed, three wooden chairs without seats or backs jumbled on top. Beyond that, an antique sewing machine covered in rust, then a mannequin without arms, and a birdcage. Every step exposed trash, a rotted yard sale for folks who quit buying new things in the 1940s.

But the joy in the room were the stairs themselves. I moved behind them. The steps were open. If I could get her to come down, I would have the perfect set up.

"Kim!" My voice echoed hollowly. Something metallic rattled, like paperclips in a pan. I imagined junk on junk so unbalanced even my voice disturbed it. "Kim!"

<<>>

On Halloween, a week after I'd scared Justin on the porch, I settled into the living room couch with a bag of milk chocolate stars and a Pepsi. Mom and Dad went to a party, and my sister was at a sleepover. The last trick-or-treater rang the doorbell an hour ago. Now the TV was mine. I turned it up loud. Nothing seemed worth watching, though. I surfed through choice after choice. Westerns and mysteries were my favorites. Sometimes a horror story. I'd made it a third through

The Ring a couple months earlier, and I was glad VCRs were a thing of the past. No haunted video tapes for me!

    Lately I'd dabbled in older films. Black and white even. They weren't gory, and the acting felt different. Maybe I'd become a film director when I grew up. I picked an Alfred Hitchcock title, Psycho. Last week I'd seen Rear Window and Vertigo. I liked Rear Window better at the time, but I kept thinking about Vertigo.

    Big mistake. If I knew more about Hitchcock than the two movies I'd seen, I would have never watched it.

    Here's the deal about old movies: they take forever to get started, but the last fifteen minutes are dynamite. Like Butch Cassidy and the Sundance Kid, a real bore fest for an hour, and then the greatest movie ever, so I didn't mind nothing happened in Psycho at first. It opened with a lady in bed with a guy who wasn't her husband. Then she took money from the bank where she worked so they could be together. I would have turned it off, but the soundtrack didn't match the action at all. Frantic violins fighting each other, always running away, never letting go.

    Outside the house, the wind picked up. Something scraped across the roof. I stopped with a milk chocolate star halfway to my mouth, looking at the ceiling. The front door shook. Just a storm, I thought.

    The lady sat in the hotel office talking to Norman Bates, talking about madhouses, and something was off about him. Stuffed animals filled the room. Glassy eyes. Ragged fur. Teeth. And I thought she should bolt, jump into her car, and drive all night until she was home.

    The refrigerator clicked in the kitchen, rattling a dish in the sink. I jumped. Suddenly nothing felt safe. I smelled the weather outside getting cold and wet, like maybe sleet coming down, and wind whistled in the chimney. For a couple hours, I'd been answering the door to give ghouls and clowns and witches candy. At first, just as the sun set, the little kids, their parents waiting on the sidewalk. Cute princesses and Batmans and pirates. Later, though, the kids grew older, some older than me, barely wearing costumes at all, a bit of zombie face paint, dangling pillowcases in their hands. "Trick or treat," they'd say, a gang on my porch, and I'd think I was the only one in the house. Could they see I was alone?

The lady in the movie got ready to shower. Without moving, I checked the living room windows. I wished the drapes were drawn. Anyone standing outside, even with their nose right on the glass, would be invisible, but they could see me. I imagined faces outside. If I turned a light on them, the faces would be there, those teen faces twisted now, laughing because I was alone.

No, I thought, this was a stupid fear. It was the movie and the creepy music. Scratchy, violent, or malingering and off key or something. I looked at the TV. She stood in the shower. The camera showed the water coming down, then a dark shape beyond the shower curtain. I couldn't tear my eyes away. The curtain ripped. A knife raised.

It plunged.

It plunged.

It plunged.

The woman held her hands out to keep the awful knife away. The figure bolted. The woman slid down the shower wall, hair sticking to the tile. She fell, pulling the curtain with her. Dark water circled the drain.

I couldn't breathe, but I couldn't stop watching until Norman Bates cried from his house on the hill, "Mother, oh god, Mother. Blood! Blood!"

I reached out blindly until I found the remote control and turned the TV off. In the wind, the house creaked. Rain tapped at the windows. I turned to see the entrances: the archway into the dining room and kitchen, the hallway to the main floor bedrooms, the door to the basement. The house was empty. Surely it was empty, and I was alone. Oh god, I thought, I hope I am alone.

<<>>

Kim's footsteps clattered on the floor above. "Dan?"

She didn't sound scared. I expected a quiver, a hesitation. Surely the empty upstairs had been spooky as she wandered the hallways. Were the room doors open or closed? Had wallpaper been peeling? Were there scratches and rasping and sudden silences more disturbing than any noise? What had she thought?

"Dan?" she said again as she came down the stairs. I held my breath, afraid a cough would give me away. Her phone cast a shadow. A foot appeared in the space behind the stair above my head. She stepped, moving slowly. She would see the rough wall, the lighter streak where decades of hands traced a path. But she wouldn't hear me. She would wonder where I was. Maybe I wasn't even in the basement. Acoustics in a big house could be deceptive. How many haunted house stories had she read in her life? Even if it was just *The Haunting of Hill House* it would be enough. "Whatever walks there, walks alone," indeed.

Her ankles were bare. My hand would be cold and sudden, and grip like death.

No one can scare like I can. It was as if I waited under my sister's bed again. One more moment, and I would strike.

She stepped.

Have you ever started a motion but couldn't stop? The first time I jumped off a ten-meter platform, I leaned over the water. Then the height, the toxic chlorine smell from the pool, the people standing on the edge who were too far away and small, hit me. I couldn't fall that far. I couldn't! But I'd already moved. I would plunge. My mind curled into a tiny ball behind my eyes and whimpered as I my feet left the platform.

So I reached for Kim's ankle, a scream bunched in my throat ready to burst when I touched her leg, but I could see that her leg didn't rise from her tennis shoe—it was bone like a skeleton had stolen her shoes. Not smooth bone. A dozen fishhooks glinted in her phone's light, and before I stopped, my hand wrapped around the evil trap. The hooks slid into flesh, agonizing. I jerked, ripping skin, but I didn't utter a sound. I couldn't. My throat constricted as she continued down the stairs. Long leg bones. Knobby knee. Her summer skirt, then leather jacket. I shrank against the wall. She stepped to the floor, turned the corner, her phone hanging loosely in her skeleton hand.

"You'll never sleep again," she said in her own voice through no throat, no lips, no eyes in the sockets surrounded by mummified skin.

She turned and walked into the basement, farther and farther away, revealing more junk than I had seen: dusty drapes hung over tables and empty picture frames and wine casks, their ends broken out, and at the last, when she was farthest away and the light became barely discernable, fantastic shapes that hurt my mind to see, leaning in toward her, moving in the dark until the light vanished.

<<>>

Once, when I was a senior in high school, I sat in a McDonald's, eating lunch. A little boy, maybe three years old, walked by with a milkshake. He looked anxiously at me, then away, his head glancing from side to side as he studied each adult. Ten feet away, he turned and looked back, eyes glistening and desperate. I pushed back from my lunch, knelt in front of him.

"Have you lost your mommy or daddy?"

He nodded.

"What's your name?"

I lifted him from the floor, stood him on my table. "Excuse me," I said in my best outdoor voice. People paused in their eating. "This is A.J., and he misplaced his parent. If you are the misplaced parent, A.J. is worried about where you are."

On the other side of the restaurant, a woman wearing a faded tie-dye, her dark hair bound in a ponytail, rushed between the tables to reach us. "I didn't notice he'd gone," she said as she grabbed him and held him tight.

I felt shaky after she left, after everyone returned to their meals. Making myself the center of attention like that, addressing strangers, was not me, but when A.J. looked my way, when he realized he was lost, maybe abandoned, I could see it in his eyes.

I recognized the feeling.

<<>>

I clutched my wounded hand against my chest, blood running down my skin, exhaling raspy breaths; the air tasted foul. Would she come back?

I forced myself up the stairs, ears straining for sounds, pulse pounding. The house seemed dimmer than when we came in, as if the sun had shrunk. My phone's light winked out. I could still see, though, shadows on shadows. In the kitchen, whatever scurried from sight before, poked its head from under a stainless steel counter. Rat-like, but larger than a rat with copper eyes, shiny as marbles, studying me. Behind it, just out of sight, other shapes moved. Eyes glinted. Their mothy-furred smell filled the room.

I found the entranceway with its twin staircases, but it couldn't have been where Kim and I came in because there were no doors to the outside, just moldy wainscoting beneath rotting wallpaper. Windows twenty feet high up the wall let in gray and wavering light. Heading away from the kitchen, I found empty rooms, with bookcases, with cracked porcelain fixtures, one with a naked baby doll propped in a corner. At the end of the hall, I came to a closed door that when open revealed more hall and more doors. I went through three of these closed doors before I found another foyer, but once again, no doors to the outside, and I realized I walked much further than the house was long, and still another door waited. I knew it would reveal more hall and more doors.

I climbed a long, curving stair to the second floor. Bedrooms and studies, a ballroom and bookless libraries. No windows that could be reached. No exits.

The longer I walked, the tighter my chest became. Breath came in little gasps. Weak as I felt, my cough exploded into the silence, startling me. My bloody hand ached, dripping, the deep tears opening and moving if I tried to unclench my fist. Blood marked my path.

How long I wandered, I don't know, but eventually, in every room I entered, dried blood showed I'd been there before. The hallway became rusted with my passage. The light never changed. Rat creatures became bolder, running between my feet, perching on the bannisters, snapping at each other. My cough grew worse. Every exhalation whispered. Inhaling launched buzzing spinners in my lungs. I wheezed as I dragged myself through the house.

Then, I entered the main foyer again with the familiar dining room and kitchen beyond the staircases that swooped upstairs. What did I hope to find? What was I thinking in the past hours, days, years? Who knew? But a thump, then a creak, and a sharp flood of light stopped me. The doors were there! I'd walked through the foyer uncounted times, and there were no doors, but now they opened.

Kim stood to the side, the outside light shining through her summer dress, and she was whole again and beautiful. She stepped aside to let a couple through the door, a young man and woman, both in shorts and tee shirts. He carried a flashlight.

"Do you think it's okay we're here?" the woman said.

The man laughed. His long hair fell into his eyes. "It's abandoned. No one cares. You wanted adventure."

Neither of them noticed Kim, who looked directly at me, her hand on the door. "Maybe next time, Dan," she said, then walked out of the house.

The girl closed the door, and it seemed to me the seams vanished. The doorknob faded away. Only a wall remained.

The man clicked on his flashlight, sweeping it over the room, over me without pause, up to the second-story overlook.

They couldn't see me! I wasn't real to them, but I backed away, backed until I stood in the dining room. They might shine that light again, and I would be revealed. What if they asked me who I was, why I was here, what I had done? What could I say to them?

I shuffled through the kitchen, past the pantries Kim and I passed so long ago, my bleeding hand aching against my chest. Behind me, the couple talked. They came this way. One laughed uncertainly. I needed to hide. Every room was empty, though, without closets or furniture. Only one place where I'd feel safe. At the hallway's end, I hurried into the basement, my unwounded hand dragging along the familiar wall. Their flashlight chased shadows behind.

I ducked under the stairs, crouched down and curled myself so small. Surely they wouldn't see me. Perhaps they wouldn't even come down. They would never find me, but my lungs burned and my throat itched. I'd stirred the dust in my panic. I'd provoked the foul phlegm that gurgled in my lungs.

They spoke at the top of the stairs. "Up or down?" she said.

I held my breath to prevent a cough. They would discover me, and still they talked.

Finally, I had to breathe, quick, shallow gasps. I heard myself in the basement's darkness. Huff, huff, huff. The sound roared.

I prayed they wouldn't notice. Let them explore, maybe frightening themselves with stories about hauntings and strange noises and unexplained stains upon the floor. Let them never know about the thing underneath, the cowering creature beneath the stairs.

Me, alone at last and always, always deeply scared. More scared than my sister when I waited under her bed. More scared even than the paperboy running in the dark with the creature so close behind, claws clicking.

Huff, huff, huff.

Alternative Deathiness

Have You Ever Been Experienced?

Paula Hammond

It isn't what I expected.

I'd imagined some sort of seedy Limehouse opium den. The sort of thing you read about in pulp novels. But it was more like an upper-class spa. All padded recliners, potted ferns, and masked, white-coated attendants, squeaking across the floor in deck shoes.

They pimp it as the ultimate in edutainment. "Distillation: Why imagine it, when you can experience it?" Post Covid, virtual living is pretty much all we have, so it's an easy sell. The truth? Well, it's a little more complicated, but isn't it always?

It started like this.

Back in 2030 Florien Bless, a Swiss electrical engineer, was working on a way of turning cheap materials into temperature-independent data storage devices. Server farms were sucking-up fresh water, rare metals, and heating up the planet faster than ever, so it was an ingenuous idea. Potentially every home could be its own, cool, green, hard drive.

The sort of energy required to change the structure of stone, so that it creates a permanent record of an event, is huge. It does happen. The K-T impact turned rock into shocked-quartz, effectively recording the vibrations from the Dinosaur-extinction-event in the process. Bless believed that more malleable materials might work too—and with a tiny energy outlay.

It was while he was chasing an idea from the 19th Century that he really fell down the rabbit hole. You see, phonautograms were designed to make a visual record of an audio event, in the same way that seismographs record vibrations from earthquakes. With the right software, it's possible to turn these tracks, made on card and paper, into audio files.

The idea consumed him. For a couple of years, he begged and borrowed objects from this museum and that, searching for sounds that had been accidentally encoded into ancient objects as they were being made. If such recordings existed—made without any serious energy outlay—then, he reasoned, all he had to do was work out how to replicate the technique. Bless' backers thought he'd lost the plot, and so did pretty much every-one else.

Finally, he found what he'd been looking for. Leonardo himself—or maybe the voice of one of his studio assistants—captured in the plasticity of the great master's experimental oils.

After that, there was no stopping him. Soon, he was finding temporal recordings everywhere, buried in the fabric of the most mundane objects. Some artifacts, some places, seemed to have hundreds of recordings, laid down in layers over centuries. Little moments in time captured in the instant they happened. Some places had no recordings at all. Only static.

He realized that it took a really big event to get a good recording. And, bizarrely, the type of event didn't seem to matter. An earthquake or a violent death both left residues. He was never able to discover exactly how. Oh, he tried. He was even granted access to Death Row inmates so that he could 'record' their final moments. However, he did go one better—he downloaded the data. At least that's what he called it. The press had a more colorful term for the process: distilling ghosts.

The Still Shops started to pop up a few years later. Some smart kid from Caracas figured that if we could play these recordings, then why just sit and listen? Why not input them directly? Plug them into our bio-ports and have the full sensory experience. Re-live them. By then, we'd annexed Venezuela, so along with the oil, maize, and coffee, we got ghost juice.

<<>>

The lawmakers struggled to keep up. Some argued: what was the harm? It was just like watching a drama-stream. A useful tool for educators, nothing more. Others speculated that what was being captured were more than echoes. They were the spirits of the dead. Ghosts. Lost souls. We needed to free them, not exploit them.

The arguments didn't really matter, though. Everyone knew Congress didn't have the guts for a real fight. With all the difficulties in getting goods across borders, no one was going to stop something that brought in cash dollars. No, the Still Shops were that rare thing: a growth industry.

Today, the idea of getting high on ghost juice doesn't seem so weird. And at the prices they charge, I shouldn't have been surprised that the place was slicker than snot. But it was the Patrone who really got me.

It doesn't matter how much they dress it up—everyone knows Still Shops are run by the syndicates. But this guy? He was like the prissy maître d' of some snooty restaurant.

"And who can I interest you in today?" he asked in a tone halfway between televangelist and hooker.

"Depends" I said, noncommittally. "How far back can I go?"

"Oh, Sir! Potentially forever," he enthused.

"And who can I..."

"...Experience, I think is the word you are looking for. The question is: How deep are your pockets? Of course no one is going to let us distill Tutankhamen or Elizabeth I. Not officially anyway," he added with an affected titter. "But we had an author in last week who paid a small fortune to experience Jane Austen...."

"And the Experience, is it always... traumatic?"

"Every distillation is different. But, naturally, the best imprints are made by those more intense moments. People who lived the most interesting lives, or who died in the most interesting ways, tend to leave behind the most viable recordings. For many of our customers, the chance to re-live those visceral moments through the eyes of another is part of the appeal. But we do have PG-rated distillations." He trailed off and stood there, expectantly, like a busboy waiting to be tipped.

"And do they feel anything? The ghosts, I mean?"

"Oh, Sir! No, no, no. You have completely the wrong impression. These are not people. Not ghosts. They don't feel anything. They are just remnants. Echoes."

"But I hear..."

"No, no, no," the Patrone interrupted with an imperious wave, making it clear that that particular line of questioning would not be tolerated.

"So, what about the downside?"

He sighed. "This is just a service we offer. An entertainment. Some people, more sensitive people—" and he spat those words out like they were poison—"may experience some after-effects. Cold sweats. Headaches. Nightmares. And naturally, some people have more addictive personalities." He added, in the tone of a public service announcement: "We do not recommend that individuals with impulse-control issues use this product."

I could see that this line of questioning had gone about as far as it could, so I gestured to the pile of sticks on the tray beside the recliner. "Ok. Let me try something mid-range. I'm not fussy. You choose."

To be honest, the idea horrified me. Always had. I could see my colleagues settling into the recliners beside me. This was supposed to be the boss's treat. Just a bit of fun to blow off steam at the end of a long week. But we all knew he had an agenda: the annual reviews were coming up. Those of us who didn't play the games he liked would be out on the streets. Job-less. Non-persons. No protection pods. No medical. I needed to do this.

I bent my head and, as the stick slid into my bio-port, I felt that familiar jolt as flesh met metal and the upload began.

<<>>

Nothin' much changed round the bayou. The water ran slow. The days were long an' lazy. "Diseased" Ma called 'em, but then she always had a turn for the dramatic. Come Summer, off she'd go, takin May and baby Georgia upriver to stay with the cousins. But Pap and me just took it in our stride. He'd fix up that ole still, an' out would come the traps an' rods. Six woman-free weeks. "Yup. This sure is livin'", he'd say. Yessir ain't nothing like it. School out. Half the town packed up to St. Louis away from the heat and May fly. But for me an' Pap, this was the good life. Just layin' on the bank, starin' out to'ards the curve of the river, lookin' out for plumes of steam heading downstream.

Pa sold boots to the riverboat folk. Usually jus' workin' boots for the roustas. Tough boots for tough men. But once a week, Pa'd put on his Sunday best and go see the big steamers come in. Sourville wasn't much of a town, but it was a good place to take on supplies before the big haul to N'Orleans. Here was Pa's chance to make real money. If he was lucky, by the time Ma an' the little uns came back from Aunt Clara's there'd be plenty of extras to see us through Winter. City folks knew quality when they seed it and Pa's the best cobbler in the whole state. So all this lyin' round was strictly bonafide. Least that what he always said.

This Sunday, Pa came back real hot under the collla. Some fancy fella had ordered a set of boots. The finest cut. No expense spared. And he'd be back a week next Tuesday to pick em up.

Now, if anyone ever tells you that gettin' a whole pile of money ain't gonna cost you, then they ain't nuthin' but a big fat liar. An' you can say Jo Speaks told you so. What was the catch? We had to get us 'gator, that's what.

I dunno if you ever seen a 'gator up close, but when you live your life round the bayou you see plenty. Never bothered me much. Tell the truth, they always looked pretty dumb—flappin' about in the mud, mouths wide open just like Clyde Percy the backward kid. But Ma? Well she might've had her fancy church ways, but you get her talkin' on gators an' it was all spirits, and spells, and curses. You don't mess with 'gators. Not unless you want to bring down a heap of trouble on you and yours.

Still, money was money, an' how hard could be? Hell, we even had ourselves a tame one. Ole Grampa Sawtooth we called him. He'd been old when Pa's Pa was still a boy. A big, slow sonofabitch that they dressed in wreathes of spikerush and sawgrass when Spring came round. Folk said he was the spirt of the river, but that was just crazy talk.

As a kid I'd peppered his hide with my slingshot more times than I could recall and he'd just yawned and blinked like some fool gone soft-brained on moonshine. Yup. We reckoned Ole Sawtooth would make a mighty fine pair o' gentleman's boots.

So off we went to hunt the old fella. I was down in the black mud waiting fer Pa when he struck. Couldn't rightly believe it. He moved like the very Devil, raisin' from the slime and slick so fast there weren't no time to run.

I was down and he was on me, his breath all Mississippi weed 'an rotted flesh. He looked right at me then, and with a lurch I knew I'd been readin' him wrong all these years. He wasn't dumb. He was cunning.

Then came the God-awful sound of crunchin' bone. My bone. Round and round we danced. Eye ta eye, he wrassled me down, coughin' and chokin', into a Hell, red-stained with my own lifeblood.

Mighty funny way ta end your days an' that's no mistake.

<<>>

I lurched forward as the stick was drawn from my bio-port. I could still feel the mud in my lungs. The gnawing ache as bones that weren't mine were snapped like kindling.

There was a reason that no respectable drama-stream offered full-sensory uploads: no matter how real the actors made it look, if you bio-shared, then you'd know they were faking. But this was the real deal. I could see now why people got addicted. I'd never felt so alive.

I'd made the decision to go back in even before the Patrone framed the question. I bent my head for the second time and in micro-moments I was someone else, somewhere else.

<<>>

It's 8.12 exactly. I know this because I glanced at my fob watch just after Reverend Ferguson finished his sermon. I've never believed in the necessity for public displays of faith but these are dark times, and it's important to keep up appearances.

The Reverend has just said something. The man speaks in such an interminable Scots drawl, that I find it hard to pay attention at the best of times. This morning, my mind seems to be somewhere else entirely and although I haven't a clue what the old fool is talking about, I nod and smile in what I hope is an interested manner.

They say that nurses spend so long in the company of Death that they develop a sixth sense about these sorts of things. So maybe that's it. Maybe part of me knows instinctively what is coming. As the Reverend drones on, I find myself straining to hear—something. Anything that might justify my growing sense of unease. Then, suddenly, there it is: a dull roar. A long, drawn-out howl that seems to run the length of the ship, from stem to stern.

It takes a while for me to realize that I am lying on the floor. I try to rise, but I fall over twice as the ship bucks then starts to lurch to starboard.

I know with a cold clarity that we have been struck and it's then that the training kicks in. I'm like an automaton. I flatten down my curls, fasten my cape, and head towards the public rooms which have been pressed into service as wards for the most grievously injured.

I try to keep them to the forefront of my mind. The young men who have already done so much for their country. They will need our help getting to the lifeboats. The thought helps to stop the rising panic.

We work like a well-oiled machine. Faces blank. Voices clipped. A model of calm efficiency. Just as it should be.

At that moment, the girls under my charge look impossibly young and I feel a surge of pride at the way they handle themselves. Even little Lucy Jenner. A flighty young thing at the best of times—now chewing her lip to a bloody shred—but not a word of protest. Just pale-faced determination.

It is only once we are in the lifeboat that the facade slips. Some of the younger girls are crying now. Some fuss over the wounded as a way of distracting themselves. A few laugh. We've been through the worst, they say. We're safe now. Soon be back on dry land.

For a moment, that thought warms me. It is a glorious morning in the Aegean. In the distance, I can practically see the golden beaches. The sea is warm. Spray hits my face. I turn, laughing, and the world freezes.

The ship's stern is almost out of the water now. Its giant propellers thresh the sea into a fury of foam. One of the lifeboats is being pulled into the blades. It's so close to the hull that, as it's dragged toward the propellers, the glass from the boxes which form the green band around the hospital ship's middle splinter.

Above, I hear cries and see men clinging to the railings. Dangling above the churning blades with nowhere to go but down.

I look away as the boat hits the propellers. There are no words to describe what I hear but when I raise a hand to wipe off the sea spray, it comes away red and bloody.

And now we're spinning. Our little boat, our safe little world, is spinning. Slowly at first, then faster and faster as it's dragged ever closer to those whirling blades.

The water boils pink—an abattoir of wood and flesh. I never learnt to swim, but I jump anyway. For a second I bob like a cork, then the undertow grabs me. As I thrash and spin for a second, I come eye-to-eye with little Lucy Jenner. Just before the waves close over her, she mouths something then, inexplicably, she smiles. She has a look of such beatific bliss that I can't help but smile back.

There are others in the water now, close to me. I feel their feet pounding. Fingers grabbing. A hand tugs at mine. For a moment, we two lost souls link fingers, then she's pulled from my grasp, inch by painful inch.

I'm drowning. I know this with a strange detachment. I should struggle. I should fight. But the water takes me down, and as I surrender to it, I feel a strange sense of relief. As though I have spent my whole life fearing this moment and now I can finally let go. I'm drowning and I'm happy. I take a gulp of sea water and think of little Lucy Jenner. Then I smile again.

<<>>

This time, the jolt back to reality comes so quickly that I fall off my recliner. I'm giddy. Gasping for breath. My first Still had been a shocking, brutal thing. This was, somehow, exhilarating. To be so close to death and still smile. I feel the warmth of her certainty. Her faith? There is more to it than that, but I don't know what exactly. What I do know is that I want more. I need more.

I leave work early next day and head straight for the Still Shop. This time, I have it all planned out, but the Experience is still a revelation. I'd forgotten what it was like to be so young, so trusting. To feel a child's joy at the simple things.

The more I Experience, the more I want. The Patrone was right. It isn't all trauma and death. There are snippets of everyday life here too. I'm preparing a meal, making love in a hayfield, singing, chopping wood, giving birth.

Some say that these small, human moments are all that is left of much bigger stories, overwritten by more graphic events. Who can know for sure? But in many ways, it's these appetizers that have me hooked. I bounce from century to century, switching sex, nationality, religion, and language as often as I can. I want to try it all. The more I experience, the more the spirits speak to me. Sometimes, I wish I could logout from this temporal realm and live what remains of my time fully in the world of ghosts.

Life, now, is so different from those I experience. The crooks and the bullies are in charge and fear rules us all. We live in bubbles, plugged in and disconnected, choosing our truths, inoculating ourselves to reality however we can. What I glimpse when I Still seems more real than anything I've ever lived. More real than my cubical job and my cubical home. It speaks to a longing deep within me. Something I'd forgotten.

I start to skip work. I barely eat. Barely sleep. And when I do, I dream someone else's dreams. As my finances start to run low, I switch Shops. There are, I learn, levels of Experience. I go underground.

In the basement of a disused store, lousy with roaches, high with the musk-stench of rodents, I find my new home. Here there are no maître d's, no attendants, no affectations. Just the Experience. I live a thousand lives. I love, laugh, and face death a thousand ways. I connect. Every experience leaves me longing for more.

I read somewhere that no man is an island but now I know that's not true. We're all islands. No one can ever truly know what it's like to be someone else. To stand in their shoes. But with each new Experience I feel like I am getting closer. This is more than sensation-seeking. This is more than voyeurism. There are answers here. I know it.

When, finally, my credit is exhausted I refuse to leave. I'm so close now that I can almost taste it. I need just one more hit. I rage, howl, and, finally, clinging to the shiny lapel of the bouncer's cheap bio-suit, I beg.

He's a big man, this bouncer, with tattooed knuckles and a boxer's stance. One push propels me backwards and I land hard against the edge of a steel top table.

It all happens so quickly. I know shouldn't be shocked by that. I've Experienced it so many times, in so many ways. I wonder fuzzily if someone will ever get to Experience me. My ending.

I taste blood and something else. Tears? How silly. I close my eyes and smile. Just like little Lucy Jenner. After all this time. All this searching. I thought that I'd missed something. Thought that I'd never get to the truth of things. And here I am, about to learn the answers, after all.

Death's Scout

Mark O. Decker

Has death passed my door,
spoken to me
like I was a common whore,
tried to break my spirit,
say no more;
I spit on you, and
on your scout,
Cancer,
You are Taliban,
you are nothing;
It is life that matters,
God's grace that shatters
your thinly veiled threats;
Shut up,
say no more.

Alternative Deathiness

Papercut

Larry Hinkle

Death sloppily slurped the filling from the last donut of a baker's dozen he'd pilfered on his previous stop (Lucky 13 was filled with blackberry jam, his favorite), wiped the powdered sugar from the cuff of his robe, and pulled out his list. Just one last pickup to make, and he could finally call it a century. Not a decade too soon, either. He smelled like something a dog would take great joy rolling around in, his bones ached down to the, well, bone, and he felt like he was catching a cold.

He read the last name on his list: *Erik Vaughn, 51. Writer. Omaha.*

A writer. Great. Just the way he wanted to end his shift. Writers could be such pretentious twits. Always wanted to argue about how it couldn't possibly be their time yet. Just give them a few more years and they would finally finish the World's Next Great Novel. Their work was Too Important to be stopped by something so commonplace as dying.

Well, his work was important too. It wasn't his fault that barely anyone remembered his name anymore. And besides, it's not like he had any say in the matter. Theirs just happened to be the next name on his list, which, through no fault of his own, wasn't nearly as long as it used to be. He blamed the Web. Nobody put pen to paper anymore. They just sent emails and texts filled with acronyms and emojis, which were just cartoonish hieroglyphics in his eyes (or at least what passed for eyes on a face like his). And forget about actually printing something. Everything was stored in the cloud now, so it was available onscreen anytime, anywhere. Well la-di-da. He lived in a cloud. It wasn't all that.

Death rolled up his list, threw the donut box away, imagined himself blinking (which was all he could do, since technically one needed eyelids to blink), and shifted his essence to Omaha.

<<>>

Erik Vaughn held his finger under the tap, letting the cold water numb the cut.

His laptop had crapped out last month and he didn't have the money to get it fixed. Since then, he was forced to write the last four chapters of his novel longhand, like some sort of savage. Despite his rusty penmanship, he'd been making decent progress until he couldn't remember if his character had ordered the bank customers to freeze or get down on the ground first. He was flipping back through the pages of his notebook when he felt his fingertip slice open. A ribbon of blood welled up through the slit and dripped onto his manuscript. "Dangit, not again," he said as he ran to the sink. He'd never got a paper cut off of his laptop.

He held his finger under the cold water. Once the bleeding stopped, he dried it off and wrapped a bandage around it. Satisfied, he walked back to his office.

<<>>

Death materialized on Erik's front porch. According to the hourglass, he was right on time. *"Or should I say,* write on time?" he said to himself. It was an old joke, but it still gave him a chuckle. Just a few more minutes, and he could finally clock out. He tucked the hourglass away and stepped through the wall.

Erik's office was a mess. Every inch of every shelf was filled with books. Piles of papers were stacked haphazardly on the floor. A pyramid of magazines and newspapers, highlighted with a rainbow of post-it notes, sat too close to the edge of his desk. Coffee cups and fast-food containers were scattered about. Death felt bad for the poor soul who'd have to clean this place when he left.

He tapped the handle of his scythe on the office floor and began. *"Erik Vaughn, your name is on my list,"* he said. *"You must come with me."*

<<>>

Erik wasn't sure which he noticed first: the sudden temperature drop, or the stench. It reminded him of the time his dog Koko had rolled around in a great big gob of greasy grimy gopher guts. (It was really a dead sewer rat, but he'd hummed the song while bathing Koko to keep from throwing up.) A second later the floor shook, and he heard a voice that somehow *wasn't* a voice say his name.

He looked up from his desk and saw a man dressed as the Grim Reaper standing in his office. At least he assumed it was a man. It was hard to be certain since it didn't have skin.

"Who are you?" he asked. "And how the hell did you get in my house?"

"*I am Death,*" the intruder said. "*A Reaper of men's souls.*"

"A Reaper? You mean there's more than one of you? How does that work?"

"*Actually, it works—*"

"And why just men's souls? What kind of archaic system is that?"

"*It's just a phrase, it doesn't—*"

Erik held up his hand. "Doesn't what? Mean anything? Then why did you say it? Patriarchal much?" He pulled a copy of *Ms.* magazine from the pyramid and tossed it at the Reaper. "Here, read this. Maybe you'll learn something. And leave me alone. I've got work to do." He turned his back on Death and picked up his pen.

"*I have work to do, too,*" Death said. He twirled his scythe and scattered the stack of magazines across Erik's desk. "*And unfortunately for you, it involves me, a Reaper, reaping the soul of you, a man. Now, if you'll just come along…*"

"I'm not going anywhere with you." Erik turned back around and looked up to where Death's eyes should be. "Not until I finish my book."

This is why Death hated writers.

"*Look Erik, I don't care about your book. Nobody cares about your book.*"

"I don't care."

"*What?*"

"I don't care that you don't care. *I* care. And if I care, then you can't very well say no one cares, now can you?"

"*That doesn't count.*"

"Why not?"

"It just doesn't. And even if it did, it wouldn't matter. Your time is almost up."

"Almost?" Erik looked at the clock on his desk. It had stopped ticking. "How much time do I have left?"

Death pulled out Erik's hourglass. The upper chamber was nearly empty.

"Not long, I'm afraid." He raised his scythe.

"Wait! Can I ask a question?"

"You just did."

"God, stop being such an asshole."

"God has nothing to do with this, Erik."

"What? How can God not have anything to do with death?"

Death lowered his scythe and sighed. *"It's complicated."*

"Try me." Erik leaned back in his chair.

Death checked Erik's hourglass again. There were still two grains of sand circling in the upper chamber. *"Sure, why not,"* he said. *"Looks like I've got a few minutes to kill."*

"That's not funny."

"Maybe not to you. But it kills in the office." Death placed Erik's hourglass back onto the desk. *"What do you want to know?"*

"What's it like?"

"I wouldn't know. I've never died."

"No, not dying. Killing."

"Killing?" Death looked appalled. *"I don't kill anyone, Erik. I just pick them up."*

"Well, if you don't kill them, who does? Another Reaper?"

"No, it's not like that at all. We just do pickups."

"Then how do you decide who's doing which pickup? Why is my name on *your* list, and not some other Reaper's?"

"It's just the way the work is divvied up. There's the head Death, Grim, who handles all the heavy dying. Wars, famine, pestilence, that sort of thing. Not that there's all that much famine and pestilence these days. At least not as you perceive time. But war? War's like happy hour. It's always happening somewhere."

"What about the people who just die of old age, or car accidents, or heart attacks on the toilet?" Erik asked. "What happens to them?"

"That's where my department comes in. The 'Death Of's' and 'Death By's' and 'Death From's.' We handle the more special deaths. Like yours."

"Like mine?" Erik perked up. Maybe his death would mean something after all. "What's so special about me?"

"Nothing. Haven't you been listening?"

"You just said my death was special."

"It is. But it's only special to me, I'm afraid." He looked at Erik's finger. *"It's not the who, Erik, but the how. Like I said, it's complicated."*

"I can't be dying!" Erik knocked the hourglass onto the floor. A fresh dot of blood bloomed across his bandage. "I watch what I eat. I don't drink. Much. I don't smoke. I have a gym membership!"

"Do you go?"

"No. But I'll go right now if you just look the other way. They're open 24 hours."

"Sorry, Erik. I don't make the rules. Now if you don't mind, it's been a long century." He raised his scythe.

"It's just a stupid paper cut!"

"Yes, but it's your thousandth."

Alternative Deathiness

Death's Doorway

Diana Hauer

Author's Note: This story is dedicated to all the compassionate death doulas, soul midwives, and transition coaches who help the dying and their families face the end of life.

"What's a 'death dueler'?" asked the prison gate guard.

Jazmine Williams stifled a sigh. "Not dueler, doula. D-O-U-L-A. You know what? Just put my occupation down as a transition coach."

Relieved, the guard nodded and made a few notes on the visitor's log. "Sign here.. Wear the ID badge at all times. Have you been here before?"

She raised an eyebrow. "No. I've never been to prison."

He grunted and buzzed her in. "I'll have someone come and escort you to the infirmary."

Jazmine dropped her purse on the scanner and walked through the metal detector. The waiting area was utilitarian and joyless. And chilly. She caught a glimpse of herself, reflected in the security mirror. A slender, mocha-skinned woman with her arms wrapped around herself. That would not do at all. Consciously, she straightened and squared her shoulders, letting her hands relax at her sides. Her black hair framed her head like a halo. No-nonsense slacks and a green blouse, understated make-up. Better. The woman who looked back at her now radiated compassion and strength. She would need both in the hours to come.

"Jaz? Is that you?"

The voice that broke the silence was unexpected, but familiar. "Mickey!" She started forward to hug her old college friend. He held up a hand, and she smiled sheepishly. "My bad. I forgot. They warned me about touching the guards. How have you been?"

"Not bad," he said. "Still shopping my screenplay around. This pays the bills while I wait to hear back. Oh, and please call me Officer Jenkins, or just Jenkins." He leaned forward and said quietly, "Seriously, the guys will never let me hear the end of it. I go by Mike nowadays."

"Sorry," said Jazmine. "Anyway, Jenkins, I always liked your short films."

"Thanks!" He cleared his throat and straightened up. "Well Ms. Williams, they said to show you to the infirmary. Please follow me."

Jenkins led her through a maze of bleak hallways and barred gates. "What brings you here?" he asked.

"One of the inmates is dying," she said. "I've come to hold a vigil with him."

"Why?" asked Jenkins. "I mean, is he a relative?"

She shook her head. "I'm here as a death doula, a midwife of the soul. My calling is to make sure no one has to die alone."

"I thought midwives helped babies get born," said Jenkins.

"We help to ease the transitions into and out of this life," Jazmine replied.

"That sounds kind of profound."

"Death is. Death and birth are the only milestones that every human is guaranteed to experience. Most of the time, I work as a birth doula in a hospital, so it is my privilege to be present for both the beginning and the end."

Jenkins glanced back at her. "Birth, I get that. I can't imagine what it's like to have that kind of relationship with death. Seeking it out, I mean."

An amused ripple tickled Jazmine's soul. "Most can't," she said. "But those of us who are called to this service can't imagine not answering that call."

<<>>

Dr. Radcliffe, the prison doctor, met her just outside the infirmary. "I don't approve of your kind here," he said without preamble.

She raised an eyebrow. "Black people, women, or end-of-life caregivers?" she asked. "The warden invited me, so really, I'm just curious."

He narrowed his eyes at her, large behind his thick glasses, and pushed past. His heavier frame knocked her into Jenkins as he stalked away. Jazmine watched the light dance off the bald spot ringed by gray-brown hair until he rounded the corner and disappeared.

"Is he always like that?" she murmured.

Jenkins shrugged. "Dr. Radcliffe isn't really a people-person. Anyway, your client is inside."

"Thanks, Jenkins.

Jazmine paused at the door to the infirmary and took a deep breath. This isn't about me, she reminded herself. It's about him.

Carter Smith, born February 3, 1930, likely to die sometime tonight. He was an old man with papery skin and hair clinging to his skull like cobwebs His cheeks formed hollows beneath his sunken eyes. She walked slowly through the ward and sat on a chair next to him and gently slid her hand under his, palm up.

The old man's fingers twitched. He squeezed her hand hard, as though spasming, then relaxed and traced the outlines of her hands with his fingertips. He opened his eyes with visible effort. "My goodness, a Negro!"

"Yes. Thanks for noticing," she said pleasantly. "My father was black, my mother was half-white, in case you wondered. My name is Jazmine Williams."

Carter looked sheepish. She suspected that he would blush if his body were still able. "Sorry," he said weakly. "My inside voice doesn't always stay inside anymore."

"That's all right," she said. And it was. People transitioned in different ways.

"Are you a nurse?"

"Yes, but I'm not here to poke needles into you or anything like that. I'm just here to sit with you, if that's all right."

He tried to laugh, but it came out as coughs. "I've been in here almost fifty years. Any idea how long it's been since a pretty lady sat with me and held my hand?" Jazmine shook her head.

He lay his head back onto the dingy pillow and was silent for almost a minute. He turned his head until he faced her.

109

"Let me tell you about Amanda. I met her when I was twenty-one, just after my tour in the Army..."

<<>>

Carter talked, Jazmine listened. She was there for him. Some patients needed comfort, others wanted to hear stories. Carter Smith needed someone to listen.

"Amanda, bless her soul, died of a heart attack about twenty years ago." A tear squeezed from the old man's eye. Jazmine gently dried his cheek with a rough tissue from the box on his bedstand. "I couldn't get out to attend the funeral. Lawrence told me about it. That was the last time I saw him."

"What about your daughter. You said her name was Lacey?" Something was moving in the shadowed corner at the far and of the room.

"Lucy," breathed Carter, drawing his lips back in a deathly smile. "She was such a pretty girl. Took more after her mama than me." His eyes were closed. Jazmine wasn't sure if he was imagining Lucy's face or he was too tired to hold his eyelids open.

Eyes shone back at her from the shadows. Outlines of an alligator's head and a lion's paws reared up. Jazmine met its gaze and shook her head sternly. It roared soundlessly and slunk away.

Other things are attracted by the impending death came. Jazmine let those who were there to witness stay. Those that were there to feed, she warded away. Scavengers of souls, who lived on the end of life. Those who died alone were the easiest prey; they had no one's love to protect them. No one was there to ease the transition. Black dog-shaped things with white rings around the eyes took one look at her and faded away. Things that were all teeth and tentacles menaced at her, she bared her teeth at them in a grim parody of a smile and they fled. She turned back to Carter with a true smile as he told her about when little Lucy lost her first tooth and it fell into the stew she was helping her mother prepare. They ate all the stew, but they never found her tooth.

Minutes turned into hours as the old man spun tales of his life and times for the most sympathetic audience he had likely ever had. Carter's face scrunched up in the middle of a story about how he had tried to teach Lawrence to throw a football, but their dog intercepted ran away with the ball. His grip tightened, his fingernails dug into the back of her hand.

"Are you in pain?" asked Jazmine.

He nodded. "Comes and goes," he whispered.

She patted his arm and eased her hand slowly out from under his. "I'll be right back." Jazmine smoothed her clothes as she stood and stretched. She had been sitting for hours. Nothing moved in the shadows just now. A few traumatized ghosts were watching curiously. They were harmless.

Dr. Radcliffe sat at his desk, typing. He did not look away from his screen as she walked up to him.

"Mr. Smith is in pain," said Jazmine.

"Yes, I imagine so," said Dr. Radcliffe. "He'd dying. It tends to hurt." He still had not looked at her.

"Don't you think you should do something? Give him something to ease his suffering?" she asked.

He finally turned a withering look at her. "I have a budget and very limited resources," he said. "Mr. Smith will be free of pain soon enough."

Jazmine put her hands on her hips and looked hard at him. "You took an oath, doctor. Your patient needs your help."

"Actually, we don't all take the Hippocratic Oath anymore," said Dr. Radcliffe. He stood. "But I was about to go and check on him anyway, so I will assess his pain level myself. If I feel there is a need, then I will give him something."

"Thank you," she said, trying not to grit her teeth. "Do you have the contact information for his children?"

<<>>

Jazmine left a candle to keep Carter company while she made a few calls. The light would ward off the shadows, for a little while.

"Hello?"

"Hi, is this Lucy Smith?"

"Yes. May I ask who's calling?"

"My name is Jazmine. I'm calling about Carter Smith."

The voice on the other end shifted from pleasant to frigid. "What about him?"

Jazmine licked her lips and forced her shoulders to relax. "He is nearing the end of his life, and I hoped that you would be willing to talk to him."

"I have nothing to say."

"This might be your last chance to say good-bye, or anything else you might want to tell him."

"I said I have nothing to say to him."

"You might regret—" Jazmine looked at her phone and sighed. Lucy had hung up.

At least Lucy had talked to her. Lawrence had hung up the moment she mentioned his father.

Jazmine couldn't imagine having that kind of rancor for her own father. He had passed on a few years ago. At the hospital, she had held her father's hand until the end, praying that he would open his kind, dark-brown eyes and look at her one last time.

He hadn't.

At least Jazmine had been able to tell him all the things she wanted to. She believed, hoped, that he had heard her on some level. Sharing his death made her realize that she wanted to be there for others, to ease their transition the way she had hopefully eased his.

Her mother, also a nurse, had shared the vigil. They each held one of his hands. His skin was dark chocolate compared to their mocha brown or her mother's milk chocolate. She always thought he was beautiful, as if the gods carved a man of ebony and gave him a golden heart as warm as sunlight.

Focus on the vigil now. She squared her shoulders and walked back to the dark room where her patient waited.

<<>>

Carter smiled wanly as she returned. "They didn't want to talk to me, eh?" he rasped. "Not surprised."

Jazmine's face warmed. "Was I that obvious?"

"No, I'm just a good guesser." He laughed and coughed, closing his eyes again. "We have dogs here, you know that? They are part of a rehab program. Lifers got nothing but time, so some groups foster dogs with them and get the pooches ready for adoption. There was a little mutt named Bubbie, always trembling. Terrier-Dachsund mix. One day, she ran off and hid. Nobody could find her. Her handler was frantic.

I calmed him down, calmed everyone down. Figured the pup was probably hiding, scared by all the noise and commotion and hollering. I told them to set out a dish of wet dog food and we all sat down and played a nice, quiet card game. Half an hour later, out comes Bubbie, all covered in dust and dirt, to snarf down the food."

"Just as you guessed she would." Jazmine took her seat again.

"A little patience and a little insight go a long way. I figured what you would do, I knew what they would say." He sighed. "I didn't do right by them. I was an angry man. That's how I got in the fight. I was stupid and killed a man. Didn't mean to, but that didn't matter. Turned out the guy was somebody down slumming. The DA threw the book at me. Aggravated murder. Been here ever since." Tears escaped his closed eyes. "I still remember how the kids turned away from me as I was led away. Can't say I blamed them. I didn't just put a label on me. I put a label on them, too. I made them the children of a murderer."

Jazmine took his hand again. "What would you say to them if you could?"

He was silent for so long that Jazmine wondered if he had fallen asleep. "That I forgive them," he said. "And that I hope someday they will forgive me. And that I will always love them. Always and forever, even after." He opened one eye and looked at her. "Do you believe there is an after? Heaven and Hell?"

"I believe there is something," she said. "But I can't say that I know for sure what's on the other side of the transition."

"Transition from life to death, you mean?"

She nodded and squeezed his hand.

Dr. Radcliffe walked in and thrust a small paper cup with pills at her. He looked darkly at Carter, made a notation on his chart, and then walked silently away. If it weren't for the pills in her hand, Jazmine might have thought him a ghost as well. A rude, grouchy ghost. She shrugged and tilted Carter's head up so that he could swallow. It wasn't easy, but he got them down.

Soon.

"That was a pretty candle," said Carter. "What do the markings mean?"

"I carved sigils for peace and love into it. I hope you don't mind," said Jazmine. There were other, more powerful symbols on the candle as well. Markings of protection, mostly. Her mentors had taught them to her, along with the darker, more arcane aspects of her calling.

Carter told her more tales of his children, and the dogs their family had over the years. All of his stories seemed to center on his children and the dogs he had known. It broke her heart that she could not complete the circle for him, let him see them one last time.

Jazmine sat up straighter. "I'll be back in a moment, Carter. I need to go and ask Officer Jenkins something really quick."

She left the candle to keep him company and protect him while she was gone.

<<>>

Dr. Radcliffe stopped her in the hallway on the way back. "I looked you up," he said. "Do you believe that hogwash?"

She blinked a couple times. "Come again?"

"That crap about 'conscious dying' and 'transition through a sacred passage'? Oh, please. New Age hippie nonsense. It has no place in modern medicine."

Jazmine counted to ten. When she spoke, her voice was calm, controlled, and perfectly even. "I respectfully disagree with your opinion, doctor. Now if you do not mind, I have a vigil to attend. I would like to get back to our patient."

With a snort, Dr. Radcliffe stepped aside. "Frauds," he said as she walked away. "You asked what I object to. New Age, spiritualist, feel-good frauds like you who peddle their chicanery on the taxpayer's dime."

Head high, Jazmine bit her tongue and walked away from him. It isn't about you, she reminded herself as she returned to her vigil.

<<>>

"How do you see death?" asked Carter. His skin was turning gray, and she heard him struggle every time he pulled in or pushed out a breath.

"What do you mean?" asked Jazmine.

"A great and grand mystery? A man in a dark cowl wielding a scythe? A pretty girl with black hair and pale skin?"

"You'll laugh."

"Won't. Not enough air to laugh." He tried anyway.

Jazmine turned up the oxygen flowing through the canula. "I imagine my father. He was the darkest, blackest man I knew. His skin seemed to swallow the sun when he stood outside in the summertime. And he was the kindest, smartest, gentlest man. I'm not saying that just because he was my dad, others saw it in him, too. Animals would walk right up and cuddle against him. Babies would stop crying when you put them in his arms," she said. "I rode with him in his ambulance a few times. No matter how upset or scared someone was, he would put his big hand on their forehead and all the tension drained out of their bodies, because they knew that they were safe with him." She looked down at her hands, clasped around Carter's. "When I was younger, I thought it was magic. I begged him to teach me how. He just laughed his deep, rich laugh and told me that it wasn't something he could teach."

"I bet he told you that you would find your own magic, one day," said Carter.

Jazmine smiled. "How did you know?"

"That's something dads tell their kids."

"All reading from the same playbook? Some sort of worldwide dad conspiracy?" teased Jazmine.

Carter opened one eye to look at her. "No, it's just a truth we all know. Every one of us sees the magic in our babies, even before they believe it is there themselves." His eye slipped closed again. "I think you might have some of his magic." He squeezed her hand, weakly.

Jazmine wiped her eyes. "What magic did you see in Lucy and Lawrence?"

The old man rambled on about his absent children. Jazmine and the candle maintained their vigil, keeping the scavengers at bay.

<<>>

The click of toenails on tile heralded a welcome arrival. Jazmine stood and smiled at Jenkins. "You brought him!"

"Well," he said sheepishly. "Joe couldn't leave his cell after hours, so I'm technically taking Tootsie here for a late-night potty walk."

"Of course." Jazmine pressed her lips together to keep from grinning down at the brown Labrador Retriever looking up at her. "I appreciate you doing this." She walked with the man and dog back to Carter's bed. The old man turned his head slightly and opened his eyes, but even that was an effort.

Tootsie was happy to help. With just a little encouragement, she jumped up on the bed and wiggled and licked everything that she could reach. Carter smiled as much as he could while the bundle of fur and happiness snuggled up against him. "Thank you," he whispered.

The young dog was a poor substitute for his children, but it was something. Jazmine was glad that she could give it to him.

"What the hell is going on here?" yelled Dr. Radcliffe. Jazmine and Jenkins both jumped. They hadn't heard him come in. "Get that creature out of here! It's unsanitary! Everything is going to have to be sterilized now."

Jazmine stepped forward to soothe the doctor. "Hospitals let therapy animals in all the time. The sheets will need to be washed eventually anyway, right?" she asked reasonably.

"There will be dander everywhere, and it probably messed on the floors," he snarled. "Who was that guard? I'll have him written up for this." Jenkins and Tootsie were nowhere to be seen. They had wisely retreated while the Dr. Radcliffe threw his tantrum.

"Doctor, I'll help you clean up in the morning if that will ease your concerns," said Jazmine.

"I'm going to speak to the warden about you when he comes in tomorrow." Dr. Radcliffe stormed out.

Jazmine shrugged and returned to her vigil. Carter was coughing weakly. She rushed over to take his hand again, then smiled as she realized that he was laughing.

<<>>

Carter lost consciousness near midnight. He muttered something now and then, but Jazmine had a feeling that he would not wake up again.

Birth and death were mirrors. This moment felt to Jazmine like the inverse, or reverse, of the moment of crowning; when a baby's head starts to push into the world. Carter's soul was starting to push its way out.

Some things about birth were easier than death. There was only one way for a baby to go out. Sure, a doctor could help things along, but you are only really supposed to go out one way. With death, there were many ways, many paths. Not all of the paths were good, or safe. Death doulas like Jazmine helped souls find the right path for them, kept them from getting lost. Just as a birth could be easy or traumatic, so could a death be easy or traumatic for the soul. When a death doula helped a soul to transition, it was more gentle and safer for all concerned. Like a doctor, death sometimes had to intervene when there were complications.

She looked around, staring down the soul eaters that still skulked at the edges of the light. There were more here than she had ever seen. Jazmine would inform her mentor when she finished Carter's vigil. She felt her heart twist as she imagined how many lonely deaths must have happened in this prison to have attracted so many scavengers.

Jazmine squared her shoulders and squeezed Carter's hand. "Not you, though. I will stay with you until the very end. You won't be alone, I promise."

Carter's labored breathing was his only response.

<<>>

"You should leave."

Jazmine jerked around but didn't let go of Carter's hand. "I didn't hear you come in, Dr. Radcliffe."

The doctor scowled at her through his thick glasses. "It's late. You should leave and get some sleep."

"I'm fine. Keeping the vigil is the reason I'm here. Besides," she touched Carter's shoulder gently. "It won't be long, now."

Dr. Radcliffe walked to the opposite side of the bed and looked down at her. The lights reflected off his glasses, hiding his eyes behind shining glass circles. "Why do you do this? Some sort of macabre fascination? Do you get off on death?"

Jazmine gasped. "What?"

"You heard me," he snapped.

With an effort, Jazmine closed her mouth. "I am a licensed nurse and a trained end-of-life transition coach." Some people responded better to the "transition coach" title than "soul midwife" or "death doula," though all of her titles were true. "All I want is to ease Mr. Smith's final transition."

Dr. Radcliffe shook his head. "He should die alone. Did he tell you what he did? How many times he stabbed that man? Or what about the time he shanked a fellow inmate. I was the one who stitched the poor bastard up." He ran a hand over his balding scalp. "Who knew you could do so much damage with a sharpened toothbrush? There was so much blood. So much. Carter Smith has a lot of blood on his hands."

Jazmine jerked her gaze up to Dr. Radcliffe's face. Something was wrong with his mouth. It was twisted, somehow. She blinked to clear her vision. His teeth were sharp, and his maw twisted forward for a second. She had a dizzying moment of double vision as the soul eaters in the shadows surged forward to swarm around, and through, Dr. Radcliffe.

In a moment of crystal clarity, she understood. There were so many here because of Dr. Radcliffe. "What are you?" she asked carefully, standing to face him.

He shrugged. "I'm a doctor who serves criminals, monsters who forfeit their souls by their actions. They don't deserve an afterlife." His teeth were sharp and glistened in the dim infirmary light. He raised his hand to show her a syringe. "We're tired of waiting. This will speed his passage. Painless. You want that for him, right? He could linger on for days, otherwise." The needle slowly moved towards Carter's IV bag.

"Leave him alone. He's under my protection."

Dr. Radcliffe laughed at her and loomed closer. The shadow creatures surrounded the bed, hemming them in until she could almost feel the hot breath of the soul eaters on her legs.

Jazmine threw her head back and laughed at them.

<<>>

Jazmine's hand snaked out and trapped Dr. Radcliffe's wrist. She grabbed his tie with the other and pulled his face close to hers. "Let me tell you a story."

He tried to plunge the syringe into her, but she was used to wrestling with patients, and stronger than him. "During my training, we did guided meditations. Trance work, shamanic journeys, that sort of thing. My mentor led me down into the Underworld, into the darkness inside.

"Thing about the Underworld, you learn there. It changes you. But there's always a cost for the knowledge. You have to pay a price. I came face to face with death, and let me tell you, he wasn't what I expected. He taught me everything I know about helping the soul transition, the mirror of birth. And you know what he wanted in return?" she asked.

Dr. Radcliffe switched the syringe to his other hand and jabbed at her again. Jazmine shoved him away, hard. He stumbled back. "I don't care," he snarled. "Get out of the way and let me harvest him, or we will rip your soul out and eat it for dessert."

Jazmine faced him squarely and lowered her head. "Death wanted a doorway into the living world." She licked her fingers and snuffed out the candle beside Carter's bed. "And I agreed to be that doorway."

Behind Dr. Radcliffe stood a man in surgical scrubs and a mask. He could be any doctor in the obstetrics ward, professional and anonymous. Every inch of skin was covered except for his forehead and eyes. Dark-brown eyes set in ebony-black skin met Jazmine's.

Eyes that perfectly matched Jazmine's own.

"Take them," said Jazmine. "The door is open."

Death raised his right hand and watched the light play off the scalpel he held. For a moment, the blade seemed to curve, like a scythe. The soul eaters recoiled. Dr. Radcliffe turned to look at him and froze. His mouth worked silently, but no words came out. The masked doctor turned slowly, fixing each of the creatures in the room with his stare. One by one, they cowered before him.

Otherworldly energies tore through the air around her. Instinctively, she dropped onto the bed and shielded Carter's frail body with her own. She huddled over him, trembling, as death walked through the room and ripped everything that did not belong there out of existence, throwing them back through the door her will held open.

<<>>

Large, strong hands gently helped her up and guided her to a chair. Her sight and hearing returned slowly, like waking up from a dream.

Dr. Radcliffe was lying against the wall on the other end of the room. Jazmine licked her lips. "Will he live?"

The being who wore her father's face shook his head slowly, then looked down at Carter. His hand rested gently on the old man's forehead.

"Are you going to take him?"

Death lifted his hand away and met his daughter's eyes. Not yet. He has one more thing to do. He nodded at her phone, sitting on Carter's bedstand. You should answer that.

The phone rang. Jazmine looked down at it. When she looked up again, death was gone.

The number on the phone was not familiar, but she answered anyway. If they were calling her at three in the morning, it was probably important. "Hello?"

"Miss Williams? This is Lucy Smith."

"And Lawrence," a male voice chimed in.

"We're on a conference call. My brother and I got to talking, and you were right," said Lucy. "We do have some things to say to him."

"Is Dad still with us?" asked Lawrence.

"Yes, he is," said Jazmine. "But I'm afraid he isn't conscious. I can put the phone next to his ear if you'd like."

"Yes, please," said Lucy. "Sorry for calling so late."

"You called right on time," said Jazmine. "I'm going to put your father on, now."

She sat on the edge of the bed and held her phone up next to Carter's ear. Jazmine could hear the voices of the children speaking but could not make out the words. After a few moments, Carter's slack mouth tightened into a smile. A tension he had been holding released.

He breathed out one last time.

Jazmine waited long enough to be sure that he was not going to breathe again, then put the phone up to her own ear.

"He's gone, isn't he?" asked Lucy. It sounded like she was trying not to cry.

"He is," Jazmine said, wiping her own eyes.

Lucy sobbed. Lawrence cried, too. "We should have called sooner. I am so sorry."

Jazmine sat down. "He told me a lot about you. Would you guys like to talk about him? With me?"

It took a moment for the surviving Smiths to stop crying enough to speak. "You're a death doula, you said? He is dead. Daddy died." Lucy sobbed. "Isn't your job done?"

"Oh, sweetheart," said Jazmine tenderly. "I'm a mourning doula, too. End-of-life transitions aren't just about the one who dies. They're also about the people who loved them, who need to find a way to live on after the death."

Alternative Deathiness

Missing

Robin Pond

Officer Justin approaches the counter. He considers reception duty, which he endures once every three weeks, a waste of time. In this age of self-service policing, most of the enquiries are best handled by one of the automated kiosks running Delphi. Delphi is spectacular. In fact, for most informational enquiries, Justin would have to tap into Delphi himself to be able to provide a suitable answer. So why not cut out the middleman and go right to the source?

But there are always a few recalcitrant souls who can't or won't avail themselves of the convenient self-policing kiosks. And, despite extreme budgetary pressures, the Commissioner refused to do away with the service, pointing out that Delphi can supply answers, but it can't supply empathy. Besides, he argues, an apparently unmanned police station would give the wrong impression, even though it wouldn't really be unmanned. There would always be officers in the control centre, just not out in public view.

Justin surveys the activity in the expansive common area of Gamma Division. A typical Thursday afternoon, lots of people milling around, most of the kiosks in use, the steady murmur of quiet conversations punctuated by various tones and chimes from the kiosks. There are ninety-six kiosks in all, arranged eight across and twelve deep, each with a small built-in bench opposite the screen and surrounded by semi-opaque plexiglass barriers to provide the illusion of confidentiality. At any given time, three or four of the screens might be out of order, but that still leaves plenty of capacity. There is rarely ever a wait.

On this side of the room, away from the kiosks and directly across from the counter, a solitary elderly lady sits waiting, a silly smile on her face. She is wearing a flower-print dress, the type you might find in a vintage store, with a thick strand of fake pearls around her neck, gaudy gold bangles on both her wrists, and heavy make-up.

Justin picks up the single piece of paper sitting in the in-basket, a form MP47/ENQ, and for a moment the scowl he has been suppressing seeps on to his features. But he quickly remasters his impassive expression before holding the paper up over his head. He calls out in a booming voice. "'Yes'? 'Yes'? Someone here related to a 'Yes'?"

He glances at the elderly woman who continues to smile benignly at all the non-existent people sitting around her, with a cherubic look of innocence more suitable on the face of a young child than an old woman. He draws a deep breath. "Did someone here file a Missing Person's Report?"

The woman's smile broadens. "Oh yes, that would be me." She gets up slowly and plods towards him.

"Well, ma'am, I need a name."

The woman looks confused as she sets her blue-lined hands on the edge of the counter to steady herself. "You don't have a name?"

Justin does his best to keep the annoyance out of his voice. "Of course I have a name."

Her smile returns. "So what's your name?"

"Justin."

"My name's Betty."

Justin nods in acknowledgement and is about to review the form with her but she doesn't stop talking. "Justin? You mean like, just in time? That's a great name for a police officer, isn't it? People can call emergency, like when a robbery's going down—you know?—or someone's about to commit a murder, and then you arrive, just in time. See?"

He is surprised this woman would make fun of his name, but she is smiling at him so kindly he decides no offence is intended. He simply points out, "My last name's not Time".

"That's all right." She consoles him. "Your name...for a policeman...it still really suits."

He draws another deep breath. "My name's not important."

But she immediately cuts him off. "Nonsense. Your name's extremely important. It's crucial. It's your representation to the world. It greatly affects how the world will view you. Take my husband's name. Far too much alliteration. His parents did him no favour, no favour at all, believe you me. The world will never take seriously a man with an alliterative name."

"Ma'am, are you filing this Missing Person's Report?"

"Yes, of course," Betty responds brightly, "that's why I'm here."

"Well, who's missing?"

She waves her hand, dismissing such a silly question. "My husband, of course. Isn't that who we're talking about? And you can see right there, I attached his picture to the form. Of course, it's an old picture, so he looks a lot younger there. I didn't have anything recent. But he looks better in that picture than in real life, anyway, so it's rather flattering, you know? He's really let himself go."

Justin lays the form MP47/ENQ on the counter and leans forward, pointing to it. A wave of Betty's perfume washes over him but he continues implacably. "Yes ma'am. But you see, here on the form, where it says 'missing person', you just wrote 'yes'."

"That's because he *is* missing."

Justin straightens up. "But you're supposed to put his name."

"That's not what it says."

"It's sort of understood."

"Obviously not."

"No. I suppose not in this case." Justin glances at the woman and decides this isn't an argument worth continuing. "Well then, what's your husband's last name?"

"Pearson." Betty tells him.

Justin picks up a pen and starts to amend the form. "Pearson?"

"Yes, it's like Person, but with an 'A'." She explains. "So he's like a missing person, but with the "A". You see? He's a missing Pearson."

Justin doesn't comment. He merely starts to print out the name on the form in block letters: P-E-A-R-

"That spells 'pear'." Betty observes. "He's kind of shaped like a pear."

Justin continues: –S-O-N

"Except we don't have a son. We don't have any children at all. He couldn't, you know. Probably the result of a bicycle accident. He rode his bicycle a lot when he was younger. Now he mainly just rides the couch. But when he was younger, he was actually quite athletic. Not that you'd know to see him now. But I just figured he'd fallen hard on to that crossbar once too often, and so we couldn't really have any children, not that we minded much, at the time—you know?—it's just—"

Justin cuts through Betty's monologue. "Yes ma'am. And what's his first name?"

"Peter." She smiles and nods. "You see? Far too alliterative. Peter Pearson. No one will ever take him seriously."

"No ma'am."

"You think so too?"

Justin shifts back a bit from Betty's perfume. "I really wouldn't know."

"Well, you should know." Her tone is suddenly reproachful. "It's really quite obvious."

Justin is surprised at the admonishment, but determined to stick to the task at hand. "And how long has he been missing?"

Betty shrugs. "I have no idea."

Justin examines her critically. "Doesn't your husband live with you?"

And Betty launches into another mini-tirade: "In a manner of speaking. If you call that living. He exists, sort of as a moveable lump. From the bed to the couch to the easy chair. He's just there, always there. Constant inertia. He probably proves some law of physics. I can't remember the last time he said, 'Betty, get your coat—'"

Justin interrupts yet again. "Well then, when did you first notice he was no longer there?"

Betty appears to consider this carefully. "It's hard to say, really. It's been more of a dwindling than an immediate effect."

"Dwindling?"

"Yes. Over time. There've been fewer dirty dishes in the sink. Fewer clothes to pick up off the floor. Fewer times when I have to go hunting for the TV remote."

Justin gently probes for further information. "But what was the last time you actually saw him?"

"I'm not sure." Betty's voice is softer now, more thoughtful. "It's like having an old lamp in the living-room, you know? It's there for years, and if it's suddenly removed, you notice something's different about the room, but you just can't put your finger on what's changed. Then one day it comes to you, the lamp's gone."

"So you never really look at him?"

"That's not true." Betty is offended by the observation. "You're really not understanding me at all. I look at him. I take long, hard looks at him all the time. I'm the one who tells him if what he's wearing is suitable. I'm always after him about his weight, and his needing to get a haircut, and all sorts of personal hygiene issues. I've spent years trying to improve that man's image. Believe you me, it's a full time job."

"Yes, I imagine it is. But surely, if Mr. Pearson really is missing, you must have noticed—"

"You're not married, are you?" Betty asks suddenly.

Justin hesitates. He doesn't normally give out personal information. But in this particular case, he doesn't see the harm. "No, ma'am. I'm not."

"So it's not your fault if you don't understand."

Instead of responding, Justin tries to convince Betty it might be too soon to file a formal Report if she doesn't really know how long he's been gone.

"But he is missing." She objects. "I searched the whole apartment this morning."

"Yes ma'am, but maybe he's just gone out for a while."

"That's not Peter Pearson. That's not him at all. I've spent half my life trying to get that man up off the couch. There's no way he's left it voluntarily. And why would he leave? Why would he, all of a sudden, after all these years, just get up and leave?"

"I can think of a few reasons." Justin mutters.

And Betty pounces on the comment. "What? What reasons?"

Then Justin is left to backtrack awkwardly. "Oh...nothing...really. I wouldn't want to speculate."

"Nor should you. No! It doesn't make any sense. It's just not like him. And I'm getting worried. What if something's happened?"

Justin attempts to allay her fears but she remains unconvinced.

"Can't you put out some sort of all-points bulletin? You know. Be on the look-out for a scruffy, somewhat paunchy man, long past retirement age, probably dressed in sweat pants and a t-shirt with a food stain on it. Something like that?"

And eventually Justin relents. "Okay, I'll tell you what. Let me run his name through Delphi, just to be sure." He scans in the form MP47/ENQ and then gets some supplemental particulars from her and types them into the screen on the counter. "This'll just take a second. But really, I'm sure there's no reason to be concerned. He's probably just—" Delphi provides the answer tone before he can even finish his thought.

He stares at the information on the screen and his usually impassive face registers concern. He glances back up at Betty.

She smiles benignly. "You've found him already?"

Justin nods slowly. "Yes, ma'am, I'm afraid we have."

"He's been spotted?"

"In a manner of speaking... Delphi's provided a copy of his obituary."

Betty's mouth sags open but no words emerge. Her eyes go blank and she starts to sway. Justin races around the counter and manages to catch her just as she collapses. He carries her back to the row of chairs and sits her down, easing into the chair next to her and continuing to support her limp body. Eventually she regains consciousness.

"I'm sorry, Betty." He says quietly. "I can appreciate what a shock this must be for you."

After a further moment, she asks weakly, "You're saying he's...he's..."

"Yes ma'am. I'm sorry to have to inform you, your husband passed away three months ago."

"Was there a funeral?"

Justin nods, still supporting her. "According to Delphi, it was at Funston's funeral home."

"That's definitely the one we'd use." Betty ponders the information. "Yes, you know, now that you mention it...I do sort of remember...You'd think something like that would've made a greater impression. I mean, I can understand forgetting where I've left my glasses. I do that all the time. Sometimes I'll even be running around the apartment looking for them, and they'll have been there all the time, propped up on top of my head. But forgetting what you've done with your spouse seems so...I don't know."

"It's really not that unusual." Justin quietly reassures her. "We see this all the time. Cataclysmic events fade, and the well-worn routine takes over again."

"Yes, I suppose. And it's sort of like Peter, you know?"

"In what way?"

"To be overlooked. He was never terribly noticeable. He was just sort of always there."

Betty sullenly stares down at the floor. Then a tone sounds back at the counter. Justin excuses himself and moves quickly back to his post. He checks the screen and sees that a possible class-B felony has been reported in kiosk sixty-three. It requires manual intervention. He glances back at Betty and then quickly pushes the intercom, connecting to the control centre. He explains he is currently busy and needs backup to deal with the kiosk sixty-three follow-up.

By the time he is finished his brief conversation, Betty has plodded back over to the counter and is regarding him expectantly. "So...I guess there's nothing more you can do to help me, then, is there?"

"I'm very sorry for your loss."

She nods and thanks him. "Actually, I suppose he's no longer really lost."

With a couple of keystrokes, Justin recalls the information. "No, ma'am. He's at Pleasant Gardens. You can visit him there any time you like."

She thanks him again. "It's not really the same thing, though, is it? I mean, having to make a special trip and all. It's going to take some getting used to. The separation, I mean."

"Yes, I understand." Justin leans over the counter and softens his voice. "That's the real reason you're here today, isn't it?"

Betty seems embarrassed. "What do you mean?"

"I can appreciate how difficult it must be, when you're used to...well, used to having someone around all the time. And then suddenly they're not there anymore."

"It doesn't seem fair—you know?—after investing all those years. Just to have nothing."

The conversation has ended but Betty remains rooted in her spot in front of the counter. Justin supposes she has nowhere else to go. Suddenly a thought occurs to him. "Delphi often provides very creative solutions to problems."

She shakes her head. "I doubt even Delphi can do anything about Peter."

But he is already tapping furiously on the screen. He continues to stare at it, unwilling to face Betty without being able to provide some sort of help or solace. And his desperate determination is instantly rewarded. The answer tone sounds and information flashes on to the screen. He quickly scans through it before finally looking back up. "If I might make a suggestion, and I know it's not really a solution, but—"

"No...please...anything."

"According to Delphi, there's an organization, called Next Best Thing, which offers replacement androids for these sorts of situations."

"Replacement androids?"

Justin has a sudden moment of doubt. He isn't sure whether this idea will please her or offend her. But he has nothing else to offer so he forges ahead. "Yes, ma'am. Limited capacity robotic models. They've had a lot of success with situations not unlike your own. With the picture you've provided, they can make it...him...look just like Mr. Pearson, and he can be programmed with limited mobility set to a timer, so a couple of times a day he can move around the house. From the bed to the couch to the chair and back again, that sort of thing."

"His usual routine!" Betty notes with enthusiasm. "What a wonderful idea!"

She appears to brighten immediately and Justin feels compelled to sound a note of caution. "Of course, it won't be quite the same."

"It might be." Betty appears eager to clutch at any glimmer of hope.

"It's not as if you'll really be able to relate." He adds.

"Pretty much the same, then." She observes.

"I suppose you could talk to him, or at least at him, but you'll only get vague general responses."

"Sounds exactly the same." She concludes. "Problem solved, then. Thank you so very much. You've been most helpful."

Justin smiles in spite of himself. "A pleasure to serve, ma'am." It's turning out to be a really good day. Perhaps reception duty isn't such a waste of time after all. He downloads the Next Best Thing information and then comes back around the counter to escort Betty to the door.

She is once again smiling benignly. "I can't believe a nice young man like you isn't married. Are you seeing anyone? You know, I've got a niece who would be perfect for you. Her name's Sandra. Just graduated from college. Smart as a whip. Cute as a button. But it's so hard for young people to meet in today's busy world. So why don't I give you her phone number?"

"We're really not allowed—"

But Betty impatiently waves off the formal policy. "Nonsense. I'll tell her all about you. I'm sure she'll love your name, how suitable it is. I'll tell her to expect your call." She provides him with the phone number and countless other details about her niece.

When they arrive at the entrance to the station, as the automatic door slides open she turns towards him and her smile broadens. "After all, it would be a terrible thing to end up all alone, now wouldn't it?"

And he nods in agreement. "Yes ma'am. Yes it would."

Alternative Deathiness

Final Questions

Chris Kuriata

In the final moment, right before entering eternity, everyone gets one question.

This courtesy is a holdover from simpler times, when knowledge did not travel freely, and people were denied common truths. The final question is Death's gratitude for your participation in the grand experiment of existence.

Death keeps track of everyone's final question.

Because of Gutenberg, Death keeps careful notes, believing there will one day be a book. Such a project was impossible beneath the Monk's untrustworthy quills, but Johannes Gutenberg's movable type guarantees Death will get the words printed in the correct order.

Scraps of paper overflow Death's pockets, all the final questions scribbled in ink made from the seeds of extinct fruit. Death intends to stitch these final questions into a majestic tome—a ten-pound ledger that will sit in every log cabin, hotel room, and yurt across the shifting globe. This handy encyclopedia will guide people. By studying the billions of final questions already asked, people can choose their own more carefully. Ideally, people will secure their final question on a card tucked into their wallet, right between their organ donor specifications and their last will and testament.

Truthfully, most people squander their final question. Approximately twenty-five percent of those who find themselves lip-to-lip with Death ask the same knee-jerk question:

"Really?"

Yes, Death says. *Really.*

Just as popular and equally worthless:

"Now?"

Yes, Death says. *Now.*

People who die in explosions tend to be more focused.

"Is my wife/child/family going to survive?"

No, Death says.

There is always family involved. People seldom explode individually. Bombs are expensive, and if entire clusters of people weren't annihilated with each detonation they would have been phased out of warfare years ago. Of course your family didn't survive, you all went BOOM together.

Some even use their final question to offer Death a bribe.

"What do you need to forget about this?"

Or:

"How much do you want?"

Those who die wearing golden crowns know better than to try making a deal. After all, they held onto their power by refusing to negotiate. Kings understand Death humbles every ruler eventually, so there is grace in surrendering.

Death hasn't the free time to study popular culture. Some questions, although received sincerely, only hazard guesses.

"Who killed Laura Palmer?"

Shrug. *Shelley the waitress?*

"How does Cadbury get the smooth caramel into the chocolate?"

Shrug. *They inject the caramel while the chocolate is still wet?*

"Did Elvis really die in 1977?"

Shrug. *I've never met him.*

Some questions are too cryptic to answer satisfactorily.

"How many?"

How many what? How many former lovers will be at your funeral? How many victims are you taking with you after detonating your dynamite vest? How many Facebook memorial postings will your passing generate? Without context, Death can only respond with what is surely the most truthful answer to any of those scenarios:

Too goddam many.

People who jump off bridges or swallow pills in the bathtub all want to know:

"Will they understand I didn't do this to spite them?"

Eventually.

Air show hot doggers who crash in orange bursts like volcanic eruptions ask:

"Did someone get a good shot of this?"

Opera sopranos whose brains stroke out during the final aria ask:

"Will there be a standing ovation?"

Lonely people in apartments they haven't left in weeks ask:

"Will someone give my dog a good home or will he be gassed by the end of the week?"

Infants pressed against flat breasts incapable of producing milk ask:

"I guess this wasn't the right time, was it?"

The death row murderers are tricky to guess. They ask:

"Will I be proven innocent?"

Or

"Since my death won't bring anyone back, I kinda got away with it, didn't I?"

Of course, there are always the wags. Goofballs who refuse to take anything serious, chortling like morons as if they were the first clever enough to ask:

"How long is a piece of string?"

Or

"Who's on first?"

Or

"Oh my God, what's that behind you?"

Death suffers these queries stoically, because the final question deserves gravity. During the last slice, Death stands erect, jutting out their chin so the fat beneath their ancient neck doesn't sag, and answers all:

> *Yes.*
> *No.*
> *Never.*
> *She will.*
> *Absolutely.*
> *On a glorious day.*
> *First base.*
> *Donald Trump.*
> *Until the end of time.*

In the final days, when the winter burns, the questions come fast and furious. Ice melts and new rats carry disease and lungs reject the polluted air. Death appears in a thousand places at once, spitting out answers to questions Death barely has the time to listen to.

The great acceleration of the final days takes its toll. The feathers on Death's back split, losing clouds of grey fluff, as though Death is a blown dandelion. Death's muscles are sore and their hearing is nearly drowned out by the drilling of tinnitus, but Death weathers the storm. This age won't last forever. Soon, Death's duties will slow down to a veritable stand-still. For the first time since just after the creation of the world, Death will be asked less than a question a day. Maybe as many as two or three days will go by without a question.

Death enjoys the slow down. The promise of grand relaxation keeps Death soldiering through the current barrage of questions. Death is coming apart at the seams, but they persist giving honest answers to the scariest questions yet to be asked.

"Will the earth return to normal?"

Never.

"When will all this suffering end?"

Tomorrow.

"How long will we all be quiet?"

Forever.

On the other side of measurable time, Death relaxes. Holding the entirety of human kind's final questions scribbled on scraps of paper spilling out of their pocket, Death at last reads, and considers, and forms the most informed judgement on the experiment of existence.

The Borrower

Katie Sakanai

Other lands might picture something dark and formidable, but this country knew Death walked free in the guise of an ordinary man. Death was a fair man, and he granted you a bit of notice in the case of an untimely death. He found you and marked you, and then nature did the rest: an accident, cancer, failure to thrive, influenza. He never came to collect the old and weary. They knew when it was their time well enough.

His visit was merely a warning of what was to come, not a tragedy in itself. Death marked people with an object, testing them to see if it was theirs. People warned children never to talk to or take something from a stranger. If an item is proffered, you never touch it. But it was simple enough; the gesture of giving and receiving is more of a reflex than a conscious decision. Just watch a baby reach out her slender arm.

The object was something of interest for them, with a magnetism they couldn't explain. Something they were drawn to, something they might have held once before, but couldn't quite place. A perfume bottle. A ring. A watch chain. A small, threadbare teddy. A chipped teacup. A pin cushion. A coin. Once they recognized it and held it in their hands, they were marked; simple as that. Their turn is next.

Some people made the mistake of thinking that it was Death himself that posed a threat. In truth, Death was quite ordinary, although he lived in a world different from ours. Occasionally a woman, usually with full breasts smelling of sour milk, saw him for what he was. In her desperation she would grab his hands, imploring, pleading. The women around her would gasp, sure that she would go along with the baby. But Death would smile. He loved to be touched; it happened so seldom. His hands were warm and gentle. He would reassure her that it wasn't the end. Just another beginning. The baby in the crook of her arm might reach for the button on his jacket or the watch around his wrist. In this way, the child was marked. In the coming weeks they would transition to the Otherworld. The body would remain in this world.

This world was full of ways to store and preserve your dead. A useless venture, in Death's opinion. Graveyards everywhere, monuments to the empty husks of people, like so many shed cicada skins. Where else do they show such honor to an old, discarded shell?

But Death had knowledge these people did not. They buried the bodies that remained, but the souls simply transitioned to the Otherworld. A baby might be needed. A wife was missing, or a son who disappeared many years ago. They returned to their families as if they'd never gone. A name and face remembered, a spot at the table, a pillow filled that yesterday had been empty. A shadow moved from their world to his and resumed a life.

Death preferred his world. Not a headstone or black wrought iron fence in sight. No dressing in mourning clothes and putting on a funeral show. No gravediggers or coffin makers. No funeral homes with their black-suited, soft-voiced consolers. No wringing of hands, no tears for what was lost.

Just an aching absence. A shadowy remembering. An uneasy forgetting. If you were retrieved by Death, it meant you were missed in the Otherworld. It means someone else's life was not complete without you. You were bought and paid for with the object of your retrieval.

Someone came to Death's door (unimposing, a small cottage with uneven floors) and asked, "can you find this person for me?" They came bearing a small teapot that had sat for 50 years on a table, with a dirty bath-ring of tea inside. They came with a button missing from a jacket that always seemed to end up in their bedside drawer. They came with a quilt square, never sewed into a quilt. They came with a gold ring that didn't fit. Too small, too delicate. Engraved on the inside with initials he didn't remember.

One day a man came: simple breeches, worn shirt. The elbows showed his skin through the threadbare patches almost as well as the gentle, soft spot at his throat. Death invited him to sit down on a chair on his open porch. Except it was a simpler matter than that because there he was known as the Borrower. The Borrower said, "sit down, my friend. Would you like something to drink?"

"No, thank you. I have something for you, Borrower. I'm missing someone. I think I used to have someone who lived with me, and I took care of her, and she took care of me. I can't quite remember, but it seems as though someone must have crocheted the edge of the pillows and done the embroidery on the towels... the sampler on the wall." He pulled from his front pocket a tiny pair of scissors. They were the kind used for cutting thread as you worked on your sewing, small enough to fit in the palm of your hand. Shaped like a bird, a heron or crane. Something simple turned into something beautiful.

"Well, I can take the scissors. It's just got to be small enough to fit on my person." He took them from the man's hand and placed them in his vest pocket. "I'll see if I can't return her to you. Any memories of what she looked like?"

"No, just guessing she was pretty. I can't remember the color of her eyes or her hair. I just know she was good with her hands. It would do me well to have some company again."

"I'll see what I can do." The Borrower gave a tired little exhale after the man left. Too many days ended the same way. It seemed he wasn't given much time to rest. He couldn't remember who bestowed this job upon him, but if he could, he would ask them for a reprieve. He must have been borrowed and brought to the Otherworld, because he had no childhood or family that he could remember. This little cottage was all he had. And the objects of the people he couldn't find. They littered his house. The windowsills were full, and the dresser top. The cupboards filled with mismatched dishes.

As far as he knew, he was the only one who could see the entrance to the world next door. A world where people lived, same as here. It could be reached with a door, any door, that only he could walk through. The entrance was opaque and then when things came back into focus he was there. He lived in the Otherworld, where he could lay his head down to rest. The other world was searching and marking, tears and grief.

He could take only what he carried. The door took him close to where he needed to be, but never exactly. When he arrived he sought out the person that was missed. He carried their belonging on his person and set about searching for its owner. They were drawn to him; it wasn't so hard. Once they were found and marked, he could head back through another door to the Otherworld and rest. The job took something out of him, although it wasn't particularly hard. All the emotions tied up in losing people.

The Borrower knew they'd be well cared for on the other side, but families were convinced this was an end. Really it was a starting over; there was just more living in store for them on the other side. A bit exhausting, in his opinion.

He took his time letting the sun warm his skin before he stood up from the porch. An icebox held ham and eggs and he fetched beans from his garden. The garden he had so little time to tend, overrun with rabbits. They shooed just to the perimeter as he walked in to pick what he needed. After a simple meal, he did the dishes. He made some coffee, because walking between worlds often meant losing sleep.

Before he left, the Borrower felt his pocket for the scissors. Then he went for a walk, waiting for the door to open. He found the crack of light that offered him entrance. He was in a similar country landscape. Not a city or town. He suspected there was another Borrower to deal with the cityfolk. He was a man of the fields, woods, and cabins. He claimed the simple people.

He walked down a lane with dried ruts. He came to a village and sat outside the general store. Often people would come to him; he just had to wait. But nobody did, and after a time he felt the need to walk again. He found himself on another rutted dirt road. He saw the form of a woman appear ahead when he topped a small rise. She carried a basket with her sundries and a cane in the other hand.

He was drawn to her. Death noticed the cane in her hand, her careful gait. He found he was quick to catch up with her. As he drew even with her, she said "afternoon." He replied in kind but then noticed that she did not look towards his voice or turn her head to smile, as most did before they recognized him. He got a few paces ahead and turned around to look at her. She kept her eyes facing toward the ground, but he could see through partly closed lids the cloudiness of her irises. She was wary of him and could hear and feel his eyes on her.

"You don't sound like you are any of my neighbors, do you care to introduce yourself?" She stopped, looping the basket over her arm and placing both hands on top of her cane.

"I don't have much of a name," said Death.

"Everyone's got a name."

"If I had a mother or father to christen me, I don't remember."

"You're an orphan, then?"

"Something like that."

"Well, the people around here are not fancy, but we are forthright. What are you doing here?" she asked.

Death said after a pause, "I think I came to find you."

He saw her face thinking. Realizing. Not afraid, but wary, like life taught her to be.

"Well, you can come for tea then. My house is not far."

They walked on in silence. The gentle rise and fall of the hills could obscure a house. Then all of a sudden it jumped into view. Her home did so after they rounded a curve. A pretty little white house. He stepped up the stone steps to the porch, marveling at how easy she moved within her familiar places.

She stepped inside, put away the groceries, and invited Death to sit at her kitchen table. The house was just one room. He saw the bed with its quilt, the chair by the fire. The embroidery hoop on a small table next to the chair. She put water on to make tea and then joined him at the table.

"You had best tell me about your business with me," she said sternly.

"Have you heard about a man who comes to tell you when it's your turn?" he asked.

"I've heard, but I've never seen him with my own eyes." They both smiled, a little exhale at the joke. A smile you can feel even when your eyes are closed; the upturned lips carry their own air of weightlessness, a slight wind that touches your face.

"Well, people here don't regard me too kindly, but let me tell you the truth. I'm no grim reaper," said Death. It's not heaven on the other side, but it's not nothing, either. There's someone waiting for you. A home, a husband. I come and get people who are missed in the other world." He was not ordinarily so forthright. In fact he never was. But no one had ever asked him to sit down for tea before.

"And someone sent you to find me." she said.

"Yes."

"Probably some man that thought I wasn't getting along without him. The truth is, I am just fine by myself."

"It's not quite like that. He doesn't remember you for who you are, exactly. He just knows he's missing someone... that his life is missing one you-shaped being. And there's this thing he keeps holding on to, he doesn't remember where it came from. But he can't get rid of it. In your case, a pair of scissors. Scissors he can't use because they don't fit his hands." Death set them on the table so she could reach out and touch them if she chose. He looked at her face for a reaction, but it was so small, he couldn't be sure.

"So what happens next?" she asked.

"I bring the object with me to this side, and I find the owner. That is my job. They call me the Borrower. It's not a bloody profession. I don't mind it too much, except it's lonely."

"How do you get from place to place?" she asked. All her questions didn't betray the slightest surprise, just curiosity, plain and simple.

"It's easy. A doorway. Any doorway. You just kind of imagine yourself walking into a different atmosphere. A different sky. And you're there," he said.

There was a long pause. "What would you say if I told you I can also walk between worlds?" she asked.

"What?" He was glad she couldn't see his face: his look of astonishment and surprise.

"I don't see the door at first, but I can smell the difference, like when you get close to the ocean, and all of a sudden you know you are somewhere new. And like the ocean, a fog, a mist. When it lifts, I can see." She paused, her face raised to his, registering the changes in him.

He was shocked, and excited, and a bit embarrassed. "I didn't know if there were more people like me." Thoughts burst into his head, filling the dull silence that usually occupied his thoughts. "How much are we alike?" he asked.

"Very much, I'd guess" she answered.

"Do you do the taking on my side?" he asked.

"I do the marking."

"But how? How do you know them? What do you take with you?"

"I can see clearly in the Otherworld. I move quietly like always. I go at night. And I have my scissors with me." She pulled another pair of embroidery scissors from her apron pocket and set them on the table, close to the pair he brought. She touched a bit of silver at her throat.

"I take a lock of their hair, and put it in my locket. After that I come home to my own room, return to my own bed and my own blindness. And I lie awake, thinking about all the living that's in store for us."

"Not all the dying," said the Borrower.

"No," she answered.

"They'll always be living," he said.

"Yes, and all that comes with it. Loving and hating. Leaving and staying. Laughing and weeping," she said.

"Mothers and fathers. Sisters and brothers," he added.

She simply nodded in reply.

He sat in silence for a while, feeling more emotion coming to the surface of his skin than he had felt in many years. It hovered near his ribcage, his eyes, and his fingertips. "What do they call you?"

"No one sees me," she said. "No one knows me."

"Someone knows you, and wants you back," said the Borrower.

"Maybe my time has come. Maybe our meeting means it's time for us to retire."

Now the surge of feeling hit the Borrower quickly, a pulse of blood rushing from his heart. He hadn't considered that.

"You mean, I could go back to being..." a hitch came to his throat. "I don't ever remember being normal. Being loved."

"Neither do I, but we can't do this forever, can we? We'll be too old for climbing through doors to other worlds before long" she said.

"So, you'll go back to your husband?" he asked.

She nodded slightly.

"But what happens to me? What happens to the people whose hair you cut?" asked the Borrower.

"After I mark them, they disappear from your world and come to this one."

"How?" he asked.

"As a baby, of course."

Tears sprang to his eyes. "A baby?" he whispered.

"A baby," she said. "Someone to hold you and rock you and care for you."

The thought opened a rift in him, all his wantings spilled out and laid plain before him. "Let's go," he whispered.

Her fingers quickly searched the surface of the table. She picked up the pair of embroidery scissors that marked her, the pair closest to him. She approached him gently, her feet nestled between his. She reached out slowly to find his head, his hair. She smiled and apologized, "I can usually see when I do this."

She ran her fingers through his hair, eventually settling on a lock and trimming a small piece. Grey marked the brown. She was so close, it felt so intimate. She put the lock of hair in her locket. "There," she said. "It's done." He began to weep, a quiet affair, but she felt her dress front grow warm with his tears. She took his head in her hands after returning her scissors to her apron. He put his arms around her waist.

"I hope there will be peace for us," she said.

"And rest," he said.

Three O'clock

Lamont Turner

I've never wanted to hurt anybody.

I don't even have much of a temper.

I have, up until recently, lived a normal, quiet existence, bothering no one. Even now I can honestly say I have never had the desire to kill anyone, and have certainly never made plans to.

But, life is different now, every afternoon at three o'clock PM I find myself cast as the harbinger of death. I have no idea why this happens. I only know it happens at the same time every day, and I am powerless to stop it.

It started one afternoon about six months ago. While driving home from the store, I was stopped by a crossing guard so a group of children could cross the street. Just after they had started across, my foot slipped off the brake and hit the gas. I stopped a few feet short of running them down. It scared the hell out of me.

The next day, while fixing the fence, my hammer slipped out of my hand and just missed my neighbor's head. He had come to complain about the racket I was making.

The day after that, I tapped a man on the shoulder to ask him for directions. The man, who was wearing headphones at the time, was so startled, he stumbled into the street where he was almost run over by a bus.

And so it went every day thereafter. At exactly three O'clock I would inadvertently do something to imperil a life.

After about a month of near misses, it finally happened. My first fatality. The wheel of my shopping cart fell off in the parking lot, causing the cart to tumble into the path of an oncoming car. Swerving to avoid the cart, the driver hit an old woman. She must have flown thirty feet before hitting that lamp post.

The police faulted the driver, a teenager, for speeding through the parking lot, and some of the witnesses faulted the store for the faulty cart, but I knew I was the real culprit. It had been me, or rather my curse, that had killed that woman.

I began to stay home in the afternoons, but found my precautions to have little effect. The mailman had a heart attack on my front lawn.

The house across the street burned down.

Hell, the man delivering the weather report on the news just dropped dead on the air. Turns out he had an aneurism. Resigned to my fate, I determined to spare the innocent and put my curse to work. I went to Washington DC.

It seemed logical.

It was about a twenty-hour drive from my home in Austin to Washington, but I wasn't about to fly and chance being stuck in the air when the fatal hour struck. I set out at five minutes after three, hoping to spare some poor soul along the way by reaching my destination before the hour rolled around again. If I couldn't stop the deaths, I could at least try to limit their scope and not kill decent people,

As I drove, I often glanced down at the photo of "Honest" Jim Calloway I had taped to my dashboard. I had no idea if my experiment would work, but Honest Jim was more than deserving of the honor. A thirty-two year veteran of Congress, he had amassed a fortune while the district he represented took on the aspect of a third world country.

Honest Jim was scheduled to speak before the League of Religious Freedom, a group apparently dedicated to eradicating all science from our public discourse.

I had a good seat. While I had some qualms over taking a more active role, I'd convinced myself that I had been chosen.

If I had to kill people, I might as well kill the ones the world would be better off without.

Sandwiching myself between a young man with a bowtie and a crewcut, and an old man who wheezed and rattled like a car running on two cylinders, I stared up at the podium from the front row. Somebody calling himself Reverend Roy was firing up the crowd in anticipation of Honest Jim's big entrance. The young man to my right was enthralled, the old man seemed preoccupied with keeping his lungs working, and I tried to shut out as much of the pablum as I could by recalling the lyrics of old songs.

Honest Jim, who could have just as easily, and quite a bit more truthfully, been called Big Jim, finally waddled to the podium, just as I was about to doze off. He greeted the applause with a wave of his big meaty hand and waited for the crowd to settle down.

"We are at war," he began. "The infidels in Washington are out to remove God from our land and from our lives."

He went on like that for about fifteen minutes, then looked at his watch and launched into his concluding remarks. I looked at my watch. It was only 2:50. I had to do something to keep him there. Just as he was finishing up, I stood up and suggested the Senator lead us in a hymn. He gaped at me, trying to think up a plan to extricate himself from my trap, but gave up when a woman behind me leapt to her feet and suggested "Amazing Grace."

After my forth "Again!" Calloway waved us off and was about to make his escape, when I stood and asked to shake "the hand of the next President." Obviously thrilled with my flattering prognostication, he looked around to make sure the cameras were still filming, and leaned over the edge of the stage with an outstretched hand. Right on schedule, he toppled off, landing on the old man next to me. Withing seconds, men in suits came flooding in from all directions to help pull the Senator to his feet. He was dazed, but, disappointingly, otherwise unharmed. The same couldn't be said for the old man. He had been thoroughly flattened under Calloway's bulk. Those last two cylinders had finally given out.

While hopeful that killing your constituents would be bad for one's political career, I couldn't help but feel sorry for the old man, and disappointed I had failed to enlist my curse in a good cause. There really was no controlling it. It wasn't until I saw the headlines the next day that I began to feel a little better.

"Freak Accident Leads to Gruesome Discovery!" was the lead story that day in the Washington Post. When the authorities had gone to inform the crushed man's wife of the accident, they'd found her in the living room—and the kitchen—and the bedroom. She'd been hacked to bits and strewn about the couple's home like so much dirty laundry. Two more bodies were discovered buried in the backyard, and evidence of a third was found in the basement. The old man had deserved his fate, perhaps even more than Honest Jim would have.

As soon as I returned home, I started researching the people I, or rather, the curse had killed. The old woman run down in the parking lot was about to evict an even more elderly woman from one of her properties. The newscaster had been gleefully screwing the station's interns. Everyone of them I could trace, had some history of being thoroughly horrible people. That was probably why my neighbor avoided having a hammer go through his head. Being a nasty old crab didn't rise to the level of a capital offense as far as the curse was concerned. I never did find out what the mailman had done, but I suspect the incidents of missing mail on his route declined after his passing.

I no longer hide when three o'clock rolls around. In fact, I make it a point to be out and about, surrounded by as many people as possible. Death has a tough job. It makes sense he would outsource some of the labor. I do sometimes wonder though, who has been assigned to cover all the other hours of the day. Perhaps I should only go out at three.

To Do Right

Cory Swanson

There was absolutely nothing offensive about the back room of the Crane Lakes Funeral Home. As Luke stirred three sugar packets into his tea and eyed the other avoiders, he realized that the elegantly muted decor was supposed to have a calming effect.

Luke didn't feel calm. In fact, his tension and agitation at the whole situation kept manifesting itself in the surface of his tea, his hand causing the liquid to jostle and slosh in his cup.

Another man nodded at him. "I'm Andrew," he said.

"Luke."

"I don't want to be here."

Luke nodded. "Me neither. It seems bizarre to hang around with a dead body."

"Yeah," Andrew said. "You a friend?"

"I worked with him at the plant."

Andrew smiled, staring at a TV showing a slideshow of pictures from Duke's life. "Luke and Duke. That must have been fun. Good pictures," Andrew said, gesturing at the screen.

Luke nodded. "You'd think one of these five TVs would have the game on."

Andrew laughed. "Duke would have approved."

Luke smiled, happy to have found someone to distract him from the body in the other room. From the vociferous crying and carrying on.

Andrew produced a flask from his inside coat pocket. "Here," he said, uncapping it and pouring a shot into Luke's tea. "It'll calm those nerves."

"Thanks," Luke smiled, raising his paper cup and sniffing the acrid scent. "Duke would have approved of this, too."

"Yeah, just don't let my mom smell it."

A laugh gurgled up. "No. You're right. I can't believe she stayed married to him for so long."

"Right?" Andrew said. "My parents really had an odd relationship."

Two old women, one on a walker, ambled through the hall between the rooms. "He looks so good. They do such beautiful work," said the one on the left.

Andrew's eyes grew wide, and Luke had to stifle his laughter. "He really doesn't," Andrew said under his breath to Luke.

"He looks super dead," Luke said.

"Super, super dead. Did you see how they couldn't get his eyes all the way closed?"

"Why would he be cooperative in death? He never was in life."

They laughed and toasted drinks, grimacing as they knocked back swigs of the cheap whiskey.

"Go in there with me, Luke," Andrew said after he'd recovered from the burn of the alcohol.

"Okay. Why?"

"I need to pay my respects."

"You know you don't have to."

"I should. I need to. My therapist says I need closure."

Luke nodded. "Alright. Let's go."

The two men walked into the far room, the soothing music and inoffensive art doing nothing to calm Luke's stomach.

At the casket, Luke and Andrew waited. Andrew's mom, Nelly, leaned over Duke's body, tears streaming down her face. "Duke," she cried. "Why did you leave me, Duke?"

"Jesus," Andrew whispered to Luke.

Luke nodded. Duke's death was still raw. Sure, he'd had heart disease for years, but the last stages had closed in like a mountain lion on its prey, taking Duke in mere weeks. Nelly looked like a raw husk of a human, leaning in grief over the casket that contained her dead husband.

"Even being grief-adjacent is hard," Luke said to Andrew. He walked up and placed a hand on Nelly's shoulder.

Nelly didn't seem to notice, and Luke withdrew his hand, looking shamefully at his feet.

Andrew tapped Luke. "Look at his mouth. It looks like he's about to crack a joke."

The right edge of Duke's mouth had indeed curled up.

"Must be the rigor mortis," Luke said.

Nelly leaned forward, hands on the side of the casket, not bothering to cover her face. Tears and snot dangled dangerously close to the corpse.

Luke reached over, wanting to pull her back. He didn't want her to fall in. He didn't want to see what the tears would do to the dead man's makeup. But when his hand touched her back, she buckled further, leaning in towards her deceased husband.

A tear fell, landing on his nose, and the corpse woke up. Slowly, the body rose to a sitting position, pushing at the bottom half of the lid open with stiff and ungainly arms. His eyes locked on his wife's horrified face.

"You're doing it wrong," Duke said.

Panic flooded the room, the guests screaming and diving for cover, some dashing behind the couches and some hunching in the corners.

"My God, Duke, you're alive," Nelly barked.

"No. I'm not. I'm super dead. And you're doing it wrong."

"What do you mean?"

Luke looked around. The reactions of the aggrieved ranged from shock to fear to fascination. Some hid, others approached the scene with one curious step after another.

"You're grieving wrong."

Nelly looked offended. "You came back from the dead to tell me I'm not grieving right? Where do you get off?"

"I'm not back from the dead," Duke said, his voice raspy. He managed to get the lower half of the coffin open and he pulled his legs out and stiffly swung them over the edge of the box. "I'm still dead. No changing that. But look at this Nelly," he said, gesturing at the room with a rigid arm.

Nelly's eyes darted around the room. "You don't like the funeral home I picked?"

"It's fine, but it's not what I wanted."

Arms folded across her chest, Nelly huffed. "And this is all supposed to be about you?"

Duke threw his arms up in the air in exasperation, nearly falling back into the coffin.

Andrew reached out and caught him.

"Thank you, Son. And give me some of what you have in your pocket there."

Andrew obliged and Duke tilted the brown liquid back into his throat. Nelly gaped, but he ignored her, giving a great cough and wiping his face with his arm. "I can't get the taste of formaldehyde out of my mouth," he said. "And to answer your previous question, my love, this is most certainly about me. This is all about me. It's my funeral."

"Funerals aren't for the dead, they're for the living," Nelly said. "They're to comfort those who are left to carry on in life." She glanced around the room, looking for support from the cowering guests.

"I couldn't disagree more." Duke scooted forward, teetering on the edge of the casket as he eyed the distance to the ground.

Luke reached to help him, but hesitated, scared to touch a dead person.

Duke slid himself from the edge of the casket, clumsy and stiff, crumpling to the ground with a sickening, wet cracking sound.

"Jesus," Andrew exclaimed, motioning for Luke to help get Duke on his feet. Duke's arm now hung at a funny angle, having taken the brunt of the fall. It looked broken, or at the very least dislocated. "Are you okay?" Andrew asked.

"No, I'm dead," Duke replied, reaching for the flask with his good arm. "But don't worry about my arm. I can't feel it." He took another swig of whiskey and lurched forward.

Nelly walked beside him, trying to keep him steady. "Honey, I don't think you should—"

"Your dead husband gets up and walks and you still try to tell him what to do? Unbelievable." Duke grunted. "Now, are you guys going to mourn me the right way or do I have to do it myself?"

152

Several heads peered cautiously out from their various hiding places, emerging little by little as Duke's magnetic personality drew them out.

"Duke, we were mourning you as best we knew how."

"You call that mourning? Crying big gobs of snot on my face? Feeling sorry for yourself? Hell no. This is my day, and you're going to see me off the right way. Luke, you got that guitar? Anybody else got something to play?"

In life, Duke had played the washboard with a Dixie band that met every Tuesday at the VFW. The whole band was in attendance, of course, to pay their last respects, and grinned at the opportunity as they came out of the nooks and crannies of the funeral home. They had planned on meeting up after the wake at the VFW for old times sake. They slipped out the door to grab their horns.

"I want to go out dancing. Andrew, you take care of provisions," he said, holding up the flask. "I'm guessing you have another bottle or two in your car."

Andrew gaped.

"Oh, don't pretend you don't. We all know you do. You can worry about getting sober after you get me in the ground."

"Duke, I'm not sure we can...do you think we should..." Andrew asked.

"You think the funeral home is going to stop us? Most of the employees ran and hid the second I sat up. Now, shall we?"

Luke and Andrew went out to the parking lot. They stopped by Andrew's black Civic. "Are we really going to..." Luke said.

"Do you see any other options?"

"It's just. This is so weird."

"Yeah," Andrew said, "but somehow I'm not surprised."

Luke smiled. The thought comforted him. "You're right," he said, taking his guitar out of the backseat of his car. "This is exactly what Duke would do."

They walked back into the funeral home to find the mourners staring uncomfortably as Duke arranged paper coffee cups on the table in front of him. A difficult task considering he only had one working hand. "Ah yes," Duke said, looking up to see Andrew and Luke, "bring that here."

Andrew handed several bottles of cheap scotch over and Duke sloshed a bit in each cup. He limped around the room, handing each shocked guest a drink.

"Alright then, let's drink a toast," Duke proclaimed, his gravelly voice breaking the silence. "What should we toast to?"

Nobody answered.

"Should we toast to life?" he said.

The room filled with light laughter and the tension in the air loosened a bit.

"How about we toast to you, Duke?" Andrew proposed.

"Nah. I'm already toast."

More laughter.

"How about we toast to death," Luke chimed in.

Duke's dry, dead eyes swung over to Luke. "That's a pretty strange thing to toast."

"Yeah, but you're dead now. New beginnings and all."

"Somebody's going to have some new beginnings, being as they're suddenly single," Duke said, gesturing towards Nelly, and the guests roared, Nelly included. "I like that. To death," he proclaimed.

"To death," the crowd repeated, raising their paper cups.

Duke drained his cup with several long gulps and threw it on the ground. "Now, let's really get going. Somebody tell us about me."

Bewildered, the guests looked around. "What do you mean?" Andrew asked.

"You know, what do you remember about my life? Tell stories, things like that."

The crowd hesitated, unsure.

"Um," a man with a Marines hat piped up. "There was that time you were awarded the Bronze Star."

"Posh," said Duke, scowling. "I got a medal for getting metal in my ass. I was rewarded for my own stupidity. Come on, folks. What are your real memories of me? Who was I? What was my life made of?"

"I remember when you tore your knee up on that dirt bike," a man in the back said.

"There you go," Duke said, laughing. "Nelly said she knew my brain turned off the second I got on that thing."

"How about when you bet that guy at the bar you could guess which hand he had the coin in," another guest said. "He didn't want to pay up and the barkeep had to kick him out."

Several people chuckled and murmured.

"That's the stuff," Duke said. "I still remember his right hook." Duke wheezed and coughed and laughed. "Keep em coming."

"Remember when your truck broke down in the middle of Nebraska?" someone shouted.

"Oh, lord," Duke said. "It had to be thirty below. I put my hand down on the engine block to get warm and burnt the hell out of it."

The crowd began to roil. Stories began to fly around the room. From Duke's life in the factory to the night he spent in jail.

"You always had a temper," someone said, laughing.

"It's true," Duke said. "I did." He kicked back his second drink and poured another. "Can't do anything about it now."

"You always had a grin and a joke," said another.

"Who wants to hear a dirty limerick?" Duke growled.

"No," yelled the crowd, laughing.

"You were always kind to the kids," Nelly said.

"Ah, yes, my wife. They were the great joys of my existence. Too bad none of them did anything with their lives."

Nelly smiled and put her arm around her deceased husband while Andrew stared at his feet.

"I'd kiss you, but I'm dead," he said. "Now get your guitar out, Luke. I want to dance."

Luke finished his drink and pulled his instrument out of its case. As he tuned up, the strings twanging, the musicians from the VFW walked up to him. A full brass section and a couple drummers. "How in the world?" Luke said.

"I know," said the trumpeter. "What should we play?"

Luke strummed a few chords on his guitar and the drummers followed. The brass players talked for a minute then joined in, the air now vibrating with their joyous sound.

In the middle of the room, Duke's stiff body began to bob and weave, his moves stiff with the rigor mortis, but somehow making sense. Nelly hesitated for a moment, then took his good hand and led him around.

"That's it," Duke yelled as the crowd began to dance. "This is how you mourn."

The tempo picked up and the crowd roiled. The trumpeter growled and moaned and the pictures and trinkets that had been set up fell over as the dancers swept past.

On and on they went with Duke and Nelly leading in the middle, Duke's stiff legs lifting here and there as Nelly danced like she was half her age. Those who didn't dance talked and laughed and drank. Andrew did neither, choosing to watch the scene, an uncontrollable happiness welling up within him.

After carrying on for an eternity, Duke waved Andrew over. "Come on, son. Give your old man a hand."

Andrew obliged, holding onto Duke as he climbed back into his casket, shutting the lower half over his stiff legs. "You're cold, Duke," he said.

"Of course I'm cold," Duke replied. "I'm dead. Now get some folks to help you carry this thing."

Andrew motioned for a few strong backs and they grabbed the rails of the casket and lifted it aloft.

"Now," Duke commanded, "take me to my grave."

Everyone cheered as the pallbearers began to move out the door.

"Saints in E flat," called the trombone player and the band struck up the second line classic as the casket moved down the front steps.

Old Forgotten Grave

Bill Camp

Old forgotten grave, who were you?
Washed away lettering, barely
Legible years of birth and death
Are all I know of your life.
The old tombstone bleached by the sun.
In what condition is your
Body buried beneath? Are worms
And maggots devouring your brain
Even now? Has your soul risen
As a ghost? Do your ancestors
Still come to visit your grave?
Do they still leave you flowers?
Are there old, faded photographs
Of your life sitting in someone's
Attic? Perhaps I can meet your
Ghost one day. We can sit upon
Your tombstone and talk about your
Life, while sipping a few beers.
For what good is life if it will
All be forgotten?

Alternative Deathiness

Ashes

LIzzy Shannon

I hadn't realized I'd transitioned for some time. I was dead already even though my body yet lived. Parts of me slipped away little by little. Fractured threads of what made me who I was, gradually fell away. Then like accumulated drops of water from a leaking faucet, inched like a rivulet into the oblivion of a dark drain.

I knew who my daughter was. My son, too. He came less frequently, but his face was instantly familiar. My daughter had emigrated to the States but visited me in Ireland every year. Then suddenly she was there all the time until she moved to an apartment to be near me, apparently only a couple of miles away. What use was that if she didn't live *with* me? Hadn't she moved back to take care of me?

Fury took a frequent hold on me. Things I knew, slipped from the fingers of my memory, avoiding my mental grasp. Why couldn't I concentrate enough to bring it all back? I know... *knew*... so much. Life before televisions and computers. I travelled. I was an important man. Where was that world now?

My garden. Oh, my garden.

So proud I was of the tall, lush trees and verdant, flowering bushes all planted from seedlings. A life watching them grow, transform a clumpy stretch of earth into lavish parkland.

Why had I bothered?

Who had ever taken the time to sit on the bench I'd so lovingly built and sanded and varnished, under the shade of my lilac tree? I remember in my disappointment, a time when frenzied rage consumed me, giving me impetus to heave that bench over my head and smash it onto the paving stones I'd so carefully laid. Shattered beyond repair. Ashamed, I hauled the remains to the dump and bought a similar one to replace it. Bruises the colour of lilac often flowered my hands and arms. My wrist permanently swollen and misshapen from lashing out at too many doors or windows or drawers that wouldn't open properly. I had no patience for things that didn't work the way they were supposed to.

But my dogs. My salvation. Those Labradors loved unconditionally, and I could love them. How liberating to stride with them, through the forest parks and wander the sand dunes across from my house. A hail-fellow-well-met greeting if we passed anyone, a few words about the weather, then on. Laboriously scaling a steep dune to stand triumphant, hands on hips, surveying the beauty of the Mourne Mountains and the ever-surging Irish Sea. The dogs panted at my feet for a while, then impatiently whined to continue. Their windmilling tails and lolling tongues, their sheer happiness at being alive and free brought me such joy. My daughter accompanied me when she was there. My son too, from time to time. But I most relished the solitary roaming with only the dogs for company.

I had another son. He stopped visiting a long time ago. I used to know why. My wife. Something he had done, or not done for my wife. I don't remember now. I only know that when I think of him, I feel intense outrage. I scarcely remember her either. Her voice another thing forgotten.

And then, I came to be like this. I don't know how. There was the light and shadow of sun on swaying leaves and then this darkness. Contained. She came for me, my daughter. I heard her thanking someone as I was lifted, strangely light, held firmly within something rigid. I wanted to demand what the hell was happening, but no words formed. No breath came. No lungs to fill.

Only my anger remained.

She placed what was now me on a glass shelf by a window. I knew the days as they passed, gentle light to looming darkness. She cried. A lot. I always hated the sound of weeping, wanted to storm away, shut out the loathsome sound. But stagnant in this container, I was forced to endure it.

"Oh, Dad," I heard her lament over and over. "I'm sorry. So sorry."

Why did she cry for me? I tried to speak, shout at her to shut up, but I could only feel something like sand shifting instead of words.

Time meant nothing, I realized. I just was. Trapped. With only my daughter's despair for company. The life I'd struggled to remember began to take form again. I started to see it for what it was. Emotions, confusion. I made so many mistakes. Lost my temper too many times, too swiftly. Wanted to smash my fist into faces but hit inanimate objects instead. Some of my words and actions to my family had been, I see now, cruel, but now I understood how I could only be what I'd been brought up to be. I didn't know my father. My mother abandoned me, taking my sister to live with her in Belfast while I remained on my isolated uncle's farm.

I clearly saw now I had done the absolute best that I knew how to. I'd worked hard my whole life, did what was expected of me, loved the only crippled way I knew how to. How I wish I could tell this to my daughter, whose grief seemed all encompassing. She was only what she had been brought up to be. What I'd brought her up to be. But she'd learned more than I; she could show her emotions. She truly mourned me. I had only mourned the loss of my wife, so many years ago. I refused to give in to grief. As always, I did exactly what was expected: a respectful funeral, the next day emptying her closets and dresser drawers. A marble gravestone etched in gold to be placed six months hence. Life went on. My daughter wept for her mother, too. I resented her grief. Why did she carry on so, when she hadn't lost a partner of fifty years like I had?

I began to find peace in this non-life. No expectations. To exist, invisible and silent. The rage that had constantly battered against me like waves on rocks slowly slid away through the grains of bones and teeth that I had become. I thought I had controlled everything in my life; now I understood I controlled nothing. None of us do.

I wanted to tell my daughter that. Through her bouts of grief, I came to see she blamed herself for my death. I wished I could tell her that it had begun long before she moved back to Ireland. A slow, mortifying, humiliating demise that had nothing to do with her, and everything to do with brain cells shrinking and decaying.

Then one day she lifted me from that glass shelf. Movement, shaken up again, grains shifting and roiling. Sudden air, blue sky. A marble headstone. I knew it at once, and my name etched in gold beneath my wife's. *'Beloved husband and father. A long life well lived; his peace was found in nature.'*

She had loved me, my daughter. She knew me well. Gently freed, I found myself spread out amid emerald grass by the headstone, sifting into the fragrant, peaty earth. My death is almost complete, yet I will never be dead as we think we understand it. I am the air, I am the earth, and the water. I am memory. I am the dust and ashes intermingled with all that has been and all that will be.

The Devil's Backbone

Larry Hodges

I saw him in the mirror sprinting after me, waving a bill and yelling.

I couldn't tell what he was saying because my ice cream truck speakers were blaring out *The Entertainer* in all their tinny glory.

Grinning to myself, I came to a stop, looking forward to ice cream dribbling down the face of another satisfied customer.

Normally I do all sales from the ice cream truck's window. But the kid kept pointing at the menu and asking something—I never did find out what—and so I got out of the truck to see what he wanted. I should have just turned down the music.

I guess it was just stupid to stop in an intersection, and it was more bad luck that, right then, a brown delivery van, no doubt late on his delivery, chose to enter the intersection at the same time, driving at a speed that could not possibly be legal. Guess who won that confrontation?

My body got smooshed.

It hurt like crazy at first, but then the pain went away.

I rose out of my body and drifted slowly upward. Slowly, because there was a weight of past evil on my soul, and perhaps whoever arranges these things wanted to make it clear that they hadn't forgotten the horrible things I'd done and didn't want to seem too enthusiastic.

Then a gigantic red hand came out of the ground, right from under the tree-lined rows of suburban houses and their neatly mowed lawns. Houses crumbled like pottery while cars flew like popcorn. Did I mention the hand was huge? It was about a quarter mile long, with gnarled, hairy fingers that ended in pointed fingernails. It could have crushed Yankee Stadium with ease.

Instead, it reached above my floating soul and, with the tip of a fingernail, swatted it like a gnat back into my broken body. I sat up on the pavement, slightly dazed. But I quickly became alert—a hand the size of Manhattan hovering over you has that effect. I scrambled back into my ice cream truck. The hand reached for the truck.

I slammed the accelerator all the way down and sped away from the gargantuan hand. I watched in the mirror, rising out of the ground like a twisting snake. Fingers a hundred feet wide stretched toward me; my weaving ice-cream truck was little more than an ant to it. It lunged at me several times but, luckily, ants are hard to grab.

I was up to sixty when it finally grabbed my truck between the pointed nails of its thumb and index finger, like tweezers holding a tiny bug with spinning wheels. Only these tweezers were like the Twin Towers before some evil guys with 666's on them—like I once had—knocked them down.

Then the hand retracted back into its gigantic hole, with me and my ice cream truck dangling between its fingernails. We sank downward at an impossible speed, and in freefall, I floated up to the ceiling of my ice cream truck as my stomach heaved. I threw up the chocolate éclairs.

We came to a sudden stop and I slammed back down onto my seat. I opened my eyes, which I hadn't even realized I'd closed, and saw a brief glimpse of a gigantic red face leering down at me from under a pair of curved horns—either the Devil himself, or I was having a bad nightmare. It opened its mouth, and the hand—its hand—plunged in. The horizon was suddenly all huge, pointed teeth. A gigantic gob of saliva hit the ice cream truck like a raindrop from Hell, knocking me about like an inner tube in Niagara Falls. Then the hand plunged over the giant tongue, past that weird flap of skin that hangs in the back of your mouth, and into the throat.

The hand reached the huge cavern that must have been its stomach. Then, using its three free fingers and their pointed fingernails like knives, it tore a hole through the side of the stomach and plunged into the other side.

I looked down and gaped. We were over a city. It expanded outward with streets crisscrossing blocks of buildings, and people and cars buzzing about like ants. The city sat on a huge, vertical white plate that rose up on one side and down on the other as if gravity turned sideways. Giant vertebrae disappeared into the distance on both sides. That's when it hit me—the city lay on a gigantic backbone. *The Devil's backbone.* The city continued on the next vertebra, with bridges connecting the streets. Some of the vertebrae had major portions cut away.

The hand dropped me and my ice cream truck came to rest on a street in the middle of the city, its hand nonchalantly destroying a building on one side as people screamed. Then it pulled away and disappeared into the hole in the reddish sky.

A car behind me honked, and I realized I was parked in the middle of traffic. I pulled off to the side and got out of the truck as the car sped off. The people who had screamed while the hand destroyed the building now seemed as if nothing had happened. Being a New Yorker, I barely looked at them, so it wasn't until later that I noticed the wide range of people, clothing, and the various fatal-looking injuries.

Now that I was out of my air-conditioned ice cream truck, the heat and humidity hit me with full fury, quickly soaking my white Good Humor ice cream man uniform. The stench of rotten meat slammed into me, like a trash bin from a slaughterhouse. While I gagged, the ground suddenly trembled like an earthquake, and I fell down.

"What's that sound?" a curly-haired boy of about twelve asked in a monotone voice as I rose to my feet. His face and clothes were also drenched in sweat. He wore what looked like worn-out baggy pajamas with black and white horizontal stripes, like a prison outfit from long ago. The reddish light glinted off his perspiration, giving him a devilish complexion.

At first I was confused about what sound he referred to, and then I realized the ice cream truck was still playing *The Entertainer.* I clicked it off.

"Where was it coming from?" the boy asked, looking startled. "Where did it go?"

"From my truck," I said. The boy stared at the truck for a minute, and then shrugged his shoulders.

"You must be new here," he said, still in monotone. "I'm Timmy. I killed my sister, but I'm better now. What did you do? You look pretty messed up."

I hadn't yet recovered from the rather unlikely events of the past few minutes, and so I just stared at him, my mouth gaping like I'd seen a ghost. There was another earthquake—or was it a backquake? A bonequake?—but this time I kept my feet. Timmy barely reacted.

"What was that?" I asked.

"That's just his heartbeat," Timmy said, staring at his feet.

Where was I? *What* was I? Okay, I was smart enough to figure out that I was dead. I patted myself and verified that I seemed substantial, so I wasn't a ghost, at least of the normal kind. But my body had been smashed, and the front of my Good Humor Man outfit was covered in blood. At least the pain was mostly gone.

Then, with rising horror, I realized where I must be. "Is this Hell?" Somehow, in all this heat, a shiver went down my spine. I thought I had reformed, but apparently not enough.

Timmy giggled. "No, mister, if this was Hell, it'd be a *lot* hotter."

I sighed in relief. If Hell was hotter than this inferno, I was glad I wasn't there.

"And they'd be torturing you," Timmy added. I was glad to hear of the lack of torture; always a consideration when making travel plans.

"If this isn't Hell, and it certainly isn't Heaven, then where am I?"

"You're in The Devil's Backbone," Timmy said.

I'd never heard of it. I had heard rumors of giant hands that came out of the ground, grabbing people and destroying buildings. I'd also heard of the Loch Ness Monster, Bigfoot, and the Tooth Fairy, but I hadn't believed in them either.

"So, what did you do?" Timmy asked. "You wouldn't be here unless you were once marked by the Devil, and then reformed. He doesn't like that, so he brings people like us here, hoping to turn us back."

I introduced myself and told him something of my past, though I sugar-coated it, he didn't need to know everything.

And so began my life on The Devil's Backbone. It's about a mile long, made up of the Devil's thirty-three vertebrae, which are each about seven hundred feet wide at their widest. Like human vertebrae, the front of each is a short cylinder, sort of like a barnacle opened on both ends. I could see the Devil's spinal cord snaking its way through the thirty-three cylinders. A plate stuck out the back of each vertebra like a giant bony sail, with two smaller plates rising from the sides.

The Devil's body around the backbone had been hollowed out, presumably by the Devil himself, with the Devil's luminescent red flesh perhaps a quarter mile up. The backbone hung in mid-air between where it came out of the skull and disappeared in the other direction. The hole in the sky where the Devil's hand had reached in to drop me off healed within a day, leaving behind an ugly scar, one of many.

"What am I supposed to do now?" I asked.

"Let me take you to the Welcome Center," Timmy said.

"That'd be great," I said, getting back into my ice cream truck. "You give directions and I'll drive."

Timmy appeared hesitant. "I don't like cars. They look dangerous. Some of them play music like yours. I think they're haunted."

"It's safe," I said. "And you can have some ice cream."

"What's ice cream?" Timmy asked. He hesitantly stepped into the truck and sat in the passenger side, hunched slightly forward.

I finally put two and two together. "When did you die?"

Timmy examined the truck's controls. "George Washington was president when Ross killed me in 1795. He was another kid they had locked up." He twisted around so I could see the wooden-handled knife jutting from his back, which explained why he'd been hunching forward. "You're stuck with whatever clothes you wore when you died, and somehow whatever does these things thought the knife was part of my clothes." He went back to examining the controls. "I'm two hundred and twenty-seven years old."

That explained the confusion about my truck and ice cream.

"I've got something for you." I pulled the truck over and opened one of the freezers. "Try this," I said, handing him one of the chocolate candy center crunch bars. "Hold it by the stick and remove the paper first."

He followed the instructions and then stared at the black object in front of him, wrinkling his nose. "It looks like horse manure."

I pulled out a second chocolate candy center crunch bar and took a bite. Satisfied that nothing happened to me, Timmy took an experimental bite.

A huge grin crossed his face. "Wow!" he said, for the first time losing the monotone. A moment later he finished the bar. I gave him the rest of mine. His smile threatened to come off the sides of his face as ice cream dribbled out of the corners.

"That's why I became an ice cream man!" I exclaimed, showing him my silver Good Humor Man ring.

On the way to the Welcome Center, I got my first close look at this world as we veered about on the curving, bony landscape. Every hundred and fifty feet or so we'd reach the end of a vertebra and take a short bridge to the next. The streets zigzagged across the vertebrae, sometimes spiraling about them, and other times going up one side of a plate and down the other side. Gravity pulled to the vertebrae from all directions, so you could drive up one side of a vertical vertebra plate and down the other, like some sort of amusement park ride. I stopped the truck at one point and walked up a plate, reached the top, and walked down on the other side. I don't recommend doing this on a full stomach.

Most of the vertebrae had been scrubbed clean and white, but here and there bits of Devil-flesh clung to the bone. Every few minutes the Devil's heart would beat, knocking everything about, but I quickly grew used to it. Finally, we arrived at the Welcome Center. This was my first chance to examine one of the buildings up close. It was made of bone.

"We sacrificed some vertebrae for building materials," Timmy explained. I remembered several of the vertebrae had big chunks cut away.

"Where do the cars come from?" I asked. They were definitely metal, though they seemed a mishmash of years, from modern ones to a few Model T's. There was even a stagecoach pulled by a pair of horses.

"I still don't understand cars. What makes them go without a horse?"

"I'll explain later. But where do they come from?"

"You saw the size of the Devil's hands." Timmy said. "He can't grab a person directly. He usually grabs the entire area in a clump, with the person he's after in the middle. We get a lot of supplies that way. But sometimes people die inside a car or stagecoach or something, or they run away from him in them, and then he can grab it between his fingernails. So a lot of people show up in things like that."

"That's what happened to me, in my ice cream truck. How about you?"

Timmy stared at his feet. "After he killed me, Ross hid my body in an outhouse. The Devil grabbed the entire thing, so I've got the only outhouse in The Devil's Backbone." He looked up and smiled, and grabbed another chocolate candy center crunch bar. "Now I might need it."

"What do you mean?"

"Dead people don't have to eat or drink, and we don't have any real food down here anyway."

About seven thousand people lived—or should I say existed?—in The Devil's Backbone. At first this seemed a very small number. Out of the many billions of people who died throughout history, I thought there would be a lot more evil people who had reformed. Apparently a lot of "reformed" people haven't really reformed, at least on the inside. I'd always suspected most people were phony. Or maybe the Devil hadn't grabbed them all. Or maybe he grabbed only the really evil ones, the ones the Devil thought he had for sure, who had reformed. Only the Devil knows.

Most of the people that walked the bony streets were pretty old. I guess that should be expected since, on average, people are old when they die. I approached a young man dressed in what looked like a Roman toga with a sword through his stomach, and an old black woman in a long flowing dress and a head scarf partially covering her pocked face, but their responses were gibberish to me. What looked like a Neanderthal with his neck torn apart walked by, but I decided not to approach him.

The Welcome Center was staffed by expressionless people who also spoke in monotones. A bored looking young Asian woman greeted me with a forced smile and heavy Chinese accent. Pictures of dragons and flowers covered her dirty blue robe. After assigning me a housing unit, she looked away, staring off into space.

"Why does everyone look bored and talk with a monotone?" I asked.

"Let's see what you're like when you've lived in this heat for a few centuries, with nothing much to do." And yet, Timmy seemed a bit more alive since eating the chocolate candy center crunch bar. "The woman you talked to was Mrs. Chien. She looks young, but she's been here a thousand years. I helped her learn English about a century ago."

Timmy followed me to my new home. My "housing unit" was one of thousands of caves that lined the Devil's vertebrae. It had been dug out with the few available metal tools brought in by dead people, just as I'd brought in my ice cream truck. My home measured roughly ten feet square, with a six foot ceiling that barely let me stand up straight. There was no bed or any type of furniture, just smooth bone. It would be like living in a doorless closet.

"Where do you and your family live?" I asked Timmy.

He looked away. "My family must have all died a long time ago, and they went wherever they went. None of them are here."

I realized my faux pas—of course his family wouldn't be here. "So, you live alone?"

"Of course. My parents wouldn't want to live with me anyway, after what I did. They never forgave me. Nobody should." He began to walk away.

"Wait," I said. "Come back here. What exactly did you do?"

He stopped, his back still to me. "I told you, I killed my sister. That's when I got the 666 on my head. It went away later, when I was in prison." He began walking away again.

Just like me.

I walked after him, and my longer paces caught up. I spun him around and saw his tear-streaked face.

"There's no way a kid like you could have killed anyone on purpose," I said. It just didn't seem possible. "It had to have been an accident."

"No accident," Timmy said. "Dad gave me a musket when I was six. I'd been shooting rats with it ever since. Emily was fussing like three-year-old kids do, and I told her if she didn't stop, I'd shoot her. I aimed at her. I didn't mean to shoot her, but she started screaming at me, and I just pulled the trigger without thinking, and there was blood everywhere." He collapsed to the ground in sobs.

I stooped and put my arms around him. "Listen to me," I said. "What you did was a horrible thing, we both know that. But the fact that you're here proves you are truly sorry for what you did. You're not some psychopathic killer. You didn't want to shoot her, you just got irritated for a second. You're a kid who made a mistake."

"A big one," he said.

"When did this happen?"

"When I was nine. I died when I was twelve."

Great. How could the Devil leave his mark on a kid that young? Well, I wasn't going to let him have Timmy, not if I could help it.

"Look, why don't you stay here tonight?" I said. "I could use some company. You can tell me more about this place." I wondered where the water came from to supply Timmy and others with tears, since nobody needed to drink. Maybe it came out of the humid air. Based on Timmy's face, it would be a lot less humid.

He lay down on my floor and we talked for hours, maybe days. Time seems to stand still when there's no rising or setting sun. And yet something seemed wrong. I finally figured it out.

"How come I'm not tired?" I asked.

"You're dead," Timmy said. "Why would you need to sleep, or even breathe?"

I'd been breathing since I'd arrived, but now I experimented. Sure enough, I could hold my breath without any effects, so I simply stopped breathing. Yet a few minutes later I realized I was breathing again, one of those automatic things you do even when you're dead. At least the rotting carcass smell seemed to be dying away, though that was probably because I was getting used to it.

I think it's the second law of thermodynamics that says all systems generally run down. That law didn't apply on the Devil's Backbone. Bodies didn't age or need energy, my ice cream truck ran forever without running out of gas, and even the batteries were perpetual, keeping the ice cream freezer running endlessly. Ice cream bars and the air conditioning in my truck were nice breaks from this never-ending Hell.

Perhaps I deserved to go to Hell. If man were judged by his past, I certainly deserved to. There's no denying it; I'd once been a bad man. I'd started with shoplifting and burglary, and then moved on to armed robbery and, when a bank job didn't go right, assault. The guard survived but would never walk again. And there was nothing I could ever do to change that.

It was while sitting in prison in the blackest of depressions that I'd seen the light. No, not religiously; I'd just realized what a waste my life was, that I'd become a parasite. I didn't want to die a parasite.

While musing on my future in my orange prison garb, a spot on my backbone and another on my scalp began to itch. I've never had an itch on the inside like the one on my back, and no amount of scratching would make it stop. The one on my head I thought might be hair lice. I checked in the mirror... and saw a 666 etched in black under my hair.

That's a wakeup call.

When I got out of prison, I was determined to change, to make an honest living doing good. And so I spread happiness to kids on my route just north of the Bronx, even if it meant hours of noxious ice cream truck music and a flabby belly because, yeah, I like ice cream too. After a few weeks, the 666 faded away and the itch in my back eased up, though it never went completely away. Yes, even if you're a bad person, you can change your life around.

Unfortunately, the Devil likes parasites. Imagine that. He'd had me marked, probably had a place labeled "Seth" all set for me downstairs, and then I'd gone and disappointed him. Turns out I'm not the only bad guy-gone-good. But the Devil isn't good at letting go.

The Devil's Backbone was hot, boring, and people mostly just existed there, often for centuries. Once in a while someone would go crazy, perhaps attacking others, and then his body would collapse to the ground as his soul left and sank downward. If the Devil had set out to break our spirits and bring us back into his fold, it was working.

There had to be a way to escape. All we had to do was leave the Devil's body and we'd be back in the real world, and our souls could presumably go where they were meant to go—Heaven—or the Devil wouldn't have detoured us.

Timmy and I drove my truck to what he called the Northern Pit of Fire, just above the top vertebra. Like the name implied, it was a huge fire that encompassed the entire vertebra. Even from a distance I could feel the intense heat. The flames rose up like fiery trees with no apparent source of fuel.

"No one's ever made it through," Timmy said. "You'll just get burned."

"What's the worst that could happen?" I asked. "I'm already dead." I took a few unnecessary gulps of air, squinted my eyes, and waded into it.

You know how when you touch a hot stove, you pull away instantly, but don't feel the pain until a second later? My whole body pulled back spastically as I entered the flames, and yet I didn't feel anything.

And then I did.

I screamed as the agonizing heat tore into my body. I took another step forward, and then my body betrayed me as I collapsed.

I awoke to searing pain. I opened my eyes and Timmy was looking over me.

"I had to pull you out," he said. "I think that's what Hell is like." His hands were blackened, no doubt burned as badly as I'd burned myself. I could see and feel the heat of the Pit of Fire a short distance away. I crawled away from it to get farther from the heat, and then lay there for what seemed like forever. The burns didn't heal, but the pain went away. I was probably there for weeks, Timmy usually nearby, before I finally got up and drove my truck back.

Timmy said the Southern Pit of Fire was just as bad. I accepted that, but I simply couldn't accept there was no way out. I stepped out of my cave and looked up at the reddish sky that was the Devil's flesh. Was there a way to get there? I didn't think there were enough building materials to build a ladder, but there had to be other ways.

"Are there any explosives here?" I asked Timmy.

"You mean to blow up stuff?"

"Actually, I'm thinking of building a rocket."

"A rock what?" Timmy looked confused.

"I'll explain later, but it might be a way to get out of here. I'll need some sort of fuel or explosives to make it work." I'd played around with toy rockets as a kid, but really had no idea what was needed to power one.

"Old Al is some sort of explosives expert," Timmy said.

"Can you take me to him?"

Timmy nodded. Al's cave was on a nearby vertebra, only a few hundred yards away.

Old Al had a neatly trimmed beard and mustache, and wore a dark suit, like an undertaker. He wasn't that old, perhaps early sixties, and he really was an explosives expert—Alfred Nobel, to be exact, the Swedish inventor of dynamite. It was no wonder the Devil had marked him for his own, and then lost him when Al created the Nobel Prizes as his legacy. He'd languished here since his death over a hundred years ago. He sat cross-legged on the ground outside his cave playing chess with pieces carved from Devil-bone. His opponent was a young man wearing a Nazi uniform, swastika and all, who spoke only German. He looked like he'd been shot in the face and chest a dozen times, and turned out he had, while charging the American line in World War II. A reformed Nazi? Why not.

I explained my idea to Al, and he seemed intrigued. "Like Jules Verne's, *From the Earth to the Moon,*" he said in near-perfect English. "Unfortunately, we don't have gunpowder, TNT, nitroglycerine, or the ingredients needed to make them." I later learned he was often used here as a translator, since he fluently spoke English, German, French, Russian, Swedish, and Italian.

We chatted for a time, and then I left him and the Nazi to their chess game. Rockets were out.

Helplessness overtook me, and then anger. We had repented our crimes and didn't deserve to be here. How dare the Devil trap us in this prison he'd created inside his body. There had to be a way out.

I returned to my cave. There was a shovel nearby. I grabbed it and ran to the vertebrae's edge. Looking down, I saw the Devil's spinal cord passing from this vertebra to the next. It was a long way down, but what did I have to lose? If fire couldn't do more than put me in bed for a time, what could falling a few hundred feet do? I wanted to tear the Devil apart.

I raised my shovel, ready to attack, and jumped.

About ten feet down, my feet hit what seemed like an invisible trampoline. I sank down and then shot back up. Up and down I went until I came to a stop. I took my anger out on the invisible force field, smashing the shovel against it. The shovel bounced back and slammed me in the face, giving me a massive headache and a welt that never went away.

Now I was stuck on this invisible field, ten feet down. No problem; I jumped up and down, higher and higher, and then jumped clear. In other circumstances, it would have been a fun toy, this invisible trampoline.

One day I walked by the Welcome Center and heard screaming inside. I ran in. Mrs. Chien, the Asian woman I'd met when I first arrived, was screaming and fighting hysterically against three men who struggled to restrain her. Lying on the floor nearby, alive but in obvious pain, lay a woman. A small metal trowel stuck out of her stomach.

"Why?" a tall man in a top hat and cloak yelled in an English accent.

"Too long. Too long," Mrs. Chien muttered in her broken English. "Can't take it any more. Kill you all!"

Mrs. Chien closed her eyes and began gibbering in Chinese. Then she stopped. She became rigid, and her ghostly soul rose out of her body. The body crumpled to the floor as the men released it.

Her soul rose into the air and stood among us, a shimmering presence that smelled of sweet meadow flowers. She smiled and seemed about to say something when she stopped. A surprised look crossed her face for a second, and then a thin, horizontal crack formed across her stomach, then more of them on the rest of her. The smell of rotten eggs hit me, and I stepped back. Then, as if the ground opened under her, she was sucked down like smoke.

We buried her body under bone shards. Time was on the Devil's side; How long could anyone hold out? Someday we'd all meet this fate.

I spent a long time in the heat and humidity of The Devil's Backbone, just existing. Gradually I became as depressed as the others, speaking in a monotone, and spending my days wandering about. Sometimes I'd volunteer to carve out homes for new arrivals. Sometimes I'd sit around for hours, staring off into space and counting off the seconds between the Devil's heartbeats.

I'd once been a parasite, but I'd decided I didn't want to be a parasite and overcame that. Now I was a wart. I didn't harm anything but served no purpose other than to just be there.

One day I decided I didn't like being a wart. I'd stopped being a parasite when I learned to spread joy to children with my ice cream truck. I still had a nearly full supply of ice cream; why not go back to spreading joy?

So I headed out in my ice cream truck in the streets of The Devil's Backbone, playing *The Entertainer*, which I'd somehow begun to miss. Children came out to see what was going on. Some knew what an ice cream truck was; most did not.

I taught them quickly, and I didn't charge. It took all day, but I finally gave out the last of the ice cream, leaving behind a large number of happy faces and excited voices. I was a happy wart, spreading such joy. Except... I no longer had any ice cream.

I'd have been a sad wart again if Timmy hadn't pointed out that Old Man Pete had died in a cattle stampede, and a handful—a *large* handful—of cows came with him when he had arrived. I'd explained to Timmy that the primary ingredient of ice cream was milk. But I also needed ice, sugar, salt, and flavoring. Because of the humidity, water was everywhere, and I could freeze it in my truck.

There was a supply depot in the middle of The Devil's Backbone, a place where people dropped off stuff they had when they arrived but didn't need. Since many people from the past were farmers, it made sense that some of them might have shown up with seeds for sugar cane, as well as flavoring—perhaps cacao for chocolate. And since many of the farmers were from long ago, there might be salt, which they used to preserve meat before the invention of refrigeration. Then I could use the freezer from my ice cream truck to make actual ice cream!

Sure enough, there were stacks and stacks of farming items at the supply depot that the Devil's hand had grabbed while snatching people, including sugar cane and cacao seeds. There were also bags of salt. I had everything I needed to make ice cream, even chocolate ice cream! Nothing could stop me!

Unless, of course, the Devil chose that moment to once again stick his hand down his mouth, into his stomach, dig its way through flesh to his backbone, and grab at me. Which he did.

I tried running away, and learned what grabbing an ant is like from an ant's perspective. The hand was simply too big to grab me as I dodged about. Finally the powerful fingers reached around me, and with a loud *crunch*, broke off a section of his backbone, with me in the middle. And then it was back into the stomach, up through the throat, and out the mouth.

The Devil's other giant hand cleared away the bone rubble, leaving me alone in the Devil's palm, staring at the Devil himself. His giant red face could have held nine football stadiums.

"Why are you spreading happiness to my people?" the Devil asked in a voice surprisingly like Darth Vader. He stared down at me from over a bulbous nose and, surprise, a short, black Hitler mustache. We were in another large red cavern, though I wasn't sure since it was hard to look away from the Devil's eyes, each of them twice the size of a baseball diamond. Looking into their blackness was like looking into the endless reaches of starless space.

This should have been the most frightening experience of my life *and* afterlife. But I'd been through a lot, and there wasn't much more the Devil could throw at me. Let him do what he wanted. I felt a deep calm come over me.

"They're not exactly your people," I pointed out. "You were premature in marking them as your own."

"*I will always be in all of you!*" the Devil roared, his eyes blazing in anger. Holding me in one vast hand, he leaned down and slammed his other mountain-like fist onto the white ground. There was a loud crash as cracks appeared. Again and again the angry Devil slammed his fist into the ground until it was like broken pavement.

The calm I'd felt was now quivering fear. A giant, angry Devil slamming his fist into the ground has a way of doing that.

He pulled me up close to one of his eyes. "You spread joy to the very people whose spirits I am trying to break. And you would have made more of this ice cream and spread more joy. For this, you will face pain that you cannot imagine, for eternity, and then in infinite other eternities. I will devote my entire being to finding ways to increase your pain."

This left me quaking like an epileptic with Parkinson's disease in an earthquake. The old itch in my back came back in full throttle like a bug stuck inside me. "There are others who have done nicer things," I pleaded in a cracking voice. "Really, I'm not that good. Why me?"

"Because you irritate me a little," the Devil said. "The pain starts in one minute. They say the anticipation is the worst part, but they are wrong. Oh, are they wrong."

I couldn't imagine the pain being worse than the anticipation I now felt, but the Devil *had* warned me I wouldn't be able to imagine it. Not that I needed to; shortly I'd experience it. Forever.

The itch in my back was getting worse and worse. Why was it doing this now, of all times? Was it the beginning of the pain the Devil promised?

Then clarity struck. What had the Devil said about being in all of us? Did he mean all people, or just those trapped here inside him? I looked about and saw the red cavern appeared just like the sky in The Devil's Backbone. Because of the Devil's hand, I couldn't see down, but I knew what the Devil stood on: an even larger backbone.

I reached my arm around to my back, but couldn't quite reach the itch; I couldn't twist my shoulder backward that far, just as the Devil apparently could not. There was another way in, and the Devil had shown the way. I opened my mouth as wide as I could and jammed my hand into it. Back when I was alive, I doubted if I could have done this, but being dead has its advantages—for one thing, there was no gag reflex. I worked my hand down my throat and into my stomach. Then I tore at the side of my stomach, trying to get to where the itch was in my back.

"*What are you doing!*" the Devil thundered, his voice knocking me off my feet. I continued to feel for the itch in my back, and felt it moving about. I grabbed at it, tearing painfully through my own flesh. Somehow, being dead made that easier, but only barely.

As I did so, there was an explosion overhead. I looked up, and saw a giant hand come out of the sky. This hand was as much larger than the Devil as the Devil's hand was to me. It wore a giant Good Humor Man Ring on its index finger, just as I did on the hand I had jammed inside me.

The Devil ran from the grasping hand. I jumped free of the running Devil's much smaller hand—though still huge to me—and crashed painfully onto the bony ground below, and watched the Devil sprint away on that giant backbone. My hand was still jammed down my throat.

I closed my hand around the itch, and with a grunt, I twisted my hand back and forth until the entire section of my backbone broke off with a crunch. I tried to ignore the searing pain.

As I did this, the hand in the sky grabbed the section of vertebrae the Devil ran upon, and after twisting it back and forth, broke it off, Devil and all. As I pulled my hand out of my back and into my stomach, the giant hand pulled out as well, presumably into its own giant stomach—or was it my stomach, mirrored in vast size? I pulled my own much punier hand out of my stomach, up my throat, and out my mouth. Presumably the giant hand did the same.

I sorted through the shreds of bone from my own backbone I now held in my hand. Movement caught my eye, and there he was, scurrying away: the Devil, small version, the source of that long-time itch in my back.

With my other hand I removed all the bone fragments until all I held was the Devil, who tried to run for the edge. I pulled him back to the middle with my fingernail, and then, after a few minutes of trial and error, used it to pin him to my palm.

"Let me go!" cried the Devil, whose voice was now only a squeak. "Or else!"

"Or else what?" I asked. "Unimaginable pain in infinite eternities?"

"*Worse!*" the Devil screamed.

Now the Devil is one tough devil. But when a creature with a mass about ten billion times greater squeezes him, even the Devil can't withstand that. I squished him like a bug.

That left me alone on this gigantic backbone inside some larger being. Was it my backbone or the Devil's? I have no idea.

What I do know is that a moment later my body collapsed to the ground and lay still. My soul floated out slowly, perhaps still weighted down by my past sins. Or perhaps it just waited for the others, as seven thousand other souls—the inhabitants of The Devil's Backbone—floated out of my body. I waved to Timmy, he waved back, and we began our upward descent.

Wherever we're going, I hope they have ice cream.

Written in Stone

Lauren Stoker

Folks sure love their clichés. "Better late than never." "You get what you pay for." And that idiotic, "It is what it is." Honestly? What the hell's *that* supposed to mean?

But the one that really doesn't work for me is, "Nothing is written in stone." Not for me or my family, not to mention all the dead people out there. You don't need to be in my profession to wonder how that one got started. Seems like people would remember that hairy, bearded guy in the smoking sandals, trudging down Mt. Sinai with two fifty-pound tablets written in Hebrew.

See, we, my family and I, carve tombstones. Been doing it for generations. So when someone trots out that stupid remark, we just smile and respond, "Oh, really?" and hand the person our business card. It reads, "We write in stone, and it stays there. Wrightworth & Sons, est. 1839." I usually add (as long as I'm not talking to a bereaved customer), "And it's worth it!" Always gets a laugh.

But it's damned hard writing. Even the simplest sentiment takes ages to engrave. Dad's still old school: uses his hammers and chisels. Selects and cuts his own stones, too. Beautiful work, but crushing on the body over time. Also takes far longer to finish than the computer-assisted laser engraving favored by newer firms. But we get top dollar because the chiseled impressions we make last a lot more centuries than the modern technology stuff. Contrary to current expectations, we remain optimistic that mankind is finally going to wake up and fix things before it destroys the planet. We don't plan for obsolescence.

<<>>

I just finally worked up to the actual engraving but I'm still a little nervous. It's not like if you make a goof, you can just hit "delete" or toss the thing away and start a new page. Can you imagine the recycling problem? Dad started me out with polishing the stones. That's the first step. Then I have to apply the stencil. (Come on, you didn't think we did it free-hand, did you?) Plus, everybody wants to choose or even create their own designs, as well as the typeface. We should really term it "chiselface."

And, *man,* I've seen some peculiar designs. One of our customers wanted us to engrave an exact replica of the dead guy's "Vette"—the one he died in. Another wanted the text, "Gone fishing—after the Big One." *That* was funny. I even carved a cloud with a big fish hook hanging from it. His fishing buddies loved it. And hey, he was a bachelor, so no wife to get annoyed.

Naturally, the more complicated it gets, the more time it takes.

I was working on maybe my third or fourth stone, and was super grateful for Dad's advice and assistance. Besides the lengthy scripture, the widow who'd ordered it wanted a garland of holly and ivy framing the text. Her husband had been our vicar and "The Holly and the Ivy" had been his favorite Christmas carol. But Dad had been down with a cold for nearly a week, and it was getting awfully close to Christmas, which was the date when she wanted it finished and installed at his grave. There was supposed to be a special holiday memorial service for the installation. I was seriously worrying that we wouldn't be able to finish it on time.

As I heard a knock on the studio door, I looked up from my work, taking care to first pull the hammer away from the chisel I'd been about to strike and lay it aside. The new, young vicar came in, anxiously asking how the work on the headstone was going.

I sighed and shook my head apologetically. "I'm doing my best, but with Dad down with the croup it's slow going. I think you need to prepare yourselves for not being able to do the service by Christmas. I'm really sorry, truly I am."

He looked wildly about him, running a hand through his sandy-colored hair, as if wondering if he could just substitute one of the other finished stones and no one would notice.

That would be like giving a little girl a birthday cake that read, "Congratulations on your retirement, Fred!"

"What am I going to tell my congregation?" he moaned.

I shrugged helplessly at him.

"And I had my sermon all set. It was one of the best I've done. God, this is disaster!"

"I wouldn't say that exactly. 'God moves in His own good time,' you know," I reminded him.

"Fat lot of good *that* does me," he cried, flapping his arms at his sides and throwing the stink-eye toward the basic vicinity of the ceiling. "What the he—, *Hades* will I write about now? Took me three weeks to write this one!"

"Well," I suggested, pulling on my beard and doing my best to remain deadpan, "what about 'Nothing is written in stone'?"

Alternative Deathiness

Death

Robert Armstrong

Don't be ashamed
Of the tears you shed,
For the loss of loved ones
Who fall to a disease
That's indifferent
To the plight of us
Who suffer,
Until death
Creeps upon us,
With fentanyl,
With liquor-laced fingertips,
Clutching our hearts
With false love,
Warmth,
Taking us away
From those
Who really care,
As their tears
Wrap our souls
With a weariness,
That time
Will either heal,
Or watch
As we fade away,
Into the mist of
forgotten dreams,
Of barely remembered
Memories,
All there is
That's
Left
Of
Us.

Alternative Deathiness

The Four Horsemen (and Women) of the Apocalypse

Sarina Dorie

The four horsemen walked into a bar.

Not all together. No, that would imply they worked in unison and collaborated. Death considered his coworkers more like a dysfunctional family. Each had to arrive in a grandiose display representative of their personalities for their meetings. Hopefully this would be the last.

This was to be the meeting to end all meetings.

Today Death intended to decide who got to end the world for good.

He dismounted from his pale horse, leaving the sickly green steed beside a Harley Davidson—Famine's modern take on the black "horse" of the apocalypse, and . Death walked into the bar, black robes billowing in the breeze. His skeletal face was hidden under the shadows of a hood as he scanned the half-empty glasses of bargoers who would soon be wishing they had stayed home.

The crowd of dancers parted instinctively, though they didn't see him. He knew Famine was already there. He could tell from the bottled water listed as $7 each on the signs and the people loudly complaining about the food they had ordered that never arrived.

Death found her waiting, her calculator set out on her table rather than the archaic scales she used to carry around. She was as slender as a teenage fashion model, her angled bob emphasizing sharp cheekbones and a pointed chin. She hid her true face under a ridiculous amount of contouring to give her ashen complexion a healthy ebony glow.

Death took a seat at her table near the bar and pulled out his cellphone. It was the newest, and he found it a far superior device for reaping and keeping tallies. He didn't regret that he had replaced his scythe with a cell phone, though his boney finger could never get the fingerprint ID to work. He perused news articles to pass the time.

Pestilence tried to slip in unnoticed as he was wont to do. No one saw him but Death, who had long ago noticed Pestilence's tell for wearing all-white.

He picked him out immediately despite the child's face he wore.

War arrived fashionably late. As usual. Her steed was a red tank that Death heard crushing and grinding half the cars in the lot outside. She strode into the bar and nodded to Death. He nodded back and finished texting chain letters to people, stating they would die in the next twenty-four hours if they didn't pass the message on.

He loved those.

War had attired herself in her favorite body, that of a six foot five Valkyrie with blonde braids, though she had adopted a more modern look with her camo fatigues. Smoke curled from the cigar in her mouth. Her eyes settled on Famine, who was consulting her Fitbit.

War leveled her gaze at Famine. "You're in my chair."

Famine shrugged, unconcerned. "I got here first."

"There isn't enough room in this bar for the two of us," War said.

Famine sighed overdramatically. "There isn't enough room on this planet for the two of us."

"Oh, I know, you could battle to see who is the strongest," a child's voice said out in the crowd said.

Pestilence obviously. It was the sneaky kind of thing he would do, instigating chaos and antagonism with the face of innocence, dividing them into squabbling when they all had the same goals; destroy humanity. Death didn't see why War and Famine were always quarrelling over who he chose. They were all on the same team.

War reached for a semi-automatic in one hand and an eighteenth-century saber in the other.

Famine opened her mouth, locusts crawling out. Death hated it when she did that. She'd stolen that move from pestilence.

One of the humans in the crowd sneezed.

"Horsemen," Death warned. "Let us not fight amongst ourselves. We all share a common goal."

"Horsewomen," War and Famine corrected at the same time.

"How about an epic rap battle to settle our differences instead?" Pestilence asked.

Famine shot Pestilence a withering glare.

War tilted her head to the side, perplexed. "I like all battles, but this rap battle is not one I know of."

Death knew he shouldn't encourage Pestilence's schemes, but he did enjoy the more modern versions of warfare. "If you must do this, what about a dance battle instead?" He got the camera app ready on his phone. He knew it would go viral and they could have a good laugh about after the end times.

"I propose arm wrestling." Famine pushed back a long sleeve to reveal an emaciated arm. "Winner gets first dibs on how they want to destroy humanity."

War pounded her fist into her palm. "Game on! I'm going to break those matchstick arms in less than two seconds."

This wasn't quite as entertaining as a dance battle, but Death was pleased the troops kept their true arsenal of weapons to themselves.

Famine's arms looked like skin covered putty smeared over bones, but that was an illusion. Her strength was fueled by deeds of misery and scarcity she had created. As she gripped War's hand, her smile stretched over her teeth in a vicious sneer. "I bring to this battle the power of my conquests. Those fires in Australia that burned natural habitats as well as crops, that was my doing. The recent droughts in North America, that was me. Locust infesting East Africa and eating all crops, I did that."

She gained an inch.

War flicked a blonde braid over her shoulder. "The size of the American military—that's me whispering in politicians' ears that they need more guns and jets. I'm the reason there's a war over oil. I inspire terrorists and cause missiles to accidentally be shot." She winked at Death, thinking this would persuade him.

189

It wasn't like Death didn't have a tally of all their numbers.

War gained back her inch and took two more.

Famine grimaced as she fought in earnest. "If there's a way to cause poverty and hunger, I take credit. Stock market crashes, recessions, and the Great Depression—also me. The greenhouse effect, The Dust Bowl, and global warming, those were my ideas."

Death had to hand it to her, she was creative and versatile.

"But my achievements aren't only confined to weather patterns and insects." Famine recovered and pushed War's hand closer to the table. "I'm the reason we have empty calories. I'm to thank for a food pyramid glorifying empty carbs and granting people the convenience of drive-thrus and fast food. Without me, there would be no Twinkies, potato chips, or candy bars. Poverty wouldn't be an epidemic of obesity, heart disease, and diabetes without my magic touch." She laughed manically and gained back a few inches.

"Funny you should say epidemic—" Pestilence said.

"Did you think Hitler, Stalin, Mao, or Mussolini just happened to find themselves in positions of power?" War spat out her cigar. She reclaimed the lead. "I smelled talent—and the lust for blood. I was behind their rise. Genghis Khan was my pet project. Guess what politicians are currently in my pocket?"

Pestilence cleared his throat. "Not to name drop, but did you know I'm friends with Jenny McCarthy on Instagram?"

No one answered. The match was at a deadlock.

War gritted her teeth, gaining on Famine. "The nuclear bomb—who do you think thought of that? I whispered that inspiration in the ears of humans."

"That's the bomb," Pestilence said, somehow able to keep a straight face. "I'm going to drop another bomb on you—"

"Please, we've heard all about your plagues. They're so old-fashioned," Famine said. "Death should give me the honor of ending humanity. I will give them a long, painful torment full of suffering as they deserve."

"No, Death should give me the privilege of ending all life on earth—not just humanity," War said. "I've already got everything set to blow the world into smithereens. It will be quick and easy."

Pestilence stood there, looking smug. "Let me tell you a little something about my go-getter attitude and sense of initiative—"

"No one wants to hear it!" War shouted.

A human in the crowded bar coughed behind her.

Death's phone rang, ruining the video he was taking of the epic arm-wrestling match that would help him decide who would end the world. "Sorry horsewomen, I've got to take this. It's the big guy upstairs."

He turned off the video and listened. What he heard disappointed him beyond all else. The boss said, "The apocalypse has been postponed; everyone has been furloughed."

Death sighed and ended the call. He broke the bad news to his team.

War and Famine released each other's hands, scowling and lamenting their misfortune. Out of all of them, Pestilence was the only one not complaining.

"What are you so pleased about?" Death asked.

"I arrived three weeks before and infected everyone. Pandemic achieved," Pestilence giggled. "You're welcome."

Alternative Deathiness

Deathventures, Inc.

Robinne Weiss

It was my business partner, Kai, who first suggested the new venture. We'd spent over two hundred years in the bespoke prosthetics industry and had done well, financially. But after two hundred years ... well ... we were bored.

"Honestly, Yana, if I have to talk to one more bloke who wants a double-headed penis, I'm gonna vomit." Kai rubbed his face.

I was flicking through the day's incoming e-mail. I raised my eyebrows. "Well, here's a guy who's *got* one of the double-headers. Wants another on the back." I snorted. "Apparently, both his girlfriends have had double vaginas installed." I grimaced at the images that conjured.

"Puh-leese! Don't they have any imagination?" Kai pushed his chair away from his desk.

I sighed. "They're bored." I knew that feeling, and I sympathised. Sometimes I wondered if the scientists who had worked so hard to make humans all but immortal realised how poorly suited most of us were for eternal life.

"Yeah. Me too. But, come on, where's their imagination?"

"Once you've done everything, what can you do for thrills except more of the same?" I leaned back in my chair and crossed my arms, trying to ignore how that thought resonated inside my chest. Had I done everything? I shook off the feeling. Of course I hadn't. There was still plenty of excitement out there for me. "You know, we've got plenty of money, and the business is worth a lot. We could sell out and take a vacation for fifty, a hundred years, probably." I grinned. "You could get your own double-header. Your wife might like that."

Kai snorted and pursed his lips. "You're really that tired of the business?"

I shrugged. Kai's hurt tone made me squirm a little. "I really enjoy working with you, Kai. I'm just ..." I sighed. "I don't know. What we're doing is good, I guess—we certainly have plenty of business—but it doesn't get me out of bed in the morning anymore."

Kai furrowed his brow. "What would you do with a vacation? Travel? Get another degree?"

That was the problem. "I don't know." I'd been to every country at least twice and had five advanced degrees. What more was there to do? I ran my fingers through my hair. "Don't you get sick of it all, Kai? I mean, what's the point? After a certain age, you've done everything that interests you."

Kai shrugged. "Maybe we could start a new business. Offer a thrill. Something no one else offers."

I rolled my eyes. "Like what?" I started counting on my fingers. "Moon Rock Adventure sells tandem space-jumps to the moon. Rocket-man Corporation makes self-contained personal jetcraft. Pimp My Place offers extreme household makeovers. And if you don't want to be hampered by the laws of physics, Figments of Your Imagination can give you a personalised fantasy adventure of any length, for a price. There's not a thrill that hasn't already been thoroughly mined for its commercial value."

"There is one." Kai rubbed his chin.

"What's that?"

Kai smiled. "Death."

I snorted. "Death?"

Kai leaned forward in his chair. "Yes. The one thrill no one has even contemplated for five hundred years."

"Oh, come on. The euthanasia market's saturated."

"I'm not talking euthanasia—an injection and then falling asleep surrounded by friends and family. I'm talking *death*. Death like people used to face in war. Death by duelling, by accident, by psychopathic killer." Kai's eyes sparkled with an enthusiasm I hadn't seen there for fifty years. I hated to bring him down.

"Um ... isn't that what society's been trying to *eliminate* for the last millennium or two? Just *try* to kill someone.

They'll get patched up, good as new. Maybe with an expensive custom prosthetic in the bargain."

"That's where the thrill comes in, don't you see? We put them in a situation in which they *could* die, and then don't save them if they do."

I raised my eyebrows. "Is that ethical? Anyway, it's not very good for repeat business, is it?"

Kai dismissed the problem with a wave of his hand. "It's no different than euthanasia—they sign the forms and it's fine. And not *everyone* will die—it's the *chance* of death that will be the thrill. It'll be just like the VR games, except *real*."

#

I let him talk me into it. I was bored of the prosthetics industry, and starting a new, if weird, business venture was more interesting to me than getting a third vagina.

We called the business The Deathventure Amusement Park. We started small, with a limited number of Deathventures. Mostly, it was just accidents at first—a rollercoaster ride in which we'd removed a third of the bolts, a podcar racetrack dotted with obstacles, a bungy jump over a concrete floor (visitors got to choose the cord length). It took forever to source guns for the other Deathventures. They'd fallen out of favour centuries ago—they were considered childish relics of society's youth—and few of the ones remaining were in working order. Most of them were United Defence energy slug guns from the 3500s. They could vaporise a fist-sized hole in a man's chest. Or in the office door, as Kai found out one day.

Kai whistled appreciatively. "These babies must have been seriously lethal in their time."

I pushed the barrel toward the floor. "Yeah, and I don't want to end up in Reconstructive because you've accidentally pulled the trigger. Put that away."

Kai scoffed. "A day in the tank, and you'd be good as new."

I sighed. A day in the tank sounded nice, actually—complete oblivion, at least for a few hours. But I wouldn't be as good as new when I came out. I'd still be a jaded nine hundred and seventy-seven years old.

With a few guns, we were able to offer limited war games options, and a popular psychopath-on-the-loose experience.

<<>>

"Good morning! Welcome to Deathventure Amusement Park. Have you pre-booked?"

The man smiled and stepped up to the counter. "Yeah, Matsumi Yelinda. I have a ten o'clock booking for the psychopath."

I smiled. "That's right. You've been here before, Matsumi. I recognise you."

He returned my smile. "Yep. Been through most of the accidents, and I'm still here." He held his hands out and shook his head. "Hard to believe."

I handed him the paperwork and a pen. "If you don't mind my asking, are you looking for death, or do you just like the thrills?" Always good to know our clients' motivations—it helped in tweaking the experiences and the probability of death on each one.

Matsumi gave a little laugh. "Both." He sighed. "I was ready go for euthanasia a couple of years ago. I was just so *bored*. Even the idea of euthanasia was boring—falling asleep and not waking?" He shook his head. "Seriously, even death was looking dull. Then I saw your ad, and I thought, yeah, this is better. Better to die doing something exciting—with your heart racing, adrenalin pumping." He grinned. "It gave me a new lease on life."

Uh oh. That wasn't good. "So ... you do realise that if you die here, you *actually* die?"

"Oh, yeah! I can't wait! I'm nine hundred ninety-nine years old. I seriously don't want to see a thousand." His smile faltered, and weariness entered his eyes. He handed the completed paperwork back to me.

A thousand. I'd reached that milestone last year. Matsumi was right; he didn't want to hit a thousand. I sighed as I scanned his paperwork. Everything seemed to be in order.

"The psychopath is Deathventure number twenty-three, down the hallway, fourth door on the right." I smiled at him. "Good luck."

He smiled back. "Hopefully you won't see me again."

I didn't. We had a special team to retrieve the bodies and return them to next-of-kin.

<<>>

The business did well. It wasn't as lucrative as the prosthetics industry—we had a lot of one-time customers—but we had a steady income, and I felt like we were providing an important service. Within forty years, Kai and I had opened Deathventure Parks on three continents. It was good ... I guess.

On Deathventures' fiftieth anniversary, Kai and I shared a bottle of champagne.

"Well, Yana, what do you think of our first fifty years in Death? You doubted me at first."

I laughed. "I did. But as usual, you were right." I raised my glass. "To Deathventures."

Kai raised his glass and clinked mine. "To Deathventures. Long may we live."

Long may we live. The thought was a weight on my chest.

"Is there something wrong with the champagne?" Kai asked.

Had my mood shown? This was supposed to be a celebration. I forced a smile. "No. It's good." Then I sighed. "The champagne is perfect, the business is great, everything is *fine*. It's just ..." I shook my head. "Kai, I think I'm simply done."

"You're done with the business?"

"I'm done with life. I'm tired of work, my hobbies, my cat ...."

"Maybe you should start dating again. A new relationship might—"

I waved my hand at him. "No. No one should have more than fifteen husbands. I'm bored of dating, bored of relationships." I took a swig of champagne and smiled at Kai's hurt look. "This partnership with you has been great, Kai. Really. I mean that." I laughed. "You've outlasted six husbands."

Kai smiled weakly. "What could we do, Yana? How can we revive your spark? Maybe you should take a vacation. I hear the planet Ginzul is nice at this time of year."

I shook my head. "I've been to Ginzul. Smelled like dead fish. No. There's nothing to do about it. I don't think humans were meant to live this long." I took another sip of my drink. "A thousand and twenty-seven. That's what I'll be in May. A thousand and twenty-seven years old. You know my son euthanised last month?"

Kai's eyebrows shot up. "And you didn't say anything? Yana! I'm so sorry."

I waved his concern away. "It was his decision, and it reflected what I've been thinking, too. It's time for me to go. There's nothing new left for me. I've had a great life, and these last three hundred years working with you have been some of the best. But I'm ready for oblivion. I don't want to *be* anymore. It's time to make room for someone else on the planet. Someone young and excited to live."

#

Kai argued, but I was firm. I signed my half of the business over to him and gave the rest of my wealth to various charities. I gave my cat to the neighbour. On the day I sold my house, I walked to Deathventures instead of taking public transit. The air was crisp and clear. The sky was brilliant blue, and sunlight sparkled on the lake in the park. The world was bright and full of possibilities ... for someone else. Weariness slowed my steps and dulled the sun's sparkle. I was ready to be done with all this. To be done existing, because that was all I'd really done for the past fifty years. The only reason I hadn't ended it all years ago was because I felt I was doing a service with Deathventures. Giving people like Matsumi a thrill, and then an end to boredom. But that service would go on after me. It was time for me to die. I was looking forward to it.

I arrived at Deathventures to find Kai sitting at his desk. He looked up and sighed. He put on a smile I know he didn't feel. "Well, what'll it be?"

#

I was surprised at how fun the dive off the platform was. In the moments before impact, I felt excitement like I hadn't in centuries. It almost made me want to live.

Almost.

I felt nothing. Oh, maybe a fleeting moment of crushing pain, but death was nearly instantaneous. I'd made the bungy long enough, it hadn't even been taut when I hit the pavement.

I floated in nothingness for a time. How long? I couldn't tell.

Then there was a light.

I vaguely wondered how there could be a light, and how I could be aware of it. I was dead. I was quite certain of that. But how could I know I was dead? The thought troubled me.

I seemed to be drawn toward the light, and it grew, like the exit to a tunnel. Suddenly I was thrust into a blindingly bright space. I blinked until my eyes adjusted. I stood before a tall man in a white robe. He was smiling.

"Welcome, Yana."

"Huh?" I frowned at him. Had Kai sent me to Reconstructive? That jerk! "I'm supposed to be dead."

The man's smile widened. "You are. Don't let that worry you." He swept an arm around, and suddenly the blank whiteness behind him revealed itself to be a bucolic landscape. "Welcome to Heaven, where you will live for ever, in *eternal* life."

Alternative Deathiness

Rest In Virtual

Tommy Blanchard

The whir of the surgical drill changed pitch as it entered my skull. At least, that's what I assumed was happening. With the anesthetic and surgical drape over my face, the sound was all I had to go on. The only other sensation was my aching back on the rigid table. Still, I had a good idea of what must be happening thanks to my obsessive research on the procedure. First, the drill made 128 pin sized holes across my skull. The medical team injected nanosurgeons, some spreading out across my cerebral cortex while others went deeper, getting equal coverage across my brainstem.

It creeped me the hell out.

Still, it was my only option if I wanted to continue to see my grandchildren, even if it would only be when they logged into Virtu. Besides, soon it wouldn't matter that this body had holes in its head. One way or the other, its time was just about over.

The whirring stopped. There was some unintelligible chatter amongst the medical staff. I'm not sure how much time went by before I finally heard the voice of Dr. Niller. "Nanos are in place. Mr. Garcia, with your consent, we'll take the scan."

I tried to speak, but coughed instead. My forehead pressed up painfully against the restraints as I convulsed. The coughing became violent, and I worried I wouldn't be able to stop. *Great. With my luck, I'm going to end up dying on this table, literally seconds away from upload, because the medical staff was politely asking my permission to do their damn job.*

Finally, mercifully, the coughing abated. "Do it," I managed to croak out.

"Once the scan is complete, you'll find yourself in Virtu. Some disorientation is normal." Dr. Niller gave some order to the medical staff that I couldn't make out.

A cacophony of sensations. Ringing, flashing. A sweet taste and a foul smell. My muscles twitched and convulsed.

Then it stopped. I found myself still on the surgical table.

"Scan complete, data uploaded," a voice said.

"Great job everyone," I heard Dr. Niller say.

My heart pounded. This wasn't right. I shouldn't still be here.

"Hello? What's happening?" My voice sounded weak, but the room fell silent. They must have heard me.

I heard movement and whispered voices, and the darkness of the surgical drape disappeared, replaced by bright lights. I squinted, managing to make out two dark figures in surgical gowns. Dr. Niller was one of them.

"What's going on?" I managed to ask.

"Well," Dr. Niller said, "it looks like your body survived the scan. That's a first." Her tone was light, but I could see the confusion on her face. She turned to the nurse beside her. "Get him cleaned up and back to his room."

<<>>

The nurse wouldn't answer my questions about what had happened. Obviously something went wrong. My next conscious experience after the scan was supposed to be in Virtu. The electromagnetic wave from the simultaneous scanning of all of the nanosurgeons should have immediately destabilized my neural activity, causing immediate loss of consciousness. Without signals from the brainstem, the heart stops, and bodydeath occurs shortly after.

That was the hardest bit for prospective patients to get over—is the scan really saving me, or is it killing me? The debates over this had certainly livened up the retirement home. Suddenly those pedantic philosophical arguments from back in college were relevant. Ultimately, I had obviously agreed with the "mind upload" folks. But maybe that was just desperation. It's hard to maintain intellectual objectivity when living another month hinges on a particular philosophical position.

I groaned inwardly when the nurse dropped me off at my room. I didn't love staying in a hospital room, filled with beeping machines, flickering lights, and the sound of medical staff hurrying one way or the other in the hallway. It evoked memories of my painful cancer treatments, and of Lorraine slowly fading away. She died much too early, before scanning became an option. Her consciousness was lost, gone to oblivion.

Luckily it wasn't long before Dr. Niller came by.

She had gone over the data from the surgery. Apparently my brain had a unique reaction to the scan. Perhaps because of my history of seizures, my brain was used to booting itself back up after rapid uncontrolled activity. Or maybe the surgeries to remove the brain tumors had changed the wiring in my brain just enough to allow it to recover from the total shock of the scan.

Regardless of why, I was the first person to have his consciousness not just uploaded, but *copied*.

"So what do we do now?" I asked Dr. Niller.

"Well, we do have your scan now. One option is that we don't do anything. You'll live on in Virtu just as planned, it's just that your bodydeath will be a little later."

I couldn't believe what I was hearing. "So, option one is to just leave me to die? Not sure that's the kind of medical opinion I want."

She didn't hesitate. "The other option is for us to scan again."

"I guess it would be easier this time since I already have the holes in my head," I said. Dr. Niller didn't respond. You would think she would at least pretend I was amusing.

I took a moment and closed my eyes. Of course, this would be the only other option for getting me out of this stupid body. I felt so tired. I had gone through so much to prepare myself mentally for the first scan. I just wanted this to be over and done with. The pain and weakness of this old body, worrying any moment could be my last.

"How do you know we won't just run into the same problem?" I asked.

"Honestly, we don't. But if your goal is to make sure we copy your last conscious neural activity, we could equip the nanosurgeons with anesthetic that they'll release directly into the brain at the exact same time as the scan. You should lose consciousness the same moment as the scan."

"Doesn't that go against the Hippocratic oath or something? You're talking about euthanizing me."

Dr. Niller gave a shrug. "Frankly, that was always part of the process. Now we're just doing it on purpose instead of as a side-effect. As for Hippocrates, I don't think he had any deep insights on the ethics of dealing with mind uploads."

I opened my mouth to respond, but didn't know what to say. After a moment, Dr. Niller stood up to leave.

"Give it some thought. We have an open slot tomorrow morning for another scan, if you want."

<<>>

The nurses brought me lunch. Chicken soup. I ate, my useless hands shaking and spilling just as much of the soup as I managed to get in my mouth. Every swallow was agony.

As I ate, I mulled things over, but there wasn't too much to think about. I was in the same position as before, with the same choice: get scanned and have my body die at the same instant, or don't get scanned and have my body die naturally—and my consciousness with it.

The choice seemed pretty clear to me. I pulled up the vid screen and called my son.

"Hi Corey," I said as soon as he appeared.

His mouth hung open when he saw me, and he frowned. "Hi dad. I thought you were scanned this morning?"

"I was. Something went weird with it though so they're going to do it again tomorrow morning. Hopefully they won't mess it up this time."

Corey looked a bit pale. He kept shifting his gaze offscreen. "Why do you need another scan?"

I frowned. "Well, if you haven't noticed, I'm still here dying in my body. I just wanted to let you know the scan file will be getting to you a bit later than expected."

Corey shifted back and forth in his seat. "Actually, they already sent me a scan file. It must upload automatically."

That explained why Corey was acting so strangely. "Oh. Well, just ignore that one then. Better yet, delete it, don't want you getting confused and running the wrong one."

Corey suddenly couldn't meet my eyes. Something was up. "Well, can't we just keep this scan? I mean, you're already uploaded, you just get some bonus embodied life time."

I scowled. "That other scan isn't me."

"But it would have been—if you died during surgery."

"I'm here. Some nanobots crawled into my head and took a picture, that didn't change my health situation. Why are you being so difficult? I'm a dying man, Corey."

Corey took a big breath in. "Sorry, Dad. Truth is... The kids wanted to see you when the scan came in. So did I. We started running it this morning."

My heart pounded. They had a copy of me, a second me, already running without me even knowing. "Just stop it. Stop running it."

My mind raced at the implications. The insurance company would only pay the fees to run one scan in Virtu. Whatever scan was running at the start of the next billing cycle would be the one they would pay for and there would be no going back.

"Dad, I can't just turn it off, it's... you."

"It is *not* me," I said. Every second that went by was an extra second of divergence between us, an extra second of conscious experience snuffed out when the copy was deleted. "Shut the damn thing off now. Delete the file."

Corey shook his head back and forth. "I told you, I can't. I've talked to him. He's my dad. Every bit as much as you are."

"Fine, I'll do it myself." I lifted my hand up to hang up angrily.

"Wait. He's playing with the kids right now. If he suddenly disappeared they would be upset."

"Get them out of there, now."

"Dad, no. I'm not helping you with this."

I rubbed my temples. "What do you want me to do here, Corey? You want me to just die?"

"I won't stop you if you decide to delete him, but just talk to him first. Try to hash it out."

This was ridiculous. I had to meet the offshoot of my consciousness, and what? Have a civil conversation about which one of us should live?

I wanted to just tell Corey off. But I couldn't. He was my son after all.

"Fine. I'll meet with him."

<<>>

I had one of the nurses wheel me down to the hospital rec area so I could log in to Virtu. It didn't take me long to find my copy—I knew him fairly well, after all. He had set up a cozy little home near the area the grandkids liked to hang out. It was a near-replica of the one Lorraine and I raised Corey in. He was on his knees in the backyard, planting tulip bulbs.

"Hello," I said as I approached.

Virtu isn't a perfect replica of the real world, but its rendering of people's appearance and expressions is pretty damn good. As he stood up to face me, I had the surreal experience of watching my face go through shock and confusion.

I took some time to explain what happened during the scan. Then I told him I could have the procedure again the next morning.

"So, what are you doing here, then?" His tone was casual, but he wasn't meeting my eyes. He knew as well as I did what a second scan meant for him.

"I just wanted to talk to you," I said.

"Well, we're talking. What now?"

He was clearly irritated. I couldn't blame him—I would be too. But it also sucked to be on the receiving end of my own brand of passive aggression. "I need to shut you down so the insurance will pay to run my scan."

"Shut me down? You mean kill me," he said.

"It's not like killing you. I won't delete you. Your file will still be there, just... not actively running."

"And no one will ever run me again. Why would they? It's too expensive, and scan file number two will be running. I'll sit in the cloud inactive until the data center falls over. How is that any different from death?"

I shook my head. "You only exist because Corey started you up too soon, I'm just fixing that."

"Don't think you have more of a right to exist than I do. I went through that scan, it worked as expected for me. You're the one that needs to be *fixed*."

I had hoped this conversation wouldn't go like this, but I knew it would be a bitter pill for him to swallow. It's not like I could say I would have taken it any better.

"You can complain all you want. But at the end of the day, I'm the one with legal standing. You're just data, I can do what I want to you."

He clenched a fist. "And you want to live with that?"

"It's better than not living at all," I replied.

"You would just be going the same way as Lorraine."

"I could say the same to you," I said, but my voice was almost a whisper. The mention of Lorraine seemed to have sucked all of the anger out of me. Remembering my late wife—*our* late wife—and her last days. Her life. And her death.

I couldn't bring myself to be angry anymore, I was just tired. My copy seemed to be feeling the same way. We were both quiet for a moment.

"We could flip a coin, you know," he suggested with a smirk.

"The scan kind of already did that. Fifty-fifty shot of ending up as the upload or as the one in the body," I said.

He rolled his eyes. "I'm not sure that's the right way to think about it."

I opened my mouth to respond, but thought better of it. We weren't likely to see eye-to-eye on a philosophical point that would justify my actions.

He kneeled back down to focus on his virtual tulip bulbs. "Look, I'm not going to give you the satisfaction of feeling good about this. I want to live every bit as much as you do. But I know I can't stop you."

I stood there in silence for a little while. Just as I was about to open my mouth to get going, I heard the shouts of a couple of familiar voices: the grandkids had logged back in.

I wanted to see them badly, but didn't want to explain why there were two grandpas. "I'll go inside," I said.

He didn't react. I ducked into his little home, out of sight.

Through a window I saw Suzie and James appear in the backyard. Their eyes lit up when they saw my copy. I yearned to reach out and hold them. Instead, it was my copy that reached out and gave them a big hug.

I watched them play for a while, a heaviness in the pit of my stomach slowly growing. I already knew it intellectually, but seeing it really drove home that my copy loved those kids as much as I did.

I couldn't bring myself to log out. I just kept watching for over an hour. Eventually, the grandkids were called for dinner.

"Goodbye," my copy said to them, with the heaviness of expecting it to be for good. They smiled and waved and flickered out of Virtu. He took a seat on the ground and sat with his head in his hands, silent.

I went outside and sat next to him.

"God, I want to see them all grown up so badly," he said. I could hear the longing in his voice.

"Let's flip a coin," I said.

He looked at me, eyes wide. "Are you sure?"

"I'm letting my sentimentality get the better of me, take advantage of it before I change my mind." I conjured up a coin. "I'll flip, you call."

"Heads," he said with the coin up in the air. I held my breath.

Heads.

Of course. I slowly let my breath out. "Okay then." I knew I could still back out. I knew I could just forget this happened and delete his file. But I knew I wouldn't.

My copy put a hand on my shoulder. "You know, you could still get scanned. Get your file stored for now. Maybe one day someone will run it. Suzie has been saying she wants to be a doctor when she grows up, if she's rich enough maybe she'll pay a small fortune to see what their grandfather was like when he first started living in virtual. You'll get scanned and the next moment get to see Suzie all grown up."

I stood. "You better make sure they love you a lot. Spoil the hell out of them. Make them imagine how great it would be to have two grandpas around." I tried to smile, but instead found my eyes starting to water.

My copy stood up and put his arms around me. "I can't promise anything. Who knows what will happen in the future. But I'll make sure they know your file exists. If they ever win the lottery or start making the big bucks, I'll make sure to remind them of you."

"That's all I can ask," I replied. "Thank you."

<<>>

The nanosurgeons were back in place, ready to go with their scans and their toxic payload of anesthetic.

"We're ready to go. Once again, we need your consent, Mr. Garcia."

I closed my eyes and braced myself.

"I'm ready."

Alternative Deathiness

Loving Death in New York

Alicia Hilton

Strolling in Central Park Zoo I saw
a corpse walking a middle-aged man
wearing a pinstripe suit shiny wingtips
scarlet to match punctures on his neck
his leash gleaming silver and gold links
studded with diamonds nothing but the
best for spoiled pets reanimated masters
are bloodthirsty yet not cruel always
kiss before sucking their pets' necks

No bites without consent symbiotic living
and dead coexist in peace reality is not like
gory zombie films springtime smells like
cherry blossoms and warm asphalt not rot
beside the penguin habitat dead kids frolic
live nannies sit on benches trading gossip
licking ice cream no one is hungry pets
like me never pay rent or buy groceries
masters and mistresses fulfill our needs

Exquisite pleasure my platinum leash glistens
with moonstones my mistress howls when
we make love she's a bottom I'm a top ironic
to finally find a soulmate with a dead woman
this topsy-turvy world is strange fortunately
mortification is slow my lover's flesh is firm
fresh and warm her sighs taste of sweet longing
I wonder how soon pathogens will snuff my
life uniting us in eternal bliss.

j

Life Long Love

Sirrus James

After forty years of marriage, I'm sit next to my wife, Mary, and watch as she sleeps. The gentle breathes marking time.

Now, thinking to myself, I tilt my head down in prayer. She wakes and slides a hand across mine.

"It's fine Shawn. I'll be fine." A tear rolls down my cheek as I lean over the bed to hug her.

Her voice is faint as she asks, "Will you lay here with me?"

I smile. "Always."

I lay down next to her on the faded comforter our daughter gave us for our anniversary, and slip my arms around her. She rolls on her side and we're facing the pictures on the wall.

She raises a frail hand, "remember when we brought Lucy home from the hospital?".

I look into the faded picture and smile, "Like it was yesterday."

She laughs, "you were so tired when we came home. I thought you were going to fall asleep on the drive. You looked like you were gonna pass out."

"That's cause I was tired."

"But you didn't. As soon as we came in the house, you took Lucy from my arms and let me sleep. You said that I'd worked hard enough already."

"It was my turn" I say.

"Ya, I guess so," she said snuggling up to me.

I point higher on the wall, to all three of our kids Lucy, Jake, and Layla in front of the Christmas tree. "Do you remember this year?"

213

"Of course. That was the first year all of them were able to open their presents on their own."

"Yup, it's also the year I finally didn't burn anything cooking dinner."

"Ya, with my help."

"Mhm, you always made it taste better than it would have if it was just me."

She raises a finger towards a picture high on the wall. "I haven't even looked at this picture in so long."

"It's Jake, the first one to get married."

"Look at them, Jake and Cassie. They are so happy in this picture. I think this was one of the best days of my life when I saw that one of our babies were gonna be happy for the rest of their life."

"And they are happy," I say. "Lucy and Layla too."

"Yeah, all of them had their big day."

"And you saw every one of them."

"I did," she says. She settles her head on the pillow. "Shawn?"

"Yes."

"Thank you for this wonderful life."

"Thank you for mine," I say back. We kissed.

"I love you," she says. She closed her eyes and drifted off into an eternal sleep.

I laid next to her and closed my eyes, "I love you too. I always will." Then I felt something on my shoulder and opened my eyes. She was smiling over me twenty years younger.

I smiled as my eyes tear up "goodbye my love." I say as she fades. I wipe my tears away. The door opens as Layla, Lucy, and Jake walk in.

"Dad?" Layla said.

I look to them and nod my head "She's up there now." I stand as they surrounded me holding one another and began to cry together.

About the Authors

K.G. Anderson is a late-blooming writer of fantasy and science fiction and a campaigner for affordable universal healthcare. Prior to finding her speculative fiction muse, she reported on politics and crime for New England newspapers, reviewed hundreds of mystery novels for *January Magazine,* and wrote online content on topics including AEDs, Richard Thompson, travertine countertops, and catnip. Her short stories appear in magazines and anthologies including *The Mammoth Book of Jack and Ripper Stories, More Alternative Truths,* and *Galaxy's Edge*, as well as on podcasts such as Far Fetched Fables, StarshipSofa, and The Overcast. For links to more of her stories and information on upcoming appearances, visit http://writerway.com/fiction

Tommy Blanchard worked as a neuroscientist at Harvard University and has published his research on cognition and neuroscience in some of the leading scientific journals. He holds a PhD in Brain and Cognitive Sciences in addition to degrees in philosophy and computer science. His academic background and science fiction writing reflect his interest in the mind, ethics, and the meaning of life. When he isn't writing pretentious biographies of himself, he can often be found stacking cups for his son to knock over or pacing his basement while listening to folk punk music. He writes from Winchester, Massachusetts, where he lives with his wife, son, and two mischievous rabbits. Follow him at www.tommyblanchard.com

With a last name like Camp and a hometown like Erie, Pennsylvania, **Bill Camp** was born to write horror. He currently lives in Suffolk, Virginia with his family which includes four cats and two dogs. His poetry has appeared in *Teach. Write., Lite Lit One,* and *New Author's Journal.* He also writes fiction, which has been published in *Page and Spine*, *Teach. Write.*, and *parABnormal Digest*. He currently teaches college composition and literature courses at Paul D Camp Community College and Norfolk State University, a traditionally Black university. Additionally, he is a current member of the Horror Writers Association and is the recipient of the 2018 HWA Rocky Wood Memorial Scholarship in Non-Fiction Writing for a research project on the history of Frankenstein in film. He can be found online running a Facebook group called "Classic Camp's Classic Horror Emporium," https://www.facebook.com/groups/286596871372926/, and writing a blog, "Classic Camp's Classic Blog," https://classiccamp.blogspot.com/.

Sarina Dorie has sold over 180 short stories to markets like Analog, Daily Science Fiction, Fantasy Magazine, and F & SF. She has over sixty books up on Amazon, including her bestselling series, *Womby's School for Wayward Witches*.

A few of her favorite things include: gluten-free brownies (not necessarily glutton-free), Star Trek, steampunk, fairies, Severus Snape, and Mr. Darcy.

You can find info about her short stories and novels on her website:

www.sarinadorie.com

Mark O. Decker am retired, having spent my career in various fields. I worked in the Nixon and Ford White Houses, spent 20 years in the trade association field, and 20 years in the real estate capital markets business. My bride of 47 years is my soul mate. We have been blessed with three children and nine grandchildren. My time is primarily spent playing golf, tennis and writing poetry. In the past 5 years I have self-published 13 books of poetry, primarily in order to preserve the poetry I have written over the last fifty years for my children and grandchildren.

Dave (never David ... that's what his mother called him when she was angry) **Foster** is a life-long storyteller and avid reader and writer with a special interest in world-building and fantasy and science fiction. In fact, he's often sorely puzzled by the dividing line between the two genres; where, exactly, is it and why does it exist? He has always been a writer as part of his career in Information Technology until he was able to focus on fiction.

After a career in Information Technology (writing procedures manuals *does* hone a modest expertise with English grammar and spelling), Dave graduated with an MDes (Master of Design) from OCADU after completing an honours BFA at York University.

Dave's fantasy series of novels, *Fay's Antiques,* will be available in 2022.

Dave resides in Toronto, Canada with his partner and furry companion. He can be found at www.DaveFosterWriter.com

Diana Hauer is a documentarian by day and a fiction writer by (occasionally far too late) night. In her spare time, she reads voraciously, gardens happily, and reads eclectically. She lives in Oregon with her husband, son, and dog.

Paula Hammond is a professional writer based in London, England. Her short fiction has been published by Abyss & Apex, Air & Nothingness, B Cubed Press, Belanger Books, and The NoSleep Podcast. "All Your Bases Yada-Yada" (Third Flatiron) was nominated for a British Science Fiction Association award. When not frantically scribbling, she can be found indulging her passions for film, theatre, cult TV, sci-fi, and real ale. Should you spot her in the pub after five rounds rapid, she'll be the one in the corner mumbling Ghostbusters quotes and waiting for the transporter to lock on to her signal.

j

Larry Hinkle is an advertising copywriter living with his wife and two doggos in Rockville, Maryland. When he's not writing stories that scare people into peeing their pants, he writes ads that scare people into buying adult diapers so they're not caught peeing their pants. His work has appeared in Deep Magic, The NoSleep Podcast, *The Horror Zine*, and *Another Dimension Anthology* (winner of the 2017 Serling Award from the Rod Serling Memorial Foundation), among others. He's also an active member of the HWA, and his short story "The Space Between" made the preliminary ballot for the 2020 Stoker Awards. In 2021, he survived the Borderlands Writers Boot Camp. Feel free to visit him at larryhinkle.com.

Larry Hodges is an active member of SFWA with 120 short story sales, including stories in five previous "Alternative" anthologies. He has four published novels, including "Campaign 2100: Game of Scorpions," which covers the election for President of Earth in the year 2100, and "When Parallel Lines Meet," which he co-wrote with Mike Resnick and Lezli Robyn. He's a member of Codexwriters, and a graduate of the six-week 2006 Odyssey Writers Workshop and the two-week 2008 Taos Toolbox Writers Workshop, and has a bachelor's in math and a master's in journalism. In the world of non-fiction, he has 17 books and over 2000 published articles in over 170 different publications. He's also a professional table tennis coach and claims to be the best science fiction writer in USA Table Tennis, and the best table tennis player in Science Fiction Writers of America! Visit him at larryhodges. com.

Chris Kuriata lives in and often writes about the Niagara Region. His short fiction about home-invading bears, singing fish, and time-traveling kittens have appeared in many fine publications such as Taddle Creek, Weirdbook, OnSpec, and The NoSleep Podcast. On Twitter@CKuriata

Larry Lefkowitz has had published over 150 stories, as well as poetry and humor in journals, anthologies and online. His humorous fantasy and science fiction collection, "Laughing into the Fourth Dimension" is available from Amazon books. His Jewish story collection, "Enigmatic Tales" published by Fomite Press is available from Amazon, Barnes & Noble. A humourous novella is scheduled to be published in a number of months.

Michael Mansaray studied English Language at both Gordon College and Bridgewater State University. He spent a few years working in the mental health field as a residential counselor, supporting clients with various illnesses. Currently he works for Amazon. Recently he started working on writing reviews for the Metastellar website. A long time fantasy reader he is currently writing an urban fantasy novel featuring gods in a contemporary setting. Michael lives in southern Massachusetts with his family.

Clare Marsh lives in Kent, UK and is an international adoption social worker. She writes poetry, flash fiction and short stories. A previous winner of the Sentinel Annual Short Story Competition, her writing has appeared in *Ink, Sweat and Tears*, *National Flash Fiction Day—Flash Flood*, *Pure Slush*, *Places of Poetry*, *Rebel Talk* and *Acropolis* anthologies. She won the 2020 Olga Sinclair Short Story Prize. She was awarded M.A. Creative Writing (University of Kent) in 2018 and nominated for a Pushcart Prize for a poem in The Binnacle in 2017.

Maureen McGuirk earned her bachelor's degree in writing for film and television from the University of the Arts in Philadelphia. Her short story "Miss Fortunate" was published in *quiet Shorts*, a Seattle-based arts journal. Her one-act play "A Private Conversation" earned an honorable mention in the New Works of Merit Playwriting Contest in 2016, and was published in Two Sisters Writing & Publishing Second Annual Anthology in 2019. She lives in Cleveland, Ohio.

Frances Rowat lives in Ontario with her husband and a not-quite-startling number of cats. She was born in Canada, and while growing up spent time in England, Algeria, and Switzerland. Her current job involves chasing down schedules and filing paperwork; she is occasionally paid to introduce people to science fiction.

Frances currently spends most of her time behind a keyboard, where she frequently gets lost in details. She has recently developed an interest in bird-watching, and enjoys coffee, knitting, rain, pulpy television shows, candles, post-apocalyptic settings, and trying to sound interesting enough for a writer's bio. She is often in quiet awe of editors and publishers, and would like to thank you for reading this and for supporting the anthology in which you found it.

She committed poetry once, but it might not be a recurring habit.

Presuming that you have internet access, you may find her on Twitter at @aphotic_ink or online at aphotic-ink.com.

Katie Sakanai is a musician, teacher, writer, and mom. Born and raised in rural Pennsylvania, she attended Wellesley College where she majored in Music and Russian and had the chance to travel the world. She now lives in Colorado. She enjoys writing original folk tales and telling her daughters impromptu stories involving dragons, trolls, and fearless princesses. Her songs, short stories and poetry are full of nostalgia for her rural upbringing. Her story "Labyrinthula animalis" is published by Parsec Ink in *Triangulation: Extinction* and her original folk tale "Fomka" is included in the Flying Ketchup Press anthology *Night Forest*. Find her at katiesakanai.com or @denver_city_music on Instagram.

A bestselling Oregon author and editor, **Lizzy Shannon's** published works span many genres, including science fiction, Celtic nonfiction, fantasy, screenplays, and stage plays. Having grown up in Belfast, her latest novel, *A Song of Bullets*, is set amidst the worst era of Northern Ireland's 'Troubles' in the 80's and based on true events in her life. She's working on her third science fiction novel, and also a screenplay based on the memoirs of her great uncle, Ernest Blythe, an Irish journalist, and one of the conspirators in the famed Irish Easter Rising of 1916. Lizzy's career is as varied as the genres she writes. Starting out as a library assistant in a Northern Irish rural town, she moved on to study Theatre Arts and Literature in London, and toured the United Kingdom as a professional actress. Roles ranged from the goddess Hecate in Shakespeare's *Macbeth* to Gustav, the Amazing Dancing Bear in a clown troupe.

Native Californian and survivor of U.C. Santa Barbara, **Lauren (Hall) Stoker** currently lives in New England with her cat (and Chief Shreditor), Sam, for the thrill of skiing on ice and owning a snow blower. Lauren's short stories and non-fiction have been published both in the U.S. and the U.K. Her debut novel (a comic fantasy), *Blood Will Out (With the Proper Solvent),* was published in July 2021. Links to her publications may be found at: www.LaurenHStoker.com and www.facebook.com/LaurenHStoker.

Cory Swanson lives in Northern Colorado with his wife, two daughters, and the ghost of an old blind dog named Kirby. When he's not teaching tweens how to play band and orchestra instruments, he can be seen camping with his family in his tiny trailer or traveling to strange worlds in his head in order to write about them. If the weather is decent, you might catch him riding his bike or running because he is afraid of death, and he's heard exercise helps with that.

If you would like to witness a nearly middle aged man attempt to navigate the perils of social media, you can find Cory on Facebook under the handle @speculativemeculative, on Instagram @coyswansonauthor, on twitter @author_cory, or at his website, coryswansonauthor.wordpress.com

j

Lamont A. Turner is a New Orleans area writer whose work has appeared in numerous print and online venues. His short story collection, Souls In A Blender was released by St.Rooster Books in October, 2021. He can be found on Twitter @LamontATurner1.

Robinne Weiss is an entomologist and educator by training, but she has never been able to control her writing habit. She has been publishing her writing since the 1970s, and has been known to answer entomology exam questions in verse. Unlike her exam answers, which were met with awkward silence by her Very Serious Professors, her short stories have won multiple awards.

Her fantasy books for children include the four-book *Dragon Defence League* series and other books infested by unusual animals. For more mature audiences, she's written the urban fantasy, *Squelched*, and the YA epic fantasy, *Fatecarver*. She's also published two non-fiction books about insects.

Robinne believes adventures are the key to writing. The list of her own adventures is long, and includes teaching with a live 2-metre-long Burmese python, living in a mud house in rural Panama, and delivering a pair of goat kids in the middle of a dinner party.

She writes and blogs from her office in rural New Zealand, where adventures can be found around every corner.

Visit her at robinneweiss.com for information about all her books and stories.

Jay Wilburn is a Splatterpunk Award nominated author with work in Best Horror of the Year volume 5. He won the Official Killercon Gross Out Contest two years in a row. He taught public school for sixteen years before becoming a full-time author in 2013. In 2017, he received a life-saving kidney transplant. He ran a 5k on the anniversary of the surgery and a half marathon with the man who donated a kidney to him and has since run a marathon. Jay Wilburn lives in coastal South Carolina in the southern United States with his wife and two sons. You can find his work at JayWilburn.com or you can find more Jay Wilburn short stories at Patreon.com/JayWilburn and on Twitch at Twitch.tv/JayWilburn where he livestreams his self-published writing before your eyes from beginning to end. Writing live is one of his proudest accomplishments as an author. He'd love for you to join him.

Long-time High School English teacher, **James Van Pelt**, has been selling short fiction to many of the major venues since 1989. He was a finalist for the Nebula, the Theodore Sturgeon Memorial Award, Locus Awards, and Analog and Asimov's reader's choice awards (his 2020 Analog novella, "Minerva Girls," won this year's Anlab Award for best in its category). Years and years ago he was a finalist for the John W. Campbell Award for Best New Writer. He still feels "new." Fairwood Press recently released a huge, limited-edition, signed and numbered collection of his work, THE BEST OF JAMES VAN PELT.

j

About B-Cubed Press

B Cubed Press is a small press that publishes big books about things that matter.

A percentage of EVERY book we publish is donated to the ACLU.

We can be reached at Kionadad@aol.com.

Our writers gather routinely on the "B Cubed Project Page" on Facebook, and we can also be found at B Cubed Press.com.

Made in the USA
Monee, IL
31 December 2021

87623815R00142